As he watched the Saurians approach, Kemp thought everything was going beautifully.

It was the perfect crowning effort to the enormously successful documentary broadcast. As the first volley of fireworks burst over the reviewing stand, however, something odd happened.

The Saurian on the podium opened its mouth, stepped forward and bit off Dr. John T. Neville's hand . . .

night of the Dragonstar

DAVID F. BISCHOFF &
THOMAS F. MONTELEONE

BERKLEY BOOKS, NEW YORK

NIGHT OF THE DRAGONSTAR

A Berkley Book / published by arrangement with
the authors

PRINTING HISTORY
Berkley edition / July 1985

ISBN: 0-425-07963-5

A BERKLEY BOOK® TM 757,375
Berkley Books are published by The Berkley Publishing Group,
200 Madison Avenue, New York, New York 10016.
The name "BERKLEY" and the stylized "B" with design are
trademarks belonging to Berkley Publishing Corporation.

PRINTED IN THE UNITED STATES OF AMERICA

This one is for
HARLAN ELLISON

Prologue

Dr. Bernard Penovich of the Institute of Biological and Paleontological Research adjusted the long-distance lens of his Leica and snapped off a series of shots of the group of grazing Camptosaurus, then looked up from the viewfinder. "It is a dream, Dr. Lindstrom," he said, absently wiping perspiration from his forehead with a bandana. "But I'm not sure if it is a pleasant dream or a nightmare."

Dr. Mikaela Lindstrom looked up from the map screen she was marking with a light pen. The two scientists sat in the back seat of an Omni Terrain Vehicle. The front seat held the driver, Lieutenant Morgan Lorkner, and Lieutenant Brian Hagermann, both of the IASA, both armed to the teeth. Lindstrom and Penovich had been outfitted with highly effective .44 magnums equipped with clips of explosive bullets. A trip out into the Mesozoic Preserve wasn't exactly a Sunday afternoon picnic in the park, even if it was just a quick preliminary survey jaunt to acquaint the distinguished guest with the lay of the land.

"What do you mean, Doctor?" Mikaela asked. "I feel like a kid in a candy store."

"Damned sight more dangerous here than in a candy store, ma'am," said Hagermann in his soft Southern accent. He adjusted his polarized goggles and shifted the weight of the rifle he kept pointed in the general direction of any fang-bearing reptiles. "The boys say the word is out 'mongst these critters that human flesh is mighty tasty."

"Goddamned monsters have had their fill," said Lorkner, a dark, morose, but always alert man in top physical trim. He grinned. "Mostly Moslem meat, praise Allah."

"Gentlemen," Penovich said. "This is a scientific expedition—my scientific expedition—and I'll have no racial slurs poisoning my research."

"Well, excuse me," Lieutenant Lorkner muttered, settling back in the seat of the idling vehicle. Foot poised on the accelerator, he was ready to take off at the first drop of reptilian drool.

"What I meant, Dr. Lindstrom," Penovich continued, "is that paleontology is a science based upon intense research and speculation. We spend years trying to prove a theory about the development of this or that species of dinosaur, we invest our lives in digging up fossils and arguing among ourselves—and then the universe drops this little surprise package on our heads. To learn of our gross errors in the very foundations of our knowledge is bad enough, but to see a life's work down the drain—That is the stuff of nightmare even given the wonder I feel at seeing these incredible creatures in the flesh."

Mikaela's gaze wandered over past the field of ginkgoes and protofirs to where the Camptosaurids used their lassolike tongues to trim the vegetation. Their name, she knew, meant "bent lizards," and they were just that, bulky bodies equipped with large hind legs and short forelimbs. Herbivorous, they had hides colored brown and green for maximum camouflage from the larger predators that prowled this encapsulated cylindrical world—and there were plenty of those. As the extant bones from Western Europe and western North America indicated, the faces of the Camptosaurus were beaklike claws—but unlike the dug-up skeletons, they had four claws on each forelimb rather than three.

"Mutation . . . evolution," Dr. Penovich had commented earlier in his visit to Artifact One. "It's surprising there's not more evidence of changes. Of course, we must take into account the various species living here whose ancestors were not kind enough to leave behind fossilized evidence of their existence."

"I think I know what you mean," said Mikaela Lindstrom, moving to a more comfortable position and wiping her short hair back. Once it had been long, but since she had been spending long periods in this hot and muggy atmosphere, she had cut it.

Phineas had complained, since he liked long hair on women; but the IASA colonel was above all a practical man, and the complaint was merely for the record, spoken with a smile. "When you're studying flesh and blood instead of dust and bones, and you look down the throat of a roaring, carnivorous theory made flesh and teeth, things can get strange."

Dr. Penovich was a squat, balding, bespectacled man from Eastern Europe, famous for his worldwide expeditions in search of the remnants of dinosaurs. Mikaela Lindstrom had met him on several occasions in the course of her duties, and whenever there had been a question he could help her with, Dr. Penovich had been happy to correspond. When this cache of wonders had come out of nowhere to land in the lap of the IASA, and Penovich got a whiff that there were dinosaurs preserved in their natural Jurassic or Cretaceous environments, he'd pulled all the strings he could and gained a position on the secondary interior survey team. Now that the alien cylinder was in a stable Lagrange Earth-Moon orbit and no longer in danger of terrorist takeover from the TWC, that team could begin its work. Though Mikaela welcomed his wide knowledge, she was finding that she resented his authoritarian wise-old-man presence; after all, she was the first paleontologist on this particular Mesozoic block.

"Enough of this maudlin meandering," Dr. Penovich said, a smile creasing his face. "We have much territory to cover today, yes? Lieutenant Lorkner, please drive on. Our new reptilian friends eagerly await us."

"Yeah, with knife and fork, no doubt," Lorkner muttered. "And I joined the IASA to see Mars!"

As they continued the tour, Mikaela Lindstrom found her mind wandering from dinosaurs to Colonel Phineas Kemp, her very own primeval plaything. She chuckled ruefully at the thought, missing him. They'd been lovers for three months, but they hardly ever saw each other. Right now, Phineas was Earthside, preparing for the introduction of Artifact One, popularly known as 'the Dragonstar,' to the general public and overseeing the funding necessary to deal with this mammoth scientific project. While she was sweating in her figurative khakis and pith helmet, he was probably in tux and tails sipping iced martinis at some state dinner, gabbing about potting T. rexes. She chuckled at the image, and the memory of his handsome, sturdy face brought flashbacks of their sturdy, emphatic lovemaking. She thought of his muscular arms around her, his serious mouth nibbling her neck, his firm hands on her hips, holding her down as he guided his—

What was that?

Mikaela blinked.

There had been a flash of color moving through a thatch of vegetation off to her left. She pulled up her binoculars. Damn! This was no time to be fantasizing about her lover. She was a scientist, and she had to pay attention, especially in this situation, despite the fact that having Phineas Kemp as a boyfriend had awoken new feelings in her.

About fifty meters off in the jungle, treetops and vines shuddered as something large brushed past them. She saw the flashes of color again, crimson and blue and—

"Stop!" she said above the din of the motors. She

BUSINESS REPLY MAIL

FIRST CLASS   PERMIT NO. 137   BOULDER, CO

POSTAGE WILL BE PAID BY ADDRESSEE

U.S.News & World Report

Subscription Department
Post Office Box 55909
Boulder, CO 80321-5909

leaned over and tapped Lieutenant Lorkner's shoulder. "Stop, Lieutenant. There's something over there."

Lorkner obeyed.

"Can you back up?" Mikaela asked anxiously.

Lorkner shrugged and obeyed. "Say when."

"What do you see, Dr. Lindstrom?" Dr. Penovich asked, lifting his Leica.

"I'm not sure," Mikaela said. "But whatever it is, it looks strange." She adjusted the binoculars, training them onto the spot where she had glimpsed the beast. "Might be worth getting a shot of, Doctor. These beasts have definitely not given up their territorial ways, and the kinds of creatures that inhabit each sector of the interior, when placed in the greater context, might give us a better idea of what we have here."

"Yes, yes, I am familiar with this idea of yours, and it is a good one," Penovich said. "But mostly now I am simply happy to see new kinds of dinosaurs."

With the OTV stopped and idling, Mikaela Lindstrom hoisted her lithe body up into a stand on the seat for a better view. "Damn! I can't see it."

She made as if to get out, but Lorkner stopped her. "Can't allow that, ma'am. This is just a survey, remember? Too dangerous to get out of the car."

"But this might be important," Mikaela said. "I want to see this thing. It looked . . . peculiar."

"Well, ma'am," Lieutenant Hagermann said, "you don't want to go traipsin' through all that undergrowth. So maybe we can raise this beastie for you. Leastways get a look at his backside arunnin'. Where'd you say you saw the critter?"

Mikaela pointed. "I'm not so sure that this—"

"My finger's crampin' anyway. Little bit of exercise might help it some."

Hagermann stood up and squinted into his highly magnified sights. "Holy shit, I do see somethin'. Just spook it out, mebbe."

The blast as Lieutenant Hagermann fired was deafening.

A loud screeching erupted from the forest.

Hagermann's hunter grin flip-flopped. "Holy shit, I musta winged it."

The tops of the trees began to sway wildly back and forth as the sound of scrabbling blended with a maddened howling.

Perspiration dripped from Mikaela's brow onto the black casing of the binoculars. "It's coming this way."

"Attacking?" Penovich asked, a mixture of excitement and fear on his face.

"No sense in taking any chances," Mikaela said, unholstering her gun and switching off the safety. She'd had only a quick course in use of the weapon, but she was fairly competent with it. Penovich, in contrast, seemed markedly uncomfortable, holding his gun in his right hand and clutching his camera in his left.

"Maybe we'd better get going," Lorkner said, a nervous twitch in his dark features.

"No. No, I want to see this thing. I want its picture," Dr. Penovich said.

"Be ready to move, Lieutenant," Mikaela said.

"Say no more." Lorkner's hands were tense on the controls, his holster unfastened.

The beast emerged from a collection of ferns like a drunk barging through bar doors. It paused for a moment, testing the air with flared nostrils, ugly gnarled head twisting about, tiny red eyes searching for its prey. Saliva misted from its mouth; blood oozed from its wounded shoulder.

Penovich raised his camera and snapped a couple of pictures, then suddenly stopped, too astonished to take any more.

Mikaela knew why.

The thing was perhaps twenty-five feet long. It stood erect at a height of something less than fifteen feet upon powerful hind haunches. The creature was colored blood crimson, with swathes of blue and green on its hide.

It was the ugliest thing that Mikaela Lindstrom had ever seen.

Open running sores abounded all over its upper body, scattered among protuberant cancers. The thing's face was scarred and marked as though with radiation burns. Its red puffy eyes gleamed with reptilian madness.

At first sight, Mikaela had assumed it was an Allosaurus or something of that ilk, but now she could see by the long snout and the longer forearms that it was not.

"It's . . ." said Dr. Penovich. "It's an Iguanodon!"

"Hell, mister," said Hagermann. "I ain't no paleontologist, but by now I know something about dinosaurs. Iguanodons ain't supposed to have claws. And Iguanodons ain't supposed to have big fangs like that."

Which was exactly the problem, Mikaela thought. And Iguanodons were also not supposed to look like lab animals after a year of cancer tests.

The dinosaur spotted them and with surprising agility leaped forward and began running through the underbrush toward them.

"Jesus!" Hagermann said, leveling his rifle and squeezing off a shot that missed. "Lorkner, get us the hell out of here!"

The command was unnecessary. Lorkner was already moving. Hagermann fired one more shot, which grazed the maddened Iguanodon in the snout, and knelt in his seat. Penovich and Lindstrom followed his lead.

"Some kind of mutant," Mikaela said. "But how . . ."

The Iguanodon made a peculiar bleating sound and fell in on the path behind the OTV, pursuing, fangs bright in the light from the Illuminator above. The monster closed in with astonishing speed, as though nothing mattered but making the survey party his lunch.

Lather and blood sprayed in its wake. Even in the wind of their passage Mikaela could hear the snorts of the creature's breathing. Hagermann motioned her and Penovich further down so that he could shoot over their heads. The explosions of the blast were incredibly loud but oddly comforting. One of the bullets caught the monster directly in the chest, blowing out a gout of blood and flesh and bone, but the thing kept on.

"My god," said Penovich, peering over the back of the open car. "That thing is like a machine."

"Maybe you'd better close the bubble top," Mikaela shouted to Lorkner.

"Yeah!" he shouted back. "I was—"

Suddenly, with a bellow that seemed to shake the world, the Iguanodon leapt. For a moment, its body seemed suspended over the OTV, casting the survey team in shadow. Lorkner slammed the accelerator to the floor and the vehicle lurched ahead.

The shadow descended.

What happened next was such a shock it all seemed a blur to Mikaela. The creature's long neck extended over the OTV, and its hideous mouth closed over Lieutenant Hagermann's arms. The creature's impact with the OTV slewed the car off the road; Hagermann was plucked from his seat, screaming.

The Omni Terrain Vehicle rocked, teetered as though it was about to fall over on one side, then steadied and stalled.

Mikaela Lindstrom fired a round into the Iguanodon's side. The creature had Hagermann in its jaws, worrying him like a dog with a bone. Showers of blood flew everywhere. Hagermann stopped screaming; his headless, armless torso fell from the Iguanodon's mouth as the beast chomped its gory meal into paste.

"Jesus!" Lorkner cried. "Jesus!" The man had pulled up his own rifle and began pumping explosive bullets into the creature's head with sharpshooter's accuracy. An evil red eye exploded, and the Iguanodon wailed with pain.

By now Dr. Penovich had recovered and was firing his own gun at the beast. "Shoot for the head!" Mikaela cried. "The head, Doctor!"

She reloaded the extra shells in the pocket of her jacket and resumed firing.

The pain-maddened Iguanodon, its body riddled with wounds, covered with blood, turned to charge its attackers—and another of Lorkner's rounds caught its remaining eye. Blinded, it stumbled about, screaming madly, while the trio of shooters placed another volley of bullets in its body.

Trembling spastically, it staggered, then fell. It trembled on the ground, its blind eyes staring into death, its jaws, unnaturally swollen with teeth, still snapping.

The survivors of the incredible and unprecedented attack could only stare numbly at the carnage. Then Dr. Penovich was sick over the side of the OTV.

"I'll take full responsibility, Lieutenant Lorkner," Mikaela said, every ounce of her strength placed in staying calm, even though she felt like following Penovich's unprofessional lead.

"We'll have to bring his body back," Lorkner said in a monotone.

"Yes. One of the larger sample bags, in the storage trunk. We can't leave him out here. Scavengers everywhere." Suddenly she seemed above it all, as though she was looking down quite calmly at the proceedings. "Dr. Penovich, are you all right?"

Sweat streamed down the middle-aged man's face. "Yes. Yes, I think so."

"I'll need your camera. We must make this fast. Predators will be here any moment." She took the Leica even as Lieutenant Lorkner, realizing the situation, jumped out and saw about the grisly task of retrieving what was left of Hagermann. "I'd like to take a sample, but there's no time."

Lorkner did his job quickly, while Lindstrom raced around the dead though still twitching thing, snapping the pictures she needed of the deformities.

"There's something coming!" Penovich cried.

With surprising calm, Mikaela helped Lorkner dump the bagged body into the back of the OTV, then jumped into the back seat, arms smeared with blood. Lorkner was right behind her. He jumped behind the wheel, started the engine, and sped the car away.

Several creatures broke from the clearing, running

toward the fallen Iguanodon to get their share of the easily obtained feast.

Lorkner closed the bubble top this time, even though they were in no apparent danger. "Who knows?" he said in a whisper. "That thing's brother may be lurking around." He couldn't contain a shudder as he looked down at his arms, smeared with Hagermann's blood.

"I've never seen anything like that before, Dr. Penovich," Mikaela said after taking a deep breath.

Dr. Penovich simply stared ahead in kind of a numb trance, clearly not hearing his colleague.

"Something is wrong," Mikaela said, the tears beginning to come. "Something is dreadfully wrong here."

One

2028 A.D.—Washington, D.C.

The Washington Sheraton Hotel on Connecticut and Woodley Northwest was the unofficial site of most official IASA conference functions and social affairs interfacing with the U.S. government. It was the natural choice for Colonel Phineas Kemp's press conference, two months after the 'Dragonstar War', as it had come to be known by the media.

Phineas Kemp was by nature a man who preferred getting around under his own steam; but because of the peculiar situation, and the attention he was getting, his IASA superiors had insisted that he arrive in a limousine, along with an armed guard.

"What we've got here, Phineas, is an ostentatious affair, so you've got to forget about your Volkswagen," General Mitchel Hopper had told him tersely. "Besides, with the amount of publicity this business has been getting, there's no telling what crazed antievolutionist is out there, ready to shoot you for the Devil."

"I just want the announcement to be heard by everyone, and I want to make the press conference as short as possible,'' Kemp had said. ''I'm going to leave it to my documentary to straighten out the whole picture. In the end, the show will be what people and posterity will remember, not all of this nonsensical hype that's been going on.''

''You can't expect people to find out that an alien artifact is floating around in the solar system, that it may be the factory for life as we know it on this planet, and not be curious,'' Colonel Waterford said in his soft but clear voice. ''We've been feeding them only the barest facts and a few pictures, and look at all the furor that's been caused. I for one wish we could dispense with the whole story right now.''

''Don't you understand, Colonel?'' Kemp's gray eyes blazed above his no-nonsense features. ''This isn't something that people are going to accept with just a story and some pictures. This may well change the course of human history. If the people of the world are not properly informed, God knows what they're going to make of it.''

''And you're going to be the one to tell them, eh Phineas?'' A dim smile played over Waterford's bland features. ''Center stage.''

''That's my duty as I see it,'' Phineas replied curtly. ''I was there. I have the command and the authority and the sources. This is what the board has decided. The project has been underway for the past month, and now that we have set a date, we can announce it and perhaps dispel some of the controversy.''

Waterford shook his head. ''Haven't changed a bit since you were last Earthside, have you, Phin?''

Damn the man! thought Phineas Kemp as the sleek, chauffeur-driven car eased up the horseshoe driveway to the front entrance of the Sheraton. Gus Waterford had always been a pain in the butt with his laconic attitudes, ever since Phineas had known him at the Academy. How he had achieved his high rank, Kemp could never understand. Perhaps the service figured they needed a token cynic to anchor their attitudes. If Phineas Kemp was the IASA's head in the stars, then Gus Waterford was the ass planted firmly on solid ground.

"What's going on up there?" Kemp said, suddenly realizing that there was a crowd of people by the entrance, all waving their arms excitedly as the black limo approached.

"No harm, sir," said a spit-and-polish corporal named Garcia, seated by him. "Just the Saurie Friends. At any rate, we've stationed the proper security, and there won't be any crazy crowds at the conference."

The car stopped. Only the armed guards prevented the large, frantic crowd from happily charging.

"That's nice to know," Kemp said with distaste as he warily eyed the motley crowd. "Saurie Friends, huh? Just who are they?"

Corporal Martin, up front, chuckled. "You must have been on the Moon, sir," he said, and they all laughed at the joke. "No, sir. The people of the U.S. have taken the news of the existence of another group of intelligent beings in an . . . interesting way. But look for yourself."

The people hailing his arrival wore T-shirts, buttons, and hats, all emblazoned with images of the Saurians, the intelligent dinosaurs Ian Coopersmith and Becky Thalberg had encountered behind that amazing wall at one end of Artifact One.

"Incredible," Kemp said. "I've been out of touch."

"Yes, sir," Garcia said. "There are Saurie toys, Saurie bubble gum—the IASA really should have put a franchise on the little guys—we could have financed our whole project for a year with the income. They've already got TV shows and movies in the works. The Saurie Friends are a group formed to welcome the critters to Earth, should they ever come."

Kemp grunted. "Well, let's get down to business."

The chauffeur opened the doors. Kemp put on his best media smile, with just the right amount of the boyish American charm that the country had come to expect from their astronauts, and made his way quickly through the path that parted the crowd.

"Tell the Sauries we love them!" a fat, breathless

woman screeched. Autograph books were waved in his
face.

A chant started. "We love Sauries! We love Sauries!"

Kemp gritted his teeth, smiled, waved, and got
through the cheering crowd as fast as he could, feeling
a curious elation at the attention. When he stepped
through the doors of the Sheraton's lobby and met with
his welcoming committee, his feeling of nervousness
and stage fright had evaporated into a definitely up
mood.

"Colonel Kemp," said a striking brunette, holding
out a welcoming hand. "I'm Kathleen Ennis of NBC.
I'm the field producer for your news conference."

Kemp took her slender hand, noting what a nice smile
she had and the sparkle of her eyes. "Nice to meet you.
Are you a Saurie Friend?"

She shook her curls, throwing her head back in a sexy
laugh. "No, I'm too addicted to men. Just call me Kate,
okay? This way, please. I'm sure you've had your fill of
reptile fanciers."

She guided him down the hall toward the room where
he would speak. People in the foyer stopped in mid-
conversation, turning his way as he passed, recognizing
him, no doubt, from pictures. "We've got a green room
with refreshments from which you'll make your entrance."

"Are all the satellite hookups functioning?" Kemp
asked.

"Yes, that manly uniform will be seen all over the
world." Her fashionable outfit swished as she walked.

"An Arthur C. Clarke special, eh?" Kemp joked,
loosening up thanks to her casual presence.

"Yes," the pretty producer said, clearly flirting with
him. "Satellite communication can be such a ball, can't
it?"

She led him to a small room adjoining the larger hall
where the podium and cameras were set up.

"Believe it or not, it's actually green," Kate said, an
attractive laugh in her voice. "And there's someone
here I believe you know, Colonel Kemp. Oh, Becky

dahling," the woman said, doing a Kathrine Hepburn imitation. "The colonel's come to call. Now you two please excuse me, I've got a dozen things to do in the next half hour."

"Hello, Phineas," said Dr. Rebecca Thalberg, getting up from a chair. She gave him a chaste peck on the cheek, which felt strange coming from a former lover. "I've decided to accept your invitation."

The news conference was as large as any the Sheraton had ever given, though representatives from the media had been restricted to one reporter per magazine, TV station, or newspaper.

As per Colonel Kemp's request, he and Dr. Thalberg were announced as simply as possible. Kemp and Rebecca made their way through a blaze of flashbulbs to the podium. Becky assumed a staight-backed seat nearby while Kemp instinctively grabbed the podium, letting the applause die down.

"Thank you," he said. "I would like to read a statement first, and then I'll welcome your questions."

Kemp pulled a piece of paper from an inside pocket, unfolded it, and carefully placed it before him.

"I'm sure you are all acquainted with the essential facts provided by the IASA concerning the discovery, the exploration of, and the subsequent conflict aboard the alien artifact popularly known as the Dragonstar. You also no doubt realize that as the Chief of Deep Space Operations for the IASA, Artifact One, the Dragonstar, is my direct responsibility.

"At the present time, I am also responsible for introducing the world to this incredible discovery. This is quite a complicated task and one that I do not take lightly; the Dragonstar and the discoveries we have made aboard it are potentially monumental in our race's development.

"Therefore, rather than content myself with a skimpy report, I have taken upon myself the task of producing a documentary in conjunction with some of the finest individuals in television and science today.

"This documentary, produced by World Media Corporation, will be shown May 15, 2028, and will be made available to all networks or television stations capable of receiving a signal from the TranSatNet, which will beam our partly recorded, partly live telecast."

Kemp looked up to see what response this announcement had brought. The reporters were literally sitting on the edge of their seats, waiting to hurl questions.

"The purpose of this telecast will be threefold:

"First, to show to the people of Earth the scope of the cylinder in audio and visual terms. Our cameras will take a tour of Artifact One, exterior and interior, complete with coverage of the denizens of the interior, both intelligent and nonintelligent.

"Second, to fully document and describe all of the events from astronomical location of the cylinder in its cometary orbit through the numerous misadventures, tragedies, and conflicts experienced before the successful placement of Artifact One in a stable position relative to the Earth and the Moon.

"Finally, to introduce, live, the intelligent life-form we have come to call 'Saurians', and to discuss the implications of what was discovered in the control sections of the ship, which are even now being explored and analyzed by the IASA scientific team headed by Dr. Robert Jakes.

"The IASA feels that the people of Earth are owed more than the basic facts, facts which hardly disclose the depth and scope of our experiences with the 'Dragonstar' and barely touch upon its future.

"This is a privilege and a challenge, and to undertake such an endeavor takes time.

"We ask only your patience. I can personally assure you that you will be amply rewarded."

Kemp smiled for the first time.

"Thank you. I'd also like to thank my colleague Dr. Rebecca Thalberg for joining me today. We will now take fifteen minutes of questions."

As Becky joined him at the podium, reporters leaped to their feet, struggling to be called upon.

Kemp picked a reporter at random. He was amused—
at presidential news conferences the President seemed to
know each of the reporters, and he, Kemp, hardly knew
a one.

"Jack Talent, Cablescope Newservices. Colonel
Kemp, the term 'misadventures' seems hardly adequate
to describe the incredible series of foul-ups and catas-
trophes experienced by the IASA, at a cost of many
lives. Will this be fully covered in your documentary?"

Kemp cleared his throat. "Yes. From the loss of the
mining snipe and its two pilots to the Dragonstar's
defense system through the massacre upon the entrance
into the rotating cylinder, through the confrontation
with the Third World Confederation over . . . ah . . .
media rights to the vessel."

The crowd laughed.

Another hand was acknowledged.

"Richard Whiting, *Washington Post*. This question is
addressed to Dr. Rebecca Thalberg. Dr. Thalberg, you,
along with Ian Coopersmith, were marooned inside the
Dragonstar after dinosaurs attacked and killed the rest
of your boarding party. Your struggle for survival while
waiting for rescue has excited much speculation. Will
you and Captain Coopersmith take part in this documentary and fully recount your experiences?"

"I can only speak for myself," Becky said. "Captain
Coopersmith is presently on extended leave from the
service and at this point does not intend to take part in
media coverage. However, in the interest of getting all
the facts straight, I have agreed to cooperate with Colonel Kemp and his crew in whatever way I can . . . yes? In
the back row . . . ?"

"Louis Stathis, HM Wireservice. Those dorks in the
TWC are still screaming bloody murder. They claim
that the IASA are imperialist barbarians who welcomed
their aid with bullets and blood. They are particularly
upset about the loss of one Marcus Jashad, leader of
their 'friendly' expedition."

Kemp snorted with laughter and anger. "Sounds like
they're talking out of their assholes to me." He colored

as he realized what he had said.

The crowd broke up as Kemp tensed and attempted to reclaim his stiff military demeanor.

"Perhaps I should rephrase that last statement," he said with the faintest of smiles. "I'm surprised that the TWC even acknowledges that such an expedition was sent. I think the record shows that Jashad and his crew were terrorists, intent upon claiming the Dragonstar —and any stardrive—for their own. The protests of the TWC are clearly a smoke screen for their embarrassment. Fortunately, the combined forces of the greater world powers are lenient, and no strong measures have been taken against that organization for its cutthroat efforts. The message the originators of the Dragonstar have placed there is for all of us. The IASA program will be available to all countries that care to accept the transmission."

More questions were hurled at the pair. Questions about the reactions of fundamentalist religions to the implications of life on Earth formed from an alien pattern. Questions as to the meaning of the Dragonstar to IASA Deep Space Exploration. Questions concerning the possibility of the alien architects of the Dragonstar (and by implication, human life on Earth) returning to visit. Kemp and Thalberg fielded them all expertly, referring any complex issues to either the upcoming documentary or the official report to be issued the following year by the IASA.

To Kemp, the proceedings seemed to go incredibly fast; to Thalberg, who enjoyed public attention much less than did her former lover, it seemed interminable. She didn't even know why she had involved herself, wishing now that she had kept to her promise to herself to continue her work as biomedical specialist on Copernicus Base, the IASA lunar colony. But something unfinished had nagged her into finally agreeing with Kemp to assist on his program.

"Well, that was quite a show," Kate Ennis said, stepping up onto the platform. Impetuously, she kissed Kemp on the cheek, then shook Becky's hand. Kemp smiled, a little dazed by her perfume. "I can see you have political designs, Colonel Kemp," she said playfully.

"Political? No, no, I'm afraid not. And just call me Phineas, please."

"Don't be so hasty, Phineas," Becky said, observing with mixed feelings the producer's clear interest in her former boyfriend. "I'm sure you'd make a fine PTA president someday."

Kate Ennis held her hand against a spray of ruffle emerging from her sharp suit and laughed charmingly. "Now, you must come and partake of the spread that your IASA Media Relations have prepared. I've seen it, and it's not bad."

"Pâté modeled after an alien cylinder, perhaps?" asked Becky as they walked to the back of the room, where the media people who had not rushed to their terminals were chowing down.

"Nothing so phallic, I'm sure." Kate lifted an amused eyebrow. "Am I interrupting anything here?"

"No, of course not, Kate," Kemp said, picking a glass of white wine off a tray after the women had taken theirs. "As a matter of fact, I wanted to talk to you. I like your style. Have you had any experience in documentaries?"

"I used to be a field producer for *Ninety Minutes*. I've no special contract with NBC and I happen to have some leave coming up, and I'd love to help you with your show. Here's my card. Perhaps we can have dinner while you're in town." She flashed a smile. "Now you must excuse me." And she was off.

"Miss Jaws, 2028," Becky said, laughing. "I do believe she has her eyes on you, Phineas, so watch out. They tell me that Swedish girls lock errant boyfriends in saunas to sweat out their sins."

"Do I hear a faint note of jealousy?" Kemp asked. Their conversation was interrupted by a number of media folk who had noticed their arrival and wanted to continue the press conference on a less formal level.

Several glasses of wine and much ego-stroking later,

Phineas found himself seated, a plate of cold cuts and olives on his lap, for a blessed time alone.

Becky saw him and had to smile. He looked like a kid at a church social, struggling with his cup of punch and chicken salad sandwich. She excused herself from the boring conversation in which she was engaged and carried her own wine glass and hors d'oeuvre over his way.

"Hey, sailor," she said.

Kemp smiled up at her, mouth full of sandwich. " 'Lo, Becky."

"Track Dragonjaws down again?"

"Uh . . . yeah. Dinner tomorrow night."

"Wonderful."

"Turns out she did a Moon story and she's got her shots and permit. Damned fine credentials, too."

"I'm sure. What are we eating this crap for? This is my college town—let me take you out to a wonderful place I know in Georgetown—my treat. For old times' sake. What do you say?"

"What do I do with my limo?"

"Send it back to the garage. I guarantee you there won't be any Saurie Friends at this place."

"Sounds wonderful to me." Kemp drained his glass. "I trust this place has good wine."

"Finest vintage, Phineas. A lot better than you can get on the Moon, let me tell you."

"Just don't let me get drunk," Kemp said, getting up.

"*Moi?*" Becky said innocently.

Two

The old man drank from his Jack Daniels bottle, belched resoundingly, then turned on his computer, keying in the dictation mode.

"The Dragonstar Adventure," he said in his rattly but resonant baritone, "by John T. Neville, King of the Hard Science Fiction Writers and the best damned lay in the universe!"

Neville chuckled to himself as he watched the phosphorous words appear on the CRT screen. His secretary would process that last bit out, of course, but it always gave him a charge to hear it and see it in print. He slurped some more from the bottle as he gazed serenely over his patio to the walls that guarded his hilltop mansion. He wished for the umpteenth time that the stuff he drank was really whiskey, but he hadn't been able to drink that wonderful nectar since his liver transplant thirty years ago, and he missed it every single day.

Tapping a single key, he told the computer not to take down his next words. He screwed the cap back on the bottle, which actually held a specially concocted geriatric preservation formula he brewed in his basement, and settled his old frail bones back in his composing chair, conveniently close to the life maintenance equipment that he kept in every room. His gaze drifted casu-

ally across the shelves holding all four hundred and
fifty-nine of his science fiction and popular science
books (no goddamn fantasy!) to the enshrined picture
of a crew-cut, bespectacled middle-aged man smoking a
cigarette in a long holder.

"What do you think about this, John?" he said to the
picture. "*Omni* called me last night for a special article
on this Dragonstar business. Aliens, you old bugger.
Aliens! Remember the talks we used to have about
aliens, you with your goddamned homosapiencentric
view of the universe! I told you we probably were just
the gunk some alien race scraped off their shoe, and I
was *right*, blast you! And you didn't have the grace to
live long enough to buy me that drink we bet."

Neville shrugged and smiled sardonically to himself.
Not that he could drink it now. And there he was, staring down at him, still with his smug smile: John W.
Campbell, Jr., himself, father of modern science fiction. Neville had been all of thirteen years old when he
had taken the bus from New Jersey to Manhattan and
plopped his first manuscript on the great man's desk.
Younger than Asimov. Better, too. Yep, John T.
Neville had sprung up right in the middle of the golden
age of *Astounding* magazine, when the likes of Heinlein
and Sturgeon, de Camp and van Vogt were forging the
vital alchemy of a great literature. A truly useful
literature, peering as it did into the future with the verve
and excitement of possibility, yet with the dark edge of
prophetic warning. A psychological mirror of the times
and a damned fine way to teach the real stuff, hard
science, more intoxicating than hard liquor. Hard
science made man the master of his universe!

And now, all this.

"It's our vindication, John. Shit, *your* vindication."
He glanced happily over at his trophy case of awards—
Hugos and Nebulas, humanitarian awards, honorary
doctorates, bowling trophies—and grinned, showing
even white surgically implanted teeth. "I got mine. But
you other guys—hell, the real pioneers always get re-
viled."

That was it, he thought happily. That would be the

slant for his article. The Dreamers Vindicated! SF Slans Victorious! We were better than all you stupid, mundane *Untermenchen* all along!

"And *I'm* going to write the definitive article, Hagar, you stupid shit!" he said to his autographed picture of Dr. Amos Hagar, the media darling who had been some lucky dinosaur's breakfast. He gave a Bronx cheer to the picture—never had liked that guy—and laughed so hard he began coughing and the warning buzzer went off on his LM unit.

His nurse scurried in almost immediately.

"Mr. Neville! Whatever are you doing?"

"Hell, I'm laughing. No harm done." He controlled his cough, and his blood pressure immediately lowered. "You don't have to treat me like a baby, damn it."

"Mr. Neville," the attractive young nurse said, "you're ninety-eight years old. You're certainly no baby, but you're much too vigorous for someone of your age and previous history of workaholism coupled with debauchery."

"You ought to at least try the latter sometime." He reached over and patted her rump. "Gave me some fine ideas for my books."

"Now, now, Mr. Neville, we want that keen mind of yours fixed on science."

"Hell, biology has always been my favorite science. I think I even got a degree in it somewhere."

After checking the equipment, Nurse Jane Wilkins was satisfied that the spry life she was charged with would rant on a while longer. "What are you working on, Mr. Neville?"

"Call me 'Doctor' today, dear. I've just remembered about my degrees."

"Certainly, Doctor." She glanced at the CRT. "Oh, the Dragonstar." Her eyes shone. "Aren't those Sauries cute?"

"Cute! Bunch of smart lizards, that's all they are. Stupid public is making them out to be Jesus's babies or something, when they'd probably eat you soon as look at you."

"Now now, Mr. . . . . Dr. Neville. That's hardly the attitude you've promoted in most of your books concerning extraterrestials. Certainly you've had any number of antagonistic aliens, but you've always explored the possibility with an open mind—and the sharpest mind in science fiction.''

"Goddamn it, woman, I'm old, and I deserve to be cranky and cantankerous if I want. Now, I'm not going to die before I finish this article, so you can just leave me be.''

Nurse Wilkins made sure the sensor field keyed to Neville's vital functions was fully operational, then departed.

Neville took another drink of his vitamin-packed brew, then rekeyed for dictation.

He started his essay off with his usual "This reminds me of the day I . . .'' anecdote, this one concerning his first first-contact story, "Streaking Eyeballs of Neptune,'' for *Thrilling Astounding Tales*, an instant classic, then proceeded to narrate the story of the Dragonstar, Neville-style, intending to finish the article up with his lengthy opinion on the subject.

"We almost had a 'Boucher's comet.'

"That's what the young IASA fellowship student Robert Boucher thought late one night at the Copernicus Base Observatory. The lunar telescopes had been running routine measurements on the Tarantula, the Great Looped Nebula in the Magellanic Cloud in the constellation Doradus, diameter eight hundred light-years, which is mighty big, folks.

"The observatory project was in photometric analysis. An array of aligned photometers was focused on a nebula feature, comparing hard UV to near infrared radiation with a three-micrometer cutoff, each photometer covering a small arc of the sky.

"Boucher noted an unexpected series of peaks at regular intervals. He called in Professor André Labate, Director of the Observatory. It didn't take long for Labate to figure out what was going on.

"Since the photometer array was aimed so far off the ecliptic, Labate knew it couldn't be an asteroid. The possibility of a new comet arose, since the object was following a nearly parabolic orbit, but spectographic analysis showed Fraunhofer absorption lines. Doppler shift on sodium D line was checked, and the spectrum proved to be only slightly shifted from the solar spectrum, which meant that solar radiation was being reflected off a spinning object, heading down the gravity well toward the sun.

"By the time Colonel Phineas Kemp, Chief of Operations on Copernicus Base, was called in, Labate and Boucher had the specifics.

"The large unidentified body was entering the main plane of the solar system at an oblique angle near the orbit of Jupiter, approximately forty degrees to the ecliptic. Measurements revealed that it had a cometary orbit with a period of about two hundred and ten years, and a velocity of thirty kilometers per second, increasing as the object approached perihelion, its closest position to the sun.

"Measurements also showed the object was not a comet but a cylinder sixty-five kilometers in diameter and three hundred and twenty kilometers in length.

"Sure as hell, nobody from Earth had shot that thing up there, and it *was* a spaceship of some kind.

"Because of the delicate political situation on both the Earth and the Moon, Kemp immediately put a top-secret classification on the information. The closest ship available for interception proved to be one of the IASA mining vessels working the asteroid belt.

Kemp selected the *Astaroth*, which immediately dispatched a surveying/prospecting craft nicknamed a snipe, manned by Peter Melendez and Charles O'Hara. These pilots guided the small vessel along an intersect course with the approaching object, armed with an arsenal of cameras and analytical instruments. Upon close approach, they discovered that the object was an immense cylindrical spacecraft turning on its longitudinal axis. Colonel Kemp ordered the snipe to touch down on the surface of the alien vessel. This maneuver triggered defensive mechanisms that destroyed the snipe, killing its crew.

"Attempts to initiate communication with any possible beings inside the vessel, now called Artifact One, proved fruitless. Aside from the destruction of the snipe, the alien vessel was silent. All telemetered data from the snipe's analysis were studied to determine the best ways to overcome Artifact One's defenses and enter the ship.

"With the approval of the IASA's joint directors, an expedition was prepared and the deep space probeship *Heinlein* was dispatched to intercept Artifact One and attempt entry. The mission was successful, and while Lieutenant Colonel Douglas Fratz and First Lieutenant Michael Bracken stayed aboard the ship, the remainder of the crew, a landing party of six, entered Artifact One.

"Inside they discovered an encapsulated world of jungle, forest, rivers, and plateaus illuminated by a thick rod that floated in zero gee along the central axis of the gigantic cylinder. The flora and terrain appeared to be an exact model of the Earth's environment during the Mesozoic Era. Ian Coopersmith, a tactical engineer whose specific mission was to neutralize Artifact One's defensive systems and gain entry into the ship, was in charge of the landing party. He placed communications officer Alan Huff by the entrance hatch and led the others on a short exploratory mission.

"They quickly learned that the alien vessel was filled not only with plant life but with dinosaurs as well. The crew was astonished to discover various species wandering about the terrain. While they watched a herd of Iguanodons feed near the edge of a lagoon, their radio helmets picked up Alan Huff's cries for help. They returned just in time to see the crewman torn to pieces by two meat-eating dinosaurs called Compsognathus.

"The scent of blood soon attracted larger, more ferocious carnivores, and the landing party was scattered. My esteemed colleague, Dr. Amos Hagar, world-renowned exobiologist, was consumed by an Allosaurus. I'm sure my dear friend, well known for his after-dinner speeches, delivered a *very* short address on the occasion. Two other crew members, Thomas Valdone and Dr. Gerald Pohl, were killed by two Gorgosaurus, leaving only Captain Coopersmith and Dr. Rebecca Thalberg, a biomedical specialist, alive. They escaped into the thick forest, unable to gain the hatch due to the continued presence of predators. They remained hidden until the illuminating rod grew dim, creating an artificial night. Nocturnal dinosaurs drove them deeper into the primordial forest, and they became lost.

"Colonel Kemp, understandably shocked—"

The door opened.

Keying out of dictation mode, the old man turned to see who his new visitor was.

A beautiful woman, large-breasted and sleepy-eyed, walked into the room, wearing only a nightgown. Her long red hair was mussed. She yawned.

"Oh, Long Jack," she said, stretching. "Last night was wonderful. I'm sooooo happy I met you. Thanks so much for inviting me to visit you here at Neville Base Alpha." She went over to kiss him.

Neville grinned. "They don't call me a hard science fiction writer for nothing." He winked over at a picture of him standing with his buddies Asimov, Clarke, Heinlein, and Pohl, all passed over into that great Valhalla reserved for brilliant SF writers. "Eat your hearts out, guys."

Three

When Colonel Phineas Kemp awoke in a hotel room, he was aware of two things. First of all, he had a hangover, which was unusual.

Second, it wasn't his hotel room.

He exhaled a groan and closed his eyes, trying to shut out the bright morning light seeping around the drapes. Slowly he groped for the memory of last night, buried somewhere in the midst of his headache.

Let's see . . .

Oh yes, the tipsy cab ride into rustic old Georgetown, to a small, relaxed French bistro with a cozy fireplace. Wonderful meal of some kind . . . lots of wine. A vague walk along the C & O canal. Talks of old times, old dreams. A trip up in the elevator of the Four Seasons hotel . . .

All with Rebecca Thalberg.

"Becky," he said and rolled over. Dark hair sprayed on the white linen of the pillow beside him. The splendid curve of a shoulder peeped from above the line of the blanket.

Oh my God, thought Kemp. Now I remember.

The sensations flooded back. It had all been so

familiar—the touch and smell of her, the sound of her voice in his ear. They'd been lovers for so long, it had been so easy, with the numbing influence of the wine, to slide back into the old feelings and needs.

Or, at the very least, the old motions of the same, which they had acted out last night with a passionate vengeance.

His movements awakened her. She sat up. The covers slid off, exposed the vaselike qualities of her naked back, perhaps Phineas Kemp's third favorite sight in the universe.

"Oh," he sighed, turning away.

"Well, good morning, Phineas. You want something from room service?"

"How about a gun?"

"For me or yourself?"

"Never mind. Coffee, juice . . . hell, Becky, you know what I like."

She made the call.

"I'd better put something on," she said as she hit the comm's off button.

"Yeah," Kemp said.

She walked to the bathroom, and Kemp utilized all his willpower not to watch. It brought up too many memories, and the memories brought up the pain he just wasn't willing to face.

When she came out, wearing a bathrobe, he was already in shirt and pants.

She dried her face with a towel. "Well, Phineas, do you want to talk before or after your coffee?"

"I had a wonderful time last night," he muttered, going to the window and looking out.

"I was afraid you'd say that."

"I'm also furious at you. And myself. We shouldn't have let that happen. Damn it, Becky, we're too grown up to let that kind of thing happen between us."

She sat on the bed, and there was a long moment of silence. "Ah, Phineas, I can always count on you to be such a comfort."

"What the hell is that supposed to mean?" He turned on her angrily. "You're the one who was screwing Ian Coopersmith in the urgency of need and survival. And you know, I might have gotten past that. But no, you had to add insult to injury. And now you come back with your tail between your legs, wanting me back."

"Tail between . . ." she said, getting angry. "Look, Phineas, last night was just as much a mistake for me as it was—"

"Oh yeah? You know I'm in love with Mikaela Lindstrom, and you drag me off to a romantic evening and drug me up and . . . You sure didn't act like it was a mistake last night. I've never heard you carry on like that before. What were you doing, imagining yourself making it again with Coopersmith in the primeval jungle?"

"Shut your goddamned stupid mouth!" she screamed at him and then helplessly began to cry.

His head pounded furiously, but his anger was spent. He took a deep breath, then sat beside her. "Look, Becky, I'm sorry. I really didn't mean that." He put his hand on her back.

"Don't touch me!" she said, face buried in her hands. "Just get away, Phineas, please."

"Becky, I guess I just haven't dealt with the pain and the anger properly. And I—"

"Just save it, Phineas, okay? I just don't want to hear it. I've heard your rationalizations for years, your explanations, your goddamned self-serving logic. Just get away from me now."

Room service chose that fortunate moment to interrupt. Kemp poured them both coffee, adding just cream to Becky's.

"Here."

"Thanks," she said, taking the cup.

"He's back with his wife, you know," Kemp said, sitting in a chair. "Wants to get away from this whole business. Won't cooperate with me or anybody. Looks like he's even thinking of quitting the service. Just wants a quiet life now. Get back with the wife and family. Still a nice place, London."

"Phineas, Ian Coopersmith and I . . . well, I told you before. That's over. That's over, we're over. But there are . . ." She sipped her coffee. "After images. Like echoes of a song."

"And so you figured you'd have a sing-along with me, Becky?"

Her dark eyes blazed at him. "I had no intention of seducing you, Phineas Kemp. Besides, you didn't seem to mind very much."

"Too, too true," he said, sipping at the coffee, letting the steam wisp up into his face. "So there's been no one else since Coopersmith?"

Becky shook her head. "I'm too knotted up inside, I guess."

"Becky, it would be different if it weren't for Mikaela. She means a lot to me. In a different way than you. Not better."

"Don't explain, I know."

"And . . . well, I try to keep my promises."

"You going to tell her?"

"I don't know. If it seems right at the time, I will."

"She'll understand, Phineas."

"Yeah. But will I?"

"You just won't give anyone a break, will you?" she said softly. "Not even yourself."

"I have . . . responsibilities."

"Yes. Responsibilities." She got up and picked up her breakfast. "Better eat yours before it gets cold, Phineas. Then you can shower and be about your 'responsibilities,' and we'll just pretend this was a little visit back in time, a sideslip . . . and forget about it. It never happened. We're just partners in this particular enterprise of yours—nothing more, nothing less. I'll do my best in whatever way I can to see that your documentary is the finest possible recording of what happened to us—not personally, of course. And you can discharge these holy 'responsibilities' of yours."

She proceeded to eat her pancakes.

Kemp went to get his plate. He looked at her, her face turned away from him, and there were things he wanted

to say that he didn't have the language for, feelings inside that he wanted to let her know about that seemed so
foolish when he thought about them. As usual, he just
pushed them back to whatever unknown parts of him
they'd emerged from and started getting some starch
into himself to soak up some of his hangover.

After a quick and silent breakfast, Becky got up to
change. "So," she said, all softness cleansed from her
tone. "You can't get Ian for your show. That's too bad.
He's very important."

"Very important, yes," Kemp agreed, wiping syrup
off his lips with a napkin. "And I've implored him. But
he's adamant. 'I just need a lot of time to myself, Colonel,' he told me. 'Yours is the only offer I'm even mar-
ginally inclined to take, and God bloody knows I've had
my share of offers. Try me again in a year or so, maybe.
I've been through too much.' I just can't figure it out,
Becky. It's his duty. To mankind."

"I think Ian has done his duty to mankind, and right
now he just wants to do his duty to himself."

"Maybe if you talked to him," Phineas said, bright-
ening. "Maybe if we both bothered him, we can at least
talk him into taping an interview. I could get my con-
tacts at the BBC to do it. Naturally, I wish he'd come
back to the Dragonstar so we'd have the proper back-
drop, but I'll take what I can get. Will you, Becky? It's
very important to me. Just give him a call."

Becky shrugged. "Sure. Why not? Since I'm on the
team now, I'll be a team player."

Kemp was shocked at how readily she agreed.

God, he thought. She really wants to see him again,
and won't even admit it to herself.

"So," Becky said from the bathroom. "Tonight's
your big dinner with that lady producer. What else have
you got on tap?"

"Oh, an appointment with the President, that's all.
And I'm going to have to get through it with this
hangover."

"Pardon me, Mr. President, while I vomit on your

shoe? Come on, you're Colonel Phineas Ironhead Kemp, Space Commander. Heroes don't get hangovers, and when they do, they can take them like men."

"You know, I never could stand your sarcasm, Becky."

"Right. I'm so good at it. Just a lot of practice, I suppose. And a wonderful target."

"Oh, yes," said Kemp, remembering. "And I've also got this wonderful idea for the show that I have to see if I can pull off. You know how I've always been a real science fiction buff."

"The nuts and bolts variety, yes."

"Well, how does this sound, Becky? For our live transmission from the Dragonstar, showing the Saurians to the world for the very first time, we include an actual live encounter between our reptilian allies and the greatest living science fiction author on Earth, a man esteemed by all countries for his accomplishments and his prophetic powers, a man who was one of the very first to dream about the possibility of all this happening."

"Who would that be, Phineas? You know I prefer historical novels."

"My favorite writer of all time, John T. Neville."

"My God, Phineas, isn't he a thousand years old?"

"No, only just short of a hundred."

"But a trip into space . . . Wouldn't it be a health risk?"

"No, we'll take care of him. You know we've got the most advanced health facilities anywhere. Besides, the guy will absolutely jump at the chance. I mean, after years and years of writing and envisioning aliens, to actually set foot on a spaceship would be the crowning moment of the man's career. Why, I bet we could even get him to write one of his nonfiction books about the whole experience."

"Sound like a good idea to me, Phineas. And this way you get to meet the nice old guy."

"Right. I'm going to call him today. I think I feel

better already, Becky. Sorry I was so upset before."

"I'm sure if we survived two years together and a spaceship full of dinosaurs, plus a hijacked freighter full of TWC terrorists, then we can survive one more night in the sack, Phineas."

Phineas sighed and went to look for his shoes.

Four

"Goddamn friggin' Commies!" John T. Neville said. He walked over to his desk, pulled open a drawer, and took out his old Marine service revolver. His usually sharp eyes were bleary as he stared at the wall. Unsteadily, he aimed his gun and pressed the trigger. The gun barked, kicking in his hand. His LM devices sounded an alarm. "Goddamn enemies of freedom! Well, we'll fight you on the DMZ and we'll fight you in space, and we'll fight—" *Kablam!* "We'll fight you until we drop. I see you, Bischoff, you pinko! You showed them the way to my home." *Kablam!* "Well, you'll not get Long Jack"—*kablam!*—"Neville!"

The apparitions wavered and disappeared. Neville blinked as he wavered a bit unsteadily himself, the smoke from the shots rising up in the room, alerting the smoke alarm, which added its deeper alarm to the strident buzz of the LM system.

Neville shook his fist defiantly toward the ceiling. "You goddamn Russkies are droppin' the big one, huh? Well you're not gonna get me! I've got a fallout shelter that can look hell in the eye. And when the winds blow away the radiation, I'm comin' for you, personally, me and my Freehold, just like in my book. And then—"

The study door was flung open: Nurse Jane Wilkins

stood there aghast, with Susie goggling over her ma-
tronly shoulder.

"Mr. Neville!" Wilkins cried. "Sit down immediately. And put that gun down!"

Shocked by the sudden arrival of these familiar faces,
Neville rocked a moment, then sat down hard in his
composing chair. "Commies," he mumbled. "Everywhere."

Nurse Wilkins advanced upon him in a huff. "Don't
worry, Susie," she said to the woman hanging back in
the doorway. "We keep blanks in the gun. No harm
done." She took the weapon away from Neville, then
checked his machines and made the proper biofeedback
adjustments. Neville immediately relaxed, drowsing a
bit. "Good. We don't have to give him any shots. He
hates shots."

"What happened?" Susie asked.

Nurse Wilkins glanced about, her eyes lighting upon
the nearly empty bottle of fluid in the Jack Daniel's
bottle Neville had been sipping. "Mr. Neville!" she
demanded harshly. "Have you been letting your vitamin fluid ferment again?" She took the bottle and
sniffed it. "No. Just a little too much vitamin stimula-
tion. No harm done. He must be getting very excited
about what he's writing here."

"It's about the Dragonstar," Susie said enthusiastic-
ally. "He's doing it for *Omni*. It looks like he's almost
finished.

"He's such a dear. So wonderfully old-fashioned."
Susie turned to the printout from the CRT and found
the place where she had stopped reading earlier.

"Colonel Phineas Kemp, understandably shocked by
the massacre of the *Heinlein* landing party," the manuscript continued, "ordered mission commanders Fratz
and Bracken to remain on board their ship and not
attempt entry into the alien vessel until a follow-up
expedition could join them. He immediately began
organizing a second team to intercept Artifact One. The
deep-space vessel *Goddard* was selected for the mission,
with Kemp as commander.

"From all indications that I have received from the

IASA, it was at about this time that information concerning Artifact One was leaked to the Third World Confederation, that pack of uncivilized wolves.

"As the *Goddard* was prepared for launch, various scientists and engineers speculated about the immense alien ship, which had assumed the informal code name Dragonstar, since it seemed to be a starship filled with 'the Dragons of Eden,' a name popularized in the twentieth century by my esteemed scientific colleague Dr. Carl Sagan, a somewhat obscure name these days since his conversion to Fundamental Christianity and his renunciation of all previous work in the 'Godless aspect' of science.

"The most popular theory concerning the vessel was that it was an alien specimen ship which visited our solar system approximately 180 million years ago, collecting a vast sample of the flora and fauna of the Mesozoic Era. Leaving our system, the theory said, there must have been an accident that either killed or disabled the crew, or disabled the main engines. In this way the Dragonstar became trapped in an eccentric, cometlike orbit that took it around the sun once every 210 years.

"Meanwhile, inside the gigantic cylindrical ship, Coopersmith and Thalberg struggled to survive, unable to find their way back to the entrance hatch.

The press had a good time with this, uncovering the fact that Rebecca Thalberg had a sexual relationship with Ian Coopersmith at that time. Of course they got it on. And so what? Good-lookin' kids, full of nature's own liquor, hormones, in a steamy environment filled with dangers. Who could blame them?

"And don't feel sorry for Phineas Kemp. From what I've heard, he immediately felt an itch for a paleontologist aboard the *Goddard* named Dr. Mikaela Lindstrom —a damned fine-formed woman, from the pictures I've seen. Anyway, the *Goddard* crew entered the alien ship and set up a base camp around the entrance hatch, using a force-field fence to keep predatory dinosaurs at bay. Lindstrom began a detailed study of the creatures, while the crew's engineers began joining outrigger impulse-engines to the Dragonstar, with which they could break

the immense cylinder from its cometary path and guide
it into a stable L–5 orbit near the Earth. From that position, scientists will study the vessel at their leisure, and
the IASA can protect the vessel from the Chinese and
the TWC.

"There was one problem with this strategy, however.
A 'sleeper' agent for the TWC, Ross Canter, had managed to be placed on the *Goddard* mission, and at the
appropriate time he sabotaged the expedition's communications gear, cutting it off from all contact with
Copernicus Base.

"Almost simultaneously, a group of TWC terrorists
led by Marcus Jashad hijacked an IASA mining vessel,
the *Andromache*, that was parked in lunar orbit. The
TWC ruthlessly murdered the mining ship's crew, except for its captain, Francis Welsh.

"Filled with one hundred trained guerrilla fighters,
the *Andromache* headed out to intercept the Dragonstar. Control of the alien vessel and its secrets of advanced technology—including its stardrive—would give
the TWC the controlling force in world affairs.

"The actual order of the events have not been fully
documented," the narration continued. "However, certain definite facts have been made available to the press.
After many encounters with the local wildlife, Coopersmith and Thalberg reached their destination, the end of
the cylinder, where they hoped they would find a passage to the control section of the mammoth ship. Instead they found a wall isolating the last fraction of the
interior from the dangerous carnivores in the wild.
Guarding this wall were what amounted to intelligent
dinosaurs, popularly known these days as 'Sauries.'
Speculation is that these creatures evolved within the
cylinder from the two-legged dinosaurs called (Sauror-
nithoides.) Slightly more than 2.5 meters tall, they are
fairly smooth-skinned with vestigial scaling. They stand
totally erect, possessing definite shoulders and arm mus-
culature and have three-fingered hands with opposable
thumbs. Their necks are thick and longish, supporting a
birdlike head. Their faces are pointed, but there is no
beak, and their large green eyes are positioned stereo-

scopically under defined brow ridges. Their skulls are large and possess sizable brain capacity.

"With a combination of luck and intelligence, the stranded engineer and doctor established communication with the species, which they found to be organized very much along the lines of the government posited in Plato's *Republic*—workers, soldiers, and scientist-kings. A breakthrough was established with one of these rulers, a 'Saurian' they dubbed Thesaurus, who had access to a passageway in the wall between the Mesozoic environment and the control section of the ship—and seemingly had suffered radiation burns as payment for the knowledge he had attained.

"Colonel Phineas Kemp soon found the lost pair, and with their help began discovering the fascinating secrets of the Saurian race—including a dioramalike teaching device left by the aliens who had constructed the ship, predicting the arrival of creatures from another world, and providing evidence that the aliens had molded the structure of life on earth. I shall return to this later with scientific musings of my own.

"Exploration of the Dragonstar ended with the arrival of the *Andromache* and its treacherous cargo. The TWC army's attempt to take over the Dragonstar failed, thanks to the cooperation of the Saurians and the hunger of the local wildlife, with which Jashad and his compatriots failed to reckon.

"Jashad himself was killed after discovering that the main intention of his mission—to own a stardrive—was fruitless. Dr. Robert Jakes had discovered that, from all signs, the Dragonstar had no stardrive; it was, in fact, what amounted to a virtual test tube for the aliens dabbling in prospective life for the planet Earth—and not, as they had thought, a specimen ship.

"The Dragonstar was placed in a stable orbit. The announcement of its discovery and arrival was made soon after by the IASA, and the rest is generally well documented.

"However, it is the importance of the Dragonstar and its contents in relation to the future that I wish to discuss here, and with this in mind, some scientific facts should be brought into focus.

"Like the hero of my novel *The Sons of Suns*, we suddenly find ourself in a new universe. What we had assumed before . . ."

Susie was distracted from her reading by the sounds of Neville rousing from his beta-wave induced sleep, brought back up by Nurse Wilkins at the LM keyboard.

"There we go, Johnny boy," she said. "I told you not to drink so much of your megavitamin punch. Too much of a good thing is sometimes very bad."

Neville rubbed his full mane of gray hair foggily and grouched, "I wish you wouldn't patronize me, woman. I just got a little too excited about what I was writing, and that's rare these days."

"All the same, please do be more careful in the future."

"This is really fascinating," Susie enthused, rattling the paper in the printer.

"Yes, and I want to get back to finishing it," Neville snarled. "Now you two skedaddle."

The phone rang. Nurse Wilkins picked it up.

"I think you'll want to take this, Johnny," she said to the old man. "Your secretary put the call through—it's from Colonel Kemp."

"What could he want?" Susie wondered.

Neville managed a smug smile as he reached for the receiver. "Good afternoon, Colonel Kemp. I was wondering when you'd call."

Five

Dr. Mikaela Lindstrom looked up hopefully from her lab table at the new arrival. "Did you get anything?"

Lieutenant Lorkner held up a bag. "Just a bit of flesh and gristle. Big as it was, there wasn't much left of that baby. Scavengers got to it last night; we had to chase off a couple of Pteradactyls as it was. I wonder if those things are the ancestors to buzzards. Ornithopter scared off most of them, but a couple were damned tenacious."

"Thank you." Mikaela soberly took the bag and placed it in a specimen freezer. "Considering the events of yesterday, you've rendered service above and beyond the call of duty, Lieutenant."

"I had plenty backing me up in that ornithopter, you can bet on that," Lorkner said, sidling up to glance at the pictures of the dinasaur that had killed his companion. "Evil-looking thing."

"Yes," Dr. Penovich said. "If evil is the unnatural, then this Iguandodon was certainly evil."

"You're sure, then, that it was an Iguanodon?" the lieutenant asked.

"Oh, yes—or at least of that family—a very large Anoplosaurus or Craspedodon perhaps," mused Dr.

Penovich. "Or a type as yet unnamed by modern pale-ontology."

Lorkner shook his head. "Doesn't figure. Where'd it get those teeth and claws, and those sores—to say noth-ing of that disposition. I've seen plenty of Iguanodons since I've been on this lost world. But nothin' like that. I don't even think T. rexes get as wacko bloodthirsty as that thing was."

"That's what we're trying to figure out," Mikaela said. "The sample you've managed to bring back will be of vital importance. In the meantime, Lieutenant, as long as your services are at our disposal, could you check the survey teams to see if any of them have ever encountered a beast looking like this. Not necessarily a bloodthirsty Iguanodon, but anything unnatural or unusual—or anything showing these kinds of cancers and sores."

"Sure. How did the meeting with Colonel Jeffries go?"

Mikaela gazed over at Penovich. "Not well. A repri-mand for recklessness, which I suppose we deserve. And God knows what Colonel Kemp is going to say when he hears about it."

Lorkner shook his head. "Well, Dr. Lindstrom, I guess the colonel knows what it's like to make mistakes that cost lives. He made a number of them concerning the Dragonstar. This damned place is unpredictable, that's all. I suppose I'll be called in for the hearing on the matter. I've made a lot of OTV trips with no fatal outcome. Hell, so did Hagermann. There was simply no way we could have known, and that's what I'm going to tell them."

"Thanks, Lieutenant," Mikaela said. "I appreciate your support. In the meantime, I think we'd better get down to making some scientific sense of what hap-pened. It could be far more serious than just the death of Hagermann, as tragic and terrible as that was."

Penovich nodded and looked down at the photos again. "Yes. I have studied these creatures all my life, and now every time I look at one I will think of yester-day's horrible . . ."

His voice broke, and he looked away.

"Well, we'll just have to be more careful in the future, won't we, Doctor? Hagermann was like me—he knew there were all kinds of risks involved in being in the IASA." Lorkner left, making sure the lab door was closed behind him.

The two paleontologists worked in the lab of the pale-ontological survey camp, located within the Mesozoic preserve, near the original hatchway of Artifact One. The room, previously used for medical purposes, had been restocked with microscopes, beakers, and refrigerators. Specimens of flora and fauna hung preserved in formaldehyde, either already analyzed and dissected or awaiting analysis and dissection. Pictures and charts of fossils hung on the walls; upon these had been tacked photos of the actual creatures they might have represented.

The chemical lab smell was curiously comforting to the paleontologists. Here was where the stuff of scientific study could be performed—safely, in controlled conditions, without their having to worry about being attacked and consumed by the objects of study.

Mikaela began to make ready the instruments she needed to analyze the specimen procured by Lorkner, switching on the electron microscope and washing and drying a slide.

"From the pictures," Dr. Penovich said, "I would judge by the creature's shape that either it was mal-formed or it grew from hatchling state at an extremely accelerated rate for a creature of its size. I'm anxious to see what you find at the cellular level."

"Signs of radiation poisoning of some kind, per-haps," Mikaela said, shutting out her grief and fear with cold duty and scientific curiosity. "I wonder if there's a leak somewhere. There's been no report of one so far."

"With such a large vessel and so few men and equip-ment, it's no wonder," Penovich said. "Something to do with the Illuminator, do you think?"

"Perhaps," Mikaela said, taking out the bag that Lorkner had brought in. "Though if it were the Illuminator, I think we'd have picked up on it a lot sooner.''

She took the hunk of flesh—a terrible mess, but suitable enough—and cut off a sliver with a scalpel, then returned the rest to the freezer. Although the specimen had already been scanned at the entryway for possible harmful viruses, she used plastic gloves and a filter mask. She placed the small sliver of flesh on the slide in a clear solution, then taped on a cover slide and carried it over to the softly humming microscope.

Just as she put the slide in place and was about to focus the microscope the lab phone rang.

"Damn," she said. The phone was closest to her, so she picked it up.

"Paleo lab," she said.

The voice on the other end seemed very distant.

"Hello. Mikaela, is that you?" Despite the amount of static, the voice was recognizably that of Colonel Phineas Kemp, beamed via satellite, with a small delay.

"Yes, Phineas, it's me. I suppose you've heard the bad news."

She had to wait some seconds before the voice responded. "Well, thank God you're okay. I had to hear about it from the President of the United States, and it didn't help my headache much. We're not exactly broadcasting Hagermann's death, but there have been leaks lately, and chances are it will get out, so I want you to prepare a statement—a statement to the effect that this was an abnormal event, and no precursor of things to come. I'm treading a thin line here before I get my presentation special together, and this isn't the kind of thing I need, so we're going to play this real low-keyed, nothing special. Hagermann died in a freak accident. Understand? I'm just telling you that in case some media maniac somehow happens to get hold of you and tries to make a big deal of it."

"Phineas, it might *be* a big deal," Mikaela said. "This was no normal dinosaur that attacked us and killed Hagermann. We're doing some tests now, and we've got pictures. Dr. Penovich can attest to all of this."

Penovich looked over at her as she waited for Kemp's

reply. "He can be terribly stubborn sometimes," she explained.

Finally, Kemp's voice erupted through the static. "Mikaela, please. I'm in a delicate situation. I need your support. How can we possibly know a normal dinosaur from an abnormal one? I'm not telling you to cover anything up. I'm just telling you not to make any waves that aren't necessary. Over and out."

Mikaela sighed with aggravation. "Very well, Phineas. But please check back with us later on this. I have uneasy feelings about it. Over and out."

She hung up the phone.

"What's the trouble?" Penovich wanted to know.

"Oh, our great leader doesn't want anything to muck up his special documentary," Mikaela said with exasperation.

"I don't blame him," Penovich said thoughtfully. "World attitude will be very vital not only in terms of funds provided for proper maintenance and study of the Dragonstar, but to contain the uneasy religious and political questions it poses."

"Too true," Mikaela said. "But a mammoth ego is also on the line, I think."

"Ah—you mean Colonel Kemp's ego. Perhaps. But only those with outsized self-images can dare great things."

"And squash other people on the way. No, wait, I'm being unfair, Dr. Penovich. I'm sure he's preoccupied and just doesn't have the time to spare for seemingly small matters. God knows, he's seen enough deaths on this ship. He's probably inured to them. Our duty is to see if indeed this represents something to be concerned about in our general attitude toward the Dragonstar."

"I sincerely hope not," Dr. Penovich said. "I should like to absorb myself in quiet study. This was my hope for my visit here. Yet already I find myself yearning to return to Prague. This is ironic, no?"

Mikaela sighed, then went back to the electron microscope and adjusted it, fitting her eyes to the viewer.

The image quickly swam into focus, and she adjusted

the controls for the clearest presentation possible. It didn't take long to note that at least half the cells seemed of an aberrant nature. She focused on the nucleus of one and increased the magnification. With this baby, you could get down to the chromosomal level. She gazed for a while at what she saw, disbelievingly, then tried the nucleus of another aberrant cell. The anomaly was consistent in both.

"Dr. Penovich," she said after taking a deep breath. "Could you come here and look at this, please?"

Six

In the backyard of his home in East Acton, London, Ian Coopersmith was trying to teach cricket to his two sons, Geoffrey, ten, and Brian, eight. They seemed less than overwhelmed by the sport.

"You see . . ." he said. "You see, Geoff, you hold the bat and guard the wicket. I try to bowl the stick off, and Brian can field, and—"

"Father, I've seen this game on telly," Brian complained, "and it's ever so boring. Geoff and I like football. Let's play that."

"But boys, cricket is my favorite," said the tall, muscular man, disappointedly gazing at the football by the garden. "And I'd really like to teach it to you. I used to play it at school. Don't you remember the pictures I showed you?"

"Oh yes," said Geoffrey, a slim and sturdy lad who seldom smiled. "Star batsman and all that, you've told us. But really, Father, cricket is just old hat, and besides, it's much too English for me. If I told my friends at school you were teaching us cricket, they'd just laugh themselves silly. I mean, cricket is the sort of game Prime Minister O'Dowd plays, and who wants to be like the old boy, with all his funny clothes?"

Coopersmith tossed the cricket ball away. He let go of his anger. After all, he was trying to get closer to his children, not alienate them. They'd grown up so much in the time that he'd been away. And many times during his absence he'd thought he'd never see Brian and Geoff—or their mother, Leticia—again. That's why he was back here at home now, why he'd made preparations to resign from the IASA and was looking for a job in London. To make up for the time he'd lost, to try to find his life back on Earth again.

He clapped his hands with an air of exasperated gaiety. "Right, then. Football it is. I suppose we can get Brian to exercise a little more—he's getting rather roly-poly of late. Eh, Brian?"

"He eats far too many sweets, Father," said Geoff.

"Oh, shut up, Geoff. I'll tell him about your little dolly girl."

They began kicking the ball around, and Geoffrey managed to plant an accidental-on-purpose kick in Brian's shin. Brian collapsed in exaggerated tears.

"Now what the devil was that all about, Geoff?" Ian demanded after making sure his youngest wasn't maimed.

"God, you look at the little wimp cross-eyed and he breaks into tears. It was just an accident anyway, Father, you needn't beat me." He looked down at Ian's tight grip on his forearm. "Mother strongly disapproves of that sort of discipline, you know."

"Well, I don't, and the next time I catch you doing anything like that, I'm going to . . ."

Suddenly he was aware of his wife's presence at the back door. Leticia was watching him expressionlessly, as though waiting to see what he was going to do next.

"Phone call, Ian," she said, her arms crossed.

"If it's another from the media, tell them simply no comment," Ian said, letting go of his oldest son's arm.

"It's Winston Arnold, Ian," she said.

"Well, in that case I'd better talk to him." Arnold was actually a friend. Coopersmith had known him a long time. They even had the same school tie, though that had just been a joke. He was with the BBC, and he seldom used his friendship with Ian to get any kind of information. Maybe this was about something other than the Dragonstar.

"You should invite Winnie over for dinner sometime," Leticia suggested, a smile coming naturally to her attractive oval face.

"Excellent idea," Coopersmith said, striding past her into their model kitchen, done in shades of blue and green. He picked up the receiver. "Hello there, Winnie. Thanks so much for the nice letter. You did a wonderful job on that story. The only decent one I've seen."

"Oh, super, Ian, because I rather have a favor to ask," came the less than cheerful voice over the phone.

"Something wrong, old boy?"

"Well, normally I wouldn't do this with you—you changing your phone number for privacy and everything—but Ian, I've been put under a bit of pressure to at least approach you on the subject."

"Subject? You mean the Dragonstar? Winnie, I told you all that I'm ever going to tell anyone."

"Yes, yes, Ian, I know. But there's been a leak concerning some incident of violence on the ship. IASA hasn't released anything official yet, and I thought you might know something specific."

"Violence? What sort of violence?"

"Then you've heard nothing about it?"

"No."

"Oh, good. Well then, I feel much relieved. I can just tell the top boys that and they'll get off my back. Believe me, it was hard to touch you up again on the subject."

Ian's voice tensed. "What kind of violence, Winston?"

"Oh, I believe some dinosaur killed some IASA member."

"Who?"

"Don't know yet . . . some lieutenant was about all that leaked."

Lieutenant. Coopersmith felt relieved. Thank God it wasn't Becky.

Winston continued, "I guess you heard about Phineas Kemp's news conference last night."

"Who could avoid it?"

"And you're still not going to become involved in the IASA's documentary?"

"Because it's my duty? I've told you, Winnie, I feel that my duty has been done. All my statements have been made. They can just read them. Get an actor to do a dramatic recreation. I just don't care. I don't want—"

"Message received, Ian. As I say, I'm really sorry to bother you like this."

"I know, I know. Pressure. You're just doing your job. That's okay, Winnie, you saved me from a bit of a row with my boys. Just a moment. As long as I've got you, maybe I could give you my truly final statement—sort of an addenda to your article."

"Oh, super! The tabloids will pee their pants. Fire away, old boy."

"As you know, Winnie, it was Dr. Thalberg and I who first made contact with the Saurians. No one else has had such . . . intimate experience with them."

"Yes, yes. So what?"

"So that makes me, I think, the authority on the subject. Correct?"

"I would say so, yes."

"Well, I've been viewing with great dismay this whole phenomenon of exploitation surrounding the creatures. It's demeaning and condescending—all these T-shirts, toys, costumes, kiddie cartoon shows. Now, I'm sure the Saurians don't really care much, even if they did know about this ruckus. But I care about it, and this is just part of the reason why I'm having nothing to do with Phineas Kemp's sideshow."

"May I quote you?"

"Maybe tone down that last bit, Winnie. I'm just not a Saurie Friend. Put *this* down for the record, though. I found the Saurians to be a fascinating, worthwhile race, from whom we have much to learn, and to whom we can teach much. But they are by no stretch of the imagination cute anthropomorphic beasts. They're sentient reptiles. Nothing more and certainly nothing less. Period.''

"Oh bravo, Ian. I can see the headline now. 'The Black Sheep of the Dragonstar Team Speaks Up.' ''

Coopersmith cheerfully extended Leticia's suggested dinner invitation, then rang off. His wife was preparing tea at the stove.

"Those two aren't at each other again, are they?" he asked as he noticed she was gazing out the window into the backyard.

"Oh, no. They're playing nicely," she said, turning her usual pleasant smile his way. She was so damned nice all the time. But how could you complain about someone being continually pleasant? That was one of the reasons he had married her—her genuine benevolence.

"I guess you heard my conversation with Winston," he said.

"Most of it. Of course, I'd heard your opinion about the Saurie Fan Clubs before. For someone who's cut all ties with the Dragonstar affair, you certainly retain strong emotions on the subject. Would you care for some tea, dear? And we've got some nice biscuits, so could you put them out? They're Brian's particular favorites.''

This frigid tone to her voice was about as nasty as she ever got, so Ian called her on it. "Right, Letty. What's troubling you?"

"I thought we'd talked all that out, Ian," she said as he rummaged through the bread box. "And I told you that I thoroughly understood what was past and what was present in regard to your commitments.''

He found the biscuits—cream-filled chocolate—and began putting them out on a plate. "I can tell by your tone, Letty.''

She paused for a moment in setting cups on saucers and then said, "I suppose it was your tone as well. You were worried about Rebecca Thalberg, weren't you? Being involved in that violent incident.''

"You eavesdrop well.''

"You were loud enough for the children to eaves-drop. Besides, that's not the point. I suppose, Ian, I'm still wondering if you really are through with the Dragonstar."

"What's that supposed to mean?" Ian asked, crinkling the cellophane up and tossing it in the garbage bin.

"It's all very well to say that you're trying to get away from it, Ian, redeem your life at home—but perhaps what Colonel Kemp says is right. It's not over, and by trying to hide from your duty, and your feelings toward those you worked with, you are ultimately tearing up the good person you are inside."

"But, Letty, you know what happened on that alien ship. I . . . I . . ."

"You fell into another woman's arms. I know, and don't think it doesn't hurt. But I really didn't care who you'd slept with when you got back—just as long as you were back. If it will help any, I should tell you that I allowed myself to be comforted once or twice while you were away."

Ian had been eating one of the biscuits, and he found himself suddenly bereft of appetite in mid-bite. "Oh. Who . . ." He couldn't finish the sentence.

Letty smiled at him. "No, maybe not. And not sexually at any rate. Though I know that's always possible. No, Ian, I've thought about this, and even though I would like you to stay far away from that Thalberg woman, and though I'd like to scratch her eyes out, reserve be damned, I know that until you are complete about all of this you'll just never be all here."

Ian thought for a moment. "You want me to stay with the IASA?"

"If that's what you want. But don't you think that a better idea would be to speak with Colonel Kemp, see what he wants? A brief return to the Dragonstar . . . a few lines spoken . . . just finish things up . . . and then you can really, I think, make up your mind as to where you really stand on your efforts to get things right at home. This will probably be your only chance, Ian, and God knows it's part selfishness that has me saying these things, because if you're here, I'd like all of you here."

"If that's the way you feel, Letty," Ian said, non-plussed.

"Ninny, it's not the way I feel that counts right now —it's the way *you* feel." She shook her head and began pouring the tea.

He thought for a moment, and then he said, "I guess you're right."

Seven

Colonel Phineas Kemp drove through the open countryside of Northern California. He had keyed in the coordinates for the home of John T. Neville, and the
on-board CPU was controlling his automobile as it
negotiated the electronic highways north of San Fran-
cisco. He was currently passing through the legislated
Agricultural Preserves of Mendocino County, and he
enjoyed watching the endless sky above him and the
gently rolling hills of lettuce and corn and other vege-
tables. Sometimes he enjoyed doing the driving himself,
if the road represented any kind of a challenge, but on a
straight-line highway like EI-State 101, driving was just
plain boring.

   His thoughts drifted back to the Dragonstar and the
international affair that had sprung up around the great
ship. Sometimes Phineas felt that the whole affair had
become a genuine, royal pain—exciting, challenging,
but a disruption in his life nonetheless. The Dragonstar
was an intruder, and it had threatened to disrupt his
grand design for success and fame. Thankfully, Phineas
had played a great part in working things out, wresting
what could have been a career-ruining fiasco from the
clichéd jaws of defeat.

Now, he thought smugly, this documentary project would put him back on the world's center stage. He had total and absolute control over the project, and he was feeling very good.

Yes, he thought with a smile, history cannot forget me now.

He had first realized that three days ago, sitting at dinner with Kate Ennis. They had been dining at a posh restaurant in the Adams-Morgan section of Washington, D.C., and Kate had been so damned effusive over his accomplishments, his career, and his future, that he had begun thinking that he truly did have "great man" possibilities. Kate had wanted to discuss his ideas for the documentary, and she had been extremely supportive of those ideas. Phineas himself had not been certain that his ideas would fly—after all, he was not a media person, a director or actor or anything of the sort. Yet he had always thought he could succeed in any of those professions without much of a problem. Nothing like running a moonbase, that was for sure. And certainly not as demanding.

He recalled their conversation with pleasure.

"What do you want the documentary to say about you in particular, Colonel?" Kate had asked over the French onion soup.

"Well," Kemp said, trying to be as modest as possible, "it's not really so important that my ego is gratified. No, I would much rather it be made obvious that I am involved in something that is invaluable to the fate of mankind. I would be happy, really, if people were to reflect back on all this and say, 'Old Phineas Kemp, he certainly did his bit.' "

Kate smiled. She certainly was an attractive woman. In fact her dark hair and striking features reminded him of Becky, not in any singular characteristic, but because they were the same type of woman.

"Well, that was well phrased, Colonel." Kate laughed politely. "But what I was thinking about was the narration. Do you see yourself in that role?"

Kemp would have loved to have narrated the worldwide broadcast, but he knew his voice was a bit on the reedy side. He was familiar enough with audio-visual presentations to know that they were always more effective when you could employ a rich, attention-getting baritone.

"Actually, no," he said. "I don't think I've got the voice for it, and I think it would be more effective if I were interviewed just like the other members of the crew."

Kate Ennis smiled and nodded her agreement at this point, so Phineas decided to push a bit further toward endearing her to him. "Besides," he said with a quick grin, "don't you think the words 'Colonel Phineas Kemp' would sound good spoken in the rolling tones of a famous dramatic actor?"

He was interrupted from his thoughts by a warning buzzer on the console of the Oldsmobile. Looking down at the colorful readout displays, he saw that he was fast approaching the off ramp for the road to Neville's home. Kemp reached out and grasped the steering wheel, resuming control of the vehicle. He eased across the lanes of the freeway and slipped onto the off ramp, following the signs to Westport, a small town on the Pacific coastline.

The town itself looked as if it hadn't changed in fifty years, and had a quaintness to it that seemed out of place in the modern world. Kemp wondered why a world-famous science fiction writer like Neville would want to live in a place like this. He would have imagined that someone like Neville would want to have his digs in a modern sky-rise condo, or even one of the new oceanic cityplexes that were so popular on the East Coast.

But as Kemp drove through the town, he could see how a writer might like a village like Westport. It was obviously some sort of artists' colony. There were countless shops and boutiques selling all manner of hand-crafted wares and *objets d'art*. The prices were stupendous, but it was getting difficult to find good artisans' work anymore. Kemp also noticed a preponderance of young people, especially young women adorned in the latest chic fashions, which was to say, very little at all. Kemp slowed to a very decent cruising speed, ogling the passersby. More than a few of the young women smiled at him. They hadn't acted like that when *he* was a college student.

Well, this was no time to be dallying, Phineas thought. He checked his map on the dashboard monitor, keying in the exact location of Neville's house and watching it light up on the screen. Kemp turned off the main boulevard, headed north along a quiet residential street, then left along a narrow road cut into the side of a sheer rock face. The road hugged the side of the cliff, winding and snaking gradually upward, finally opening up on a small plateau topped by a sculptured mound of earth.

Atop this mound was "Neville Base Alpha," as the estate-fortress of John T. Neville had been named by the well-known author, raconteur, and television personality. He had another home in Manhattan dubbed "Neville Base Beta," and Phineas assumed that if the eccentric man ever decided to set up a third residence it would be called "Gamma."

The estate was an architectural dream—the confluence of many planes and angles, great panes of passive solar glass, clerestories, heat stacks, and decks. The main building was surrounded by a moat filled with water and protected by an electrified fence. There was a single entrance, overlooked by a small guardhouse and a single oriental fellow in a security uniform which looked suspiciously like the uniform of the "dreaded Hardji of the planet Darskath." The Hardji were a concoction of Neville's, having appeared in one of his most famous tetralogies, *The Darskath Interregnum*.

Phineas had read that series of novels when he was a young lad in Canada, and he had assumed since then that he had seen the last of the dreaded Hardji—until he pulled up to the guardhouse.

"Colonel Phineas Kemp, IASA. I'm here to see Mr. Neville," he said casually to the guard, who peered

down at him through the black glass of his helmet visor
while training what looked to be some sort of disintegra-
tor weapon at his face.

"Yes, sir, Mr. Neville is expecting you. But first I
must see some identification."

Phineas smiled as he reached for his billfold in his
breast pocket.

"Easy," said the Hardji. "Now bring it out reeeeeal
slow."

"For Christ's sake," Phineas said, handing over his
IASA ID plate, "it's just my fucking wallet."

Ignoring the comment, the guard studied his ID, then
nodded as he handed it back. "All right, sir. Mr. Neville
will be waiting for you on the lower deck. Just follow
the drive around to the left and pull up in the space
marked Earth Visitors."

"Right-o," Phineas said. "Earth Visitors it is."

Accelerating and cutting hard on the wheel, Phineas
moved quickly away from the guardhouse, crossed over
the drawbridge and moat, and followed the perimeter of
Neville's house until he found the parking lot adjacent
to the lower deck.

As he rolled to a stop, he saw the sliding glass doors
open on the lower deck and an odd-looking figure appear. After all these years, he was finally meeting the
author who had thrilled and inspired him as a boy.
Despite his case-hardened exterior, Phineas felt a surge
of emotion race through him, and he would have sworn
his heartbeat jumped just a tad.

Stepping from the car, he watched Neville approach.
The writer was a tall man with broad shoulders and a
moon face. He had a large, loose-limbed frame, and his
clothes hung upon him as if they were still dangling in a
closet. Neville had long hair that frizzed out in all directions, and his eyes had a bulging, hyperthyroid aspect.
He walked with an arm-swinging, rollicking gait that
suggested that he had suffered a stroke or two, but there
was a free-spirited energy radiating from him like sunlight.

"Colonel Kemp, welcome to Neville Base Alpha!"

The writer extended a large, bony hand and shook
Kemp's. There was surprising strength in his grip.

"Sir, it's a pleasure to meet you. Please, call me
Phineas." He looked carefully at the old man. In one
moment Neville looked every bit of his ninety-plus
years, and in the next he appeared decades younger.
There was a mercurial aspect to him—he seemed to be
forever changing.

"Glad to, Phineas. Why don't we come inside?"

Neville led the way into a room filled with
memorabilia from long ago—framed paintings of book
covers, original magazine illustrations, plaques, photographs, and other pieces of the past. Phineas felt like he
was walking through a wing of a museum. He spotted a
painting of a familiar cover—a book he had read in the
eighth grade called *The Scaling of the Xedrin*. He had
never forgotten the wonderful intricacies of the plot or
the ingenious aliens Neville had dreamed up for that
one.

"You know, I remember reading this one when I was
twelve years old," Phineas said, pointing to the painting.

"Ah yes, the golden age," Neville cried.

"What's that?"

Neville chuckled. "The golden age of science fiction."

"Oh, you mean back in the nineteen forties?" asked
Kemp.

"No, dear fellow. The golden age of science fiction is
twelve. That's the time when most of us discover it, and
that's when it's best for us, right?"

"Yes, I suppose so."

"Nothing to suppose. Look at all the adolescent male
fantasies we used to write about. All those spaceships
that looked like our dongs? Do you think that was an
accident? Fuck, no!"

Neville wheeled erratically and began walking down a
long hall, motioning Phineas to follow. They entered a
large room decked out with the latest communications
and media gear—laser decks, computer consoles, tele-

com centers, monitors, hologrammers. It looked like
the bridge of a movie spaceship from the eighties. At the
opposite end of the room was a desk where a middle-
aged woman dressed in nurse's white was sitting studying a computer monitor.

"This is the nerve center of the whole operation,"
Neville said. "I call it the bridge. Pretty nifty, eh?"

"Impressive, yes." Phineas was getting a kick out of
the old guy, and smiled easily.

"And that old bag over there in the white clothes is
my nurse, Ms. Jane Wilkins. Say hello to the colonel,
Nurse Jane."

The woman stood up and smiled wanly. "You'll have
to forgive Dr. Neville, Colonel. He's just had his nap,
and he's always a bit high-strung when he first gets up."

"High-strung? Listen, Colonel, Ms. Wilkins thinks I
reached this ripe old age by playing by the rules, see?
She doesn't realize that I smoked a couple of packs a
day for sixty years. That I could hold more Jackie D.
than any writer since Dick R. Gordon."

Phineas laughed politely and searched for a place to
sit down, selecting a couch in front of what was obviously Neville's command chair and desk console.

"Ah . . . Dr. Neville, I think I'd—"

"Listen, Phineas, don't bother with the 'Doctor'
business. I only make Nurse Wilkins do that when I'm
feeling feisty." Neville laughed at his small joke,
reached down behind the desk, and produced a two-liter
bottle of Jack Daniels. When he noticed Kemp watching
him with an expression of genuine surprise, he smiled
and paused before putting it to his lips. "Hah! Don't
worry about this. It's not really Jackie D. I just keep my
vitamin gruel in the old bottles. Kinda makes me think
of the good old days when I could keep a fifth of that
shit next to my chair leg and type out a whole book in
one sitting. Sometimes I'd sit there for twenty-four,
maybe forty-eight hours straight, just to meet a
deadline. And ole Jack would always see me through.
Some people said they were my best works—the ones I
wrote when I was blind drunk. Funny how literature is,
isn't it?"

"Yes it is," Phineas said. "Now, I was wondering if we might get the particulars of this event ironed out."

"What's to get ironed out? You want me to star in your documentary, right?"

Phineas cleared his throat. "Well, not exactly star, but you would play a significant role. I'd like to arrange for you to meet with the leaders of the Saurians, and we would record the historic event live for a worldwide television audience."

Neville rolled his slightly bulging eyes for a moment, then smiled broadly. "Of course. I knew I wasn't the star, but I wanted to have a bit of fun with you."

"Very well." Phineas was beginning to have enough of the old gaffer's humor and just plain nuttiness. "What we have planned is for you to be picked up next week by one of our IASA limo-jets. You would then be flown down to Vandenberg AFB and taken on board one of the lunar shuttles. You would be met at Copernicus Base by some of my officers and staff, and we would personally escort you up to the Dragonstar, which is orbiting at Lagrange Point 5. You would arrive in plenty of time—enough to afford you ample opportunity to tour the lunar installations as well as a complete inspection of the Dragonstar itself."

Neville did not reply, but simply sat watching him with a strange look on his face.

"Is there something wrong?" Phineas asked.

"Wrong? No, of course not. It's just that I've never been in space before. Seems kind of silly, doesn't it? The world's greatest SF writer, and he's never been in space."

Neville threw back his head and laughed somewhat maniacally. Then he stopped suddenly and stared at Phineas with a look of mock seriousness. For a moment, the man looked quite mad.

Phineas didn't know what to do. "Well, there's a first time for everything," he heard himself saying.

"What's the matter, Doctor?" Nurse Wilkins asked. "You're not becoming afraid in your declining years, are you?"

This seemed to ignite something in Neville. He

erupted like a dormant volcano. "What? Long Jack Neville afraid of anything?"

The writer moved to his feet quickly. Some lights on a console by Nurse Wilkins started blinking, and a warning klaxon began to bleat out its insistent message that something was amiss.

"Watch it, Doctor," nurse Wilkins said. "You're setting off your life-support monitors."

She made a few radio-remote adjustments to her console and Neville started to calm down. The klaxon died out, and Neville stared solemnly at Phineas.

"Never let it be said that Long Jack Neville was afraid to go out into fucking space." The writer's face was somewhat contorted, and the life-support monitors chimed lightly. Then he relaxed again.

Phineas had to laugh openly as he watched and listened to old Neville. The guy was a real character, that was for certain. "Please, sir," Phineas said softly. "Take it easy. No one's going to be saying anything of the sort."

"Of course not," Neville gathered his composure once again. "If the truth be known, I'd be ready to go instantly. When am I supposed to get down to Vandenberg?"

Phineas grinned. "ASAP, sir. I can have a limo-jet up here within the hour if you'd like."

"That fast, eh? Well, I suppose I'll have to pack, and things like that . . . and I'll be needing to take along my life-support monitors, and probably the old bag over there as well."

"No problem with that," Phineas said. "Have you ever wanted to take a trip to the Moon, Ms. Wilkins?"

The nurse giggled appreciatively, and for a moment appeared to be a young girl again. "God, yes. You won't have to ask *me* twice. Do you think I'll be able to see the Sauries?"

Phineas winced at the mention of the media word for the Saurians, but he covered it quickly with a smiling nod. "Oh yes, if you're going to be accompanying the good doctor, I don't see how you could miss them."

Neville took a long pull from his Jack Daniel's bottle and seemed to sink a little deeper into his command console chair. "Well, then, I guess there's not much else to discuss, is there, Colonel?"

"Just when you would like to leave?"

"Couldn't I wait until you're ready to go back, and just ride with you?" For the first time Neville seemed to be less manic, more concerned and serious.

Phineas sighed audibly. "Normally, perhaps, but I have some additional business to take care of here on Earth. I'm going to be running from place to place for the next few days, and I didn't want you to be bored—being dragged around with me. That's why I arranged the private jet and the rest of your itinerary."

"Oh, I see. That was very thoughtful of you."

"Well, we tried to think of everything. Believe me, Dr. Neville, the IASA and the World Media Corporation would be honored to have you participate in our project."

Neville's eyes brightened a bit. "Yes, you're right, Colonel. It is only fitting that I be part of the programming." The writer stood up and walked to a collection of photographs of men in baggy suits, white shirts, and skinny ties. Everyone had short haircuts, horn-rimmed glasses, and pear-shaped bodies. Neville pointed to several of the framed photos. "You know who these guys are?"

Phineas looked closely at the old black-and-white prints. The men appeared to be standing on some forgotten street corner in Brooklyn. "No, I can't say that I do."

"That collection of first-class nerds is First Fandom. I came along a little too late to really be a part of them, but they soon adopted me and all the other great writers of the forties and fifties. They knew brilliance when they encountered it, and they accepted me into their select fold, Colonel. They believed in the Future with a capital F! And I *owe* it to them to be a part of your documentary project. Don't you see that?"

Phineas wasn't certain what the old man was getting

at, but he did the most diplomatic thing he could think of and nodded with a great show of affirmation.

Neville sucked in a long breath, filling his bony chest with air, and exhaled grandly. "Very well, Colonel, let's be off on our great adventure. Ms. Wilkins, pack all my shit! We're going into Space—The Final Frontier."

"Well," Phineas said as Neville eased into his command console chair. "I think I'll be leaving now. I've got plenty of work to do before getting back up to Copernicus Base."

"Are you sure you won't stay for lunch? My servo-kitchens are preparing a wonderful lunch of vitamin-paks and pureed fruits. But I'm sure we could dig up a hamburger for a red-blooded astronaut like yourself."

"I appreciate the offer, Doctor, but I have a previous engagement. Thank you just the same." Phineas realized that he had suddenly had quite enough, thank you, of Long Jack Neville.

The writer was struggling to his feet once again. "All right, then. I know a busy man when I see one. But at least I can give you a copy of my newest novel, *The Robots of Sphereworld*."

Before Phineas could reply, Neville was moving across the room to an immense series of glass-fronted bookshelves. He pressed a button, one of the segments slid open, and the shelf slid forward. The writer reached up and pulled a hardcover book down from the shelf and handed it to Kemp, who noticed that the cover illustration was garish and brightly colored.

"Here you are, Colonel. And if you'll notice, it's already autographed for your convenience, and mine.

Phineas could not resist opening the book to the first page, which was inscribed in a bold but spidery hand:

> *To My Good Friend, Best Wishes,*
> *Long Jack Neville*

Interesting that we've become such good friends so quickly, Phineas thought.

"Why, thank you, sir. I'll read this on my way back

to Vandenberg. And now, I'm afraid I must be going. Ms. Wilkins, here is a card with the coded exchange for Vandenberg. Call when you're ready to depart, and they'll scramble up a limo-jet for you.''

The nurse took the card and nodded as she escorted Phineas from the room and down the hall. He could hear the shambling footsteps of Neville close behind. When they reached the sliding glass doors of the lower deck, Phineas shook the author's hand, waved politely to his nurse, and moved to his vehicle.

God, it was good to get out of there. Almost a hundred years old and getting more senile by the minute. How in hell did he still write coherent books? He must have periods of lucidity followed by mental lapses when his thoughts went banging around like Ping-Pong balls in a vacuum chamber.

Phineas exhaled slowly as he flipped on the electric engines of the Oldsmobile and eased down the driveway past the guardhouse. The Hardji warrior waved at him, and Phineas accelerated away from the zany place as quickly as he could.

Eight

So much had happened since the first time Dr. Robert Jakes had stepped inside this place.

He stood at the entrance to the aft section of the giant alien ship called the Dragonstar. When his team of IASA scientists had first found the entrance, it was disguised as part of a temple, which was overseen by the priest class of the Saurians.

The Barrier, a great wall which the Saurians' ancestors had constructed more than a thousand years earlier, separated their pre-electric culture from the wild jungle that occupied the majority of the immense cylinder's interior. The Barrier also fenced in the control section of the Dragonstar—the end of the ship that housed the alien crew quarters, the ship's great engines, and other command functions.

The section in which Jakes and his team now worked and lived was in fact the heart of the Dragonstar. It was a vast area laced with corridors and shafts and honeycombed with cells and compartments, which to this day had not been completely investigated. Because of the immense size of the alien vessel, it might take years to fully discover all that might be contained within its myriad cells.

And yet, in a surprisingly short time, Dr. Jakes and his team had been able to discover a significant number of facts about the ship, and some tenable theories to accompany the facts. First thought to be a specimen-collecting ship, the Dragonstar was soon discovered to be a seed ship: a gigantic star-faring life factory which possibly had moved from one stellar system to the next, seeding suitable planets with life forms which had been produced within the confines of the ship.

It was Robert Jakes himself who had discovered the alien dioramas—great kinetic, three-dimensional displays that sensed the presence of intelligent brain activity and then began doling out information in visual displays. Jakes called them "teaching devices," but their original function may have been something altogether different.

Yes, thought the scientist, in the beginning this whole damned place was my playground—now I've got to share it with a whole army of others. *C'est la vie.*

Indeed, there were now specialists in such diverse fields as paleontology, archeology, anthropology, biology, microbiology, and botany—as well as chemists, physicists, and engineers of all types swarming about the aft section like bees in a hive.

This division of labor freed Jakes to conduct his investigations and experiments without trying to worry about other questions that might be outside his area of expertise.

What most intrigued Jakes were the huge clusters of engines affixed to the rear of the giant cylinder. Each giant cone was more than a kilometer in length, and there were twelve clusters of ten cones in each. His initial assessment that these engines were of a conventional design and function was now under serious question, both by himself and his chief project assistant, Dr. Mishima Takamura. Although the engines seemed to be totally inert and incapable of function, Dr. Takamura's people had been able to conduct some preliminary tests that indicated the possible existence of an interstellar drive.

Faster than light. Every time Jakes considered the concept he felt chills up and down his spine. Logic told him that it was plainly impossible.

But, of course, an alien ship 320 kilometers long and 65 kilometers in diameter was also an "impossibility," until one showed up falling down the gravity well.

Dr. Jakes was pulled from his thoughts by the approach of several technicians, who were riding in an electric van up a large ramp from the old Saurian temple. The van stopped beside Jakes, and a young woman climbed out. She was lean, blond, and pale. The name COWAN was stenciled on the breast pocket of her coveralls.

"Excuse me, Dr. Jakes, I was wondering if you've got a minute," the young woman said.

"Sure, Angie." Jakes smiled, wishing that he wasn't feeling as old as his sixty-six years. "What can I do for you?"

The woman hesitated for a second, then continued. "Well, it might not be anything, but I thought you might want to know about it anyway. Sam and I were down in the village this morning, and we saw a couple of the Saurians kind of 'razz out,' if you know what I mean. Really go nuts right in the middle of the outdoor marketplace. It took about twenty other guys to take 'em down. I think they had to kill one of them. It was pretty bad."

Jakes shrugged. "Well, I'm no expert on those kinds of things, but maybe it's just part of that R-complex ritual that Captain Coopersmith observed."

Angie Cowan shook her head. "I don't think so, Dr. Jakes. I've been up here with the Sauries for six months now, and I've seen the cycles they go through. They seem real prepared for them, what with the special tunics and all. It all seems pretty ordered. This was more like a . . . like a psychotic episode, you know?"

"All right, why don't you make out a report and send it up to my lab. I'll see that it gets to Dr. Lindstrom's people. You never know, there might be something to it."

Angie Cowan smiled and moved back toward the van. "Thanks, Doctor. The whole thing was kind of upsetting, and I thought somebody ought to know about it. Catch you later."

Dr. Jakes waved as the van wheeled off, leaving him at the entrance to the aft section. He was due back at the laboratory for a meeting with Mishima, and he hated to be late for appointments.

The chief engineering labs had been set up in a large series of rooms adjacent to the section they called the engine rooms. It was the last series of cells before the superstructure of the engines themselves. The chief engineering labs represented the only area inside the Dragonstar in which Jakes and his people had tampered with the original equipment. They had remodeled the area to suit their purpose of experimentation and testing. Portable power-paks, generators, racks of electronics, bubble chambers, control consoles, and recording gear filled every available space.

This was the place where all the basic research was going on, and Jakes often said that if there were going to be any great breakthroughs on the many mysteries of the Dragonstar, most of them would begin in the lab.

It was a quiet series of rooms. The staff went about their assignments determined to do the best they could under the circumstances. New equipment and gear were almost constantly being shuttled in, and with each passing week the research team became better armed in the battle against ignorance.

The biggest problem, mused Jakes as he entered his office, a small area sealed off by portable screens, was attempting to contemplate the alien mind. Everything he and his people discovered on the monstrous ship would be interpreted through the human experience—and 90 percent of the time that interpretation would be wrong. The idea that you were dealing with a totally different way of looking at the universe took some getting used to.

"Ah, there you are," said a familiar voice, interrupting Jakes's thoughts. Mishima Takamura stood at the doorway. Jakes removed his glasses and slowly massaged his temples. Glasses were an anachronism in the twenty-first century, but Jakes had been wearing them since he was five years old, and he felt absolutely naked without them. Besides, they made him look a bit eccentric, and he was so damned ordinary that he believed he needed something to make him stand out. At least this way he was always remembered as the guy with the glasses.

Takamura took a chair opposite the desk. Jakes liked Mishima very much, and he was pleased when he had been able to pry the young physicist loose from his work at Caltech and bring him up here. Hundreds of physicists had applied to work on board the Dragonstar, but Takamura had been Jakes's only choice as chief project assistant. Not only was Mishima brilliant, but he was a cultured man and a great conversationalist.

"The esteemed Dr. Takamura," Jakes said with a smile. "You've been leaving E-mail for me all over the place. What the hell can I do for you?"

Takamura looked at him with his dark brown eyes, brushing his boyishly long hair away from his forehead. The young scientist had the good looks of a media star, but he never noticed how the women and some of the gay men seemed to be attracted to him.

"I think we've found some new evidence to support Mac's idea that maybe there is some kind of new radiation in the central chamber."

Jakes leaned forward, replacing his glasses on his seamed face. "Really? What kind of evidence?"

"We've been doing a Sheffield Analysis on the VLF spectrum, and there's something on the core graphs that has no known antecedents."

Jakes smiled. "Mishima, that hardly qualifies as evidence, does it? Sounds like just another mystery to add to the others."

"No, I don't think so. Its presence is correlated to the other new activity the sensors have been picking up."

"You mean the tachyon pulse we received last

month?'' Jakes picked up a light-pen and began twid-
dling with it on the desktop.

"Of course," Takamura said. "It all makes sense,
doesn't it, Bob? When you and your team first entered
the aft section, you found that burned-out transmitter,
remember?"

Jakes could only nod his head as his assistant continued.

"You yourself theorized that it had been a tachyon
message, a one-shot burst out into the galaxy telling the
creators of this tub that we had finally arrived."

"That was just a theory. There was no way to test my
assumptions. There still isn't."

"No, but that big burst of nonrandom signal we intercepted last month was no accident. It was a tachyon
pulse, and it was directed, and it was full of ordered
phenomena. Bob you know in your heart of hearts that
it was a messge from Out There somewhere—a message
that was received by this ship."

Jakes nodded slowly. His assistant was only verbaliz-
ing what he himself had been thinking for weeks. But
after all they had been through, he had wanted to think
it was all over, that from this point on it was simply
going to be playtime for all the scientists excited with
their new toy. Jakes didn't want any more adventure,
any more disruptive elements to wreck his plans for a
quiet lifetime of new discovery.

"I know, I know," Jakes said. "But it just raises
more questions. If this ship actually received a message
from out there somewhere, that implies a few things
that frankly scare me."

Takamura grinned. "You're not alone in feeling that
way. It means that the ship wasn't dead in the water
after all. It occurs to me that we may have been drawn
into an elaborate kind of trap."

"Trap? Are you sure that's the right word?"

"I certainly hope it's the wrong word, but I'm convinced that the ship received an answer to the pulse you
detected leaving this ship when you first walked in the
door."

"And of course this new VLF radiation is part of the whole involved story, right?"

Mishima nodded. "I think we would be fools to ignore it. Something is going on here. Something we don't yet understand."

"Damn! I wish Kemp were back up here. That fucking documentary has got him by the ass just when we need his input."

"I don't see why Kemp is so necessary. I think we'd better inform the Joint Chiefs ASAP."

Jakes smiled. "Well, I think we should go through proper channels on the way. Kemp has got to be made aware of what we're thinking before it gets spread all over the ship. How many of your people know about this?"

"About the radiation? Just Mac and Greta. I told them to keep a lid on things for the time being."

"You're convinced there's nothing harmful?"

The assistant shrugged. "I am convinced of nothing up here. That is always the best policy, don't you think? But there's more."

"What?"

"I was down at the base camp in the interior yesterday, and I ran into Dr. Penovich. He was a teacher of mine in undergraduate school—it's a small world, isn't it? Anyway, he told me that the accident they had down there with one of the dinosaurs had some funny implications."

"Like what? Christ, this is starting to sound like a damned mystery novel."

"He told me that the beast that killed one of the servicemen was some kind of mutation. A herbivore that had acquired a taste for meat. Penovich also said that there was evidence of accelerated growth. *Very* accelerated."

"Listen, we don't know anything about the biology of this place—it's too early yet. We're all just scratching the surface, and maybe we're jumping to conclusions." Jakes listened to himself talk and was embarrassed at how unconvincing he sounded.

Mishima frowned. "If the biology of the ship behaves in a significantly different way than what we are accustomed to, then we must investigate it thoroughly. It means that we are dealing with something unpredictable and therefore unstable—and possibly dangerous."

Dr. Jakes nodded slowly, pretending to be casually digesting his assistant's words. Actually, his mind was a jumble of chaotic thoughts. How the hell could they really know what was going on? How could they have assumed they knew everything after such a short time on board? All of a sudden everything seemed like it was on the verge of falling apart. He recalled the words of Angie Cowan earlier that morning and wondered if the incident with the Saurians had anything to do with Takamura's VLF radiation.

"Well, what do you think we should be doing?" Mishima asked.

Jakes sighed audibly. "Christ-on-a-crutch, I don't know. I really don't know what to do. Kemp would blow his mind if we went over his head to the Joint Chiefs, though."

"Then let's get in touch with Kemp now," Mishima said.

"That's going to be tough."

"But not impossible, I presume."

Jakes smiled. "You know, Mishima, you drive a tough bargain. In fact, you're no bargain at all. I have the feeling you're going to stand here and bug the shit out of me till I call Colonel Kemp."

Dr. Takamura grinned and reached for the phone.

"All right," said Jakes, taking the receiver from his assistant's hand. "Let's see what's going on."

He pushed through the preliminary clearance codes and waited for one of the functionaries on Copernicus to track Kemp down. He was in transit from Northern California by limo-jet to Vandenberg AFB. A few moments passed as the proper connections were made.

"This is Colonel Kemp." The voice of the Chief of

Deep Space Operations sounded crisp in the receiver. There was the high-pitched whine of jet engines in the background.

"Phineas, this is Bob Jakes."

"Jakes, what're you doing calling me down here? I'm in the middle of a thousand and one things."

"We've been having some problems up here, Phineas, and I wanted to talk to you about them before we went any further."

"What kinds of problems?" Kemp's voice was suddenly softer, more concerned.

Jakes outlined the observations of Takamura's team, the test results, and some of the theories that were beginning to take shape. He also threw in the incident with the Saurians and the death of one of Lindstrom's team.

There was a pause at the other end of the line as Kemp considered what he had heard.

"Phineas, did you read me on all of that?"

"Yes, damnit, I heard you Bob. What the hell is going on up there? Can't you people get along without me for a couple of weeks?"

"It's been close to a month, Colonel, but that's not the point. Some of my people are convinced that we're dealing with some new developments that won't wait. Mishima thinks the ship has received a transmission from the folks who made this lovely terrarium, and that's the reason why we've been picking up some strange phenomena. Heaven knows what we may have missed."

"Why the hell does this have to happen now? I've got a whole damn movie crew coming up on the shuttle tomorrow. They've got a schedule to keep for World Media Corporation."

"Well, if you ask me, Colonel, this VLF radiation increase seems a sight more important than a bunch of reporters' fucking schedules." Jakes let slip what he had been thinking. He had noticed a reluctance on Kemp's part to really involve himself in the things he'd been hearing. That goddamned documentary was filling his head with delusions of grandeur.

"I haven't asked you, Dr. Jakes. And I'll remind you that it isn't your job to worry about the priorities of this project. I'm glad you had the presence of mind to alert me to what's been happening, and I appreciate the vigilance and responsibility of your people. But please, Doctor, leave the priorities and the decision-making to me."

Jakes was getting hot, but he did his best to control himself. "Well, what do you want us to do about everything?"

"Listen, Bob, I can tell you're upset. Why don't you just relax and put this thing on a back burner for a week or so? This documentary crew will be in and out of here in ten days. Then we can all get back to business, all right?"

"I'm sorry, Phineas, but I think that attitude is plain stupid, and I'll go on record to that effect."

Kemp laughed. "What the hell's gotten into you, Bob?"

"I was about to ask you the same question."

There was a pause at the other end of the line. Then: "Listen, we're getting ready to touch down at Vandenberg, and I don't have time to get into an argument with you. Things will keep for at least another day or two until I'm back on board. I promise I'll see you as soon as I get back. Sorry, Bob, but I've got to sign off."

Jakes hung up the receiver angrily. "Goddamn it, sometimes that guy pisses me off!"

"I can see that," Mishima said. "What are we going to do?"

Jakes shook his head and ran his fingers through his thinning gray hair. "There's not much we can do till he gets back on board."

"I don't like it. I say we contact the Joint Chiefs." Mishima stood up, and reached for the phone again.

"No, wait. We're only talking about a day or two. Let's spend that time getting all the facts straight. Have your team put together a detailed report, and I'll get my own speculations about the engines into readable form.

I'll contact Dr. Lindstrom and see if she'd like to contribute to the paperwork.''

"All right, I can go along with that.''

"If we're going to go against Kemp, we may as well be as prepared as possible.''

Takamura grinned weakly. "Pasteur said that 'Fortune favors the prepared mind.' I guess we don't have any other choice.''

Nine

Standing on the observation deck of the control tower, Ian Coopersmith could see the heavy air traffic at Vandenberg kiting and wheeling about the sky like gulls above their rookery. The flight from Heathrow was a blur in his memory, so consumed had his thoughts been with the whole Dragonstar mess. There was so much to clear up, so much business left undone, that he couldn't take it any longer.

Lying back in the quiet countryside of England hadn't been the curative endeavor he had envisioned. In fact, it had been bloody awful. Not that he didn't get along with the boys and Letty, but he quickly discovered that he was not the kind of person who could spend all his time with them. Ian Coopersmith was a man who needed to be in action, solving problems, completing tasks, heading up a mission.

A mission.

That was how he saw life: as a series of missions, of things that needed to be accomplished. And when he had returned to the warmth and security of his nest, he had found that he couldn't live with the boredom of being so safe, so . . . ordinary.

That realization had taken time to settle in. But when

it did, you beat cheeks to do something about it, right, lad? Ian allowed himself a small personal grin, and was thankful that he hadn't totally lost his sense of humor.

Of course the worst part of the whole bloody situation had been the fucking *guilt*.

He had had no conception of the word until he fell into Leticia's arms upon his triumphant return to Earth and suddenly realized that he couldn't look her straight in the eye. He had assumed that he would be a perfect adult about the whole thing and plainly state what had gone on between Becky Thalberg and himself. Ian knew that the media had picked up on the "marooned in Paradise" theme and had played it like a squeaky violin in all the tabloids and newsfaxes and video programs, and he assumed that Letty would have been prepared for the worst.

And yet, when it came time to discuss the whole affair with her, he had been locked up tighter than a fused bolt on a decompression chamber. All that emotion—the fear and the guilt—became bottled up in him like a vile mix of bad juices, juices that would eventually ferment and turn to the worst of all acids—the kind that ate you up from the inside out. Slowly, inexorably.

The whole thing got barmy in a big hurry. Letty knew what he was thinking, and he knew what she was thinking, but neither of them would initiate the conversation that would have cleared the air.

Until this week. Until Ian heard the quietly spoken rumors that there was something queer going on aboard the Dragonstar. It was then that he knew the charade, the solemn game he and his wife had been playing, needed to be ended. One night, an hour after they had gone to bed and presumably fallen asleep, Ian had spoken aloud into the darkness that he was sick of being eaten alive by his own feelings and trapped emotions. He announced that he was going back on active duty and that he would face his fears in the only manner he knew how: through the challenge of work that must be done.

If he still had any conflicting feelings about Becky

Thalberg, it was time to get them worked out. If he had any scores to settle with Phineas Kemp or any of those big beasties out in the floating jungle, well, then, now was the time to get them settled.

"IASA Flight 616 now touching down on Pad Seven. Attention all personnel. Limo-jet 616 on Pad Seven."

The intercom announcement jarred him from his thoughts. Flight 616 was the one he was waiting for, and he directed his gaze leftward toward Pad Seven, where a black VTOL ship was slowly settling onto the octagonal landing platform. It looked like some kind of mutated insect as it came to rest. Ian continued to watch as a gangway oozed up from the platform like a multi-segmented worm and attached itself to the opening hatch. The moment he had been waiting for was now close at hand, and he mentally rehearsed the conversation. He walked across the lounge, heading for the set of double doors through which the occupants of Flight 616 would pass.

Just relax, old boy. Nothing to get excited about. Just like old times, that's all.

The door swung open and a short, handsome man in dress blues with the insignia of a colonel stepped into the lounge. Phineas Kemp had a handsome, unlined face and bright blue eyes. It was a face that Ian knew extremely well. A crowd of underlings accompanied the colonel, and he was speaking to several of them as they entered the lounge. Consequently Kemp did not at first notice Ian.

Suddenly Kemp looked away from his assistants and stared at the man standing in front of him in an IASA captain's uniform. Displaying an expression of true surprise, Phineas Kemp stopped in his tracks as his jaw dropped open.

"Jesus Christ! Ian, what're you doing here?"

Kemp extended his hand, and the two men shook hands. They stared at each other for an instant, and Ian felt a conflux of emotions course through him. He was simultaneously embarrassed, pleased, and angry. Kemp seemed to be playing up the moment for the benefit of

the others in the group, and Ian felt as though he might
be playing a part in a show.

"Ian, I thought you were in England."

"Oh, yes . . . well, I decided that I'd had enough of
the good life, you know? Had to come back to the real
world for a while."

Ian smiled, and everyone chuckled at the small joke.
But then he leaned closer to Kemp and spoke in a softer
voice. "Actually, Phineas, I need to speak to you in
private, if you could arrange it."

Kemp looked at him with a solemn expression.
"Now?"

"Can you think of a better time? What's your
schedule?"

Kemp checked his chronometer. "I've got a briefing
in an hour, then I'm to meet Jack Neville for a shuttle
flight up to Copernicus Base."

"All right, let's go to your office. This shouldn't take
long."

Phineas Kemp considered the proposal for an instant,
then nodded his head. Waving off his liaison officers,
he told them he'd meet them in the briefing room. "All
right, Ian, let's go. This way."

The colonel led him down a long corridor, into an
elevator crowded with other staff personnel, and then
down another hall. They walked briskly, and neither
man spoke. Ian felt awkward and overly officious as
they passed AFB staff, and he suppressed the urge to let
loose with some nervous laughter. He was afraid Kemp
would think he was losing his grip.

Finally they reached a small, Spartanly furnished office. Kemp took a seat behind a large, old-fashioned
wood desk. "This is just a temporary office," he said.
"I'm not here that often." He paused and smiled
weakly. "Well, what's up, Coopersmith? Did Becky
Thalberg get in touch with you?"

"Becky? No. Why?"

"Well, to tell you the truth, I've been thinking about
you lately, and I asked her to get in touch—for me, that
is."

"Really? Well, no, I haven't heard from her."

"And yet here you are. So what is going on, Captain?"

"I've decided to come back aboard," he said in a soft but forceful manner.

Kemp grinned. "What makes you think I need you?" The question was asked as though in jest, but Ian detected the underlying hostility. *He's still pissed at me for planking his old girlfriend, that's for certain.*

"You just said you wanted Becky to get in touch with me. Besides, I've got this . . ." Reaching into his pocket, Ian produced a piece of E-mail. "This is a letter from Chris Alvarez, Joint Chiefs. It says I'm welcome back to active duty whenever I choose."

Kemp's expression changed quickly to something near indifference. "Oh yes, I seem to remember them sending that off. They wondered why you never even deigned to reply."

"My silence was a reply in itself."

"Yes, I suppose it was." Kemp stood up and walked to a window. He looked out as though interested in an incoming VTOL. "So you think you're ready to get back to work, eh?"

Ian nodded. "I think so. It's been difficult to stay at home. I was never cut out to live like that, I'm afraid."

Kemp smiled. "Too sedate for you, eh?" He continued to stare out the window.

"What's that?" Ian could sense the slight sarcasm in Kemp's voice.

"Much rather be running through the jungle playing out some Edgar Rice Burroughs fantasies, right?" Kemp turned around and smiled.

"Is that supposed to be a joke?" Ian was still willing to give him the benefit of the doubt. "Listen, Colonel, this whole thing isn't very easy for me. I'm trying to explain myself, and I'd appreciate your listening instead of badgering me."

"Badgering you? Captain, I wouldn't think of such a thing."

Ian had always wondered what he would do if Kemp

started in on him like this, and he could feel anger rising up in him like a hot column of vomit. It wasn't going to take too much more before things got ugly.

"Captain Coopersmith, I haven't got all day for your little display," Kemp said after Ian had failed to respond. "If you have something to say, let's get on with it."

The smug bastard. Using his rank to play off our personal differences.

"You won't need all day, Colonel. Is it so hard to understand that I want to go back aboard the Dragonstar?"

"I expected that. Isn't there anything else?"

"What else could there be?" Ian truly had lost Kemp's train of thought. What the hell was he getting at?

Kemp smiled. "Oh, come now, Captain. Don't you want to be working closer to your new love?"

Goddamn the bastard! Who does he think he is? "That's uncalled for, Colonel." Ian stood up and leaned across the massive desk, glaring at Kemp.

"Touched a raw nerve, eh?"

"It sounds like you're the one with the raw nerve. What's eating you, Colonel?"

"You destroy a relationship between me and Rebecca Thalberg and you have the balls to ask me what's *eating* me?" Kemp laughed derisively.

"I didn't destroy anything. Are you going to tell me that if you were in the same position you would have acted differently?"

"That's hard to say, Captain."

"Bullshit!" Ian cried, moving away from the desk, hoping to blow off some of the growing tension by pacing a bit. He turned quickly and faced Kemp again. "You would do the same thing under the same circumstances . . . unless you're a fucking wooden Indian! And if that's the case, it's no wonder Becky threw you over. Nobody wants to be involved with a goddamned automaton!"

The words stung Colonel Kemp like a swarm of angry

insects. "Take it easy, Captain," was all that he could manage to say.

Ian was bristling with pent-up rage now. He paced more vigorously about the tiny office, afraid to look at Kemp for what it might inspire in him. He drew a deep breath, tried to relax, then spoke in a hard, even voice. "You get me all frothed up, and then you tell me to take it easy. You're a real character, Colonel. Now let's get something straight, all right? I did not 'snake' your girlfriend, do you understand that? Whatever happened between us occurred out of necessity, out of the expediency and the existential aspects of the moment."

Kemp managed a small grin. "That's quite a philosophical way of looking at plain old lust."

"It was part of what we needed to survive, Colonel. Since you weren't there you'll just have to take my word for it. Listen, I didn't come here to fight with you, I came here to get back to work."

"I'm right in the middle of a documentary project. I could certainly use you up there." Kemp's mood seemed to be changing.

"Phineas, we never were what you would call close friends, I realize that. But at least we always respected one another, and we always worked well together. It wasn't until this whole mess with the Dragonstar that things became sticky, you know."

"I agree." Kemp seemed to relax a bit as he changed position in his seat behind the wooden desk. "I suppose it is silly to carry grudges."

"Is that what you're doing?"

Kemp shook his head slowly, appearing to let down all his defenses now. "I don't know what I'm doing. I guess I don't know how I feel about you, Ian. Or about Becky, or any of this."

"Does it really matter? Now that it's all over?"

"It's never over," Kemp said. "I thought you would have realized that.

"Perhaps you're right, but I just want you to understand that I want to get back to my work as soon as possible, and that it's for *me* that I need to get back up

there, Colonel, not Becky or anybody else. I heard that
there's some trouble, and maybe I can be of some use. I
feel so useless down here. That's the biggest problem."

Kemp looked at him sharply, his blue eyes sighting in
on him. "What did you say about trouble? What have
you heard?"

Ian filled him in on the rumors he'd picked up from
his friend, the news correspondent.

"Goddamned reporters," Kemp said. "Christ, they'll
dig up anybody's bones, won't they?"

"Well," Ian asked, "is there any truth to it? Has
there been any trouble? A man killed is always news,
especially if he was eaten by a dinosaur."

Kemp shook his head slowly in total disgust. "I'll be
honest with you, Captain. I'm not really sure what's
going on up there. I've been so damned busy with this
media event, this worldwide documentary thing, that I
haven't been keeping close enough tabs on what's been
happening on the Dragonstar."

"That doesn't sound good," Ian said, hoping he
wasn't going to touch any more raw nerves.

"No, it's not, but I just want this thing to come off
flawlessly, and I guess maybe I've had my priorities
wrong."

"Sounds like you need me up there as soon as possible. At least I could kind of substitute for you until the
documentary's over with and things are back to normal—whatever *that* might be."

Kemp nodded grimly. "That might be the best thing
you could do for me right now. There isn't a man alive,
except for Jakes maybe, who knows that ship as well as
you."

"While we're on the subject, what did happen up
there? A man was killed by a beastie, wasn't he?"

Kemp nodded. "Yes, he was out on a routine paleontological mission with Mikaela. She called me right after
it happened, and I told her to keep a lid on the whole incident until we got this documentary finished."

"Jesus! Are you sure that was the right thing to do?"

The colonel looked at him thoughtfully. "You know,

now that I'm thinking about it more objectively, perhaps you're right. Maybe it needed to be evaluated more fully. I don't want anything dangerous to affect the broadcast.''

"What exactly happened?"

Clearing his throat, Kemp started talking in a professorial tone. "Mikaela stumbled upon a new species of dinosaur, or at least some kind of mutation. It looked like an Iguanodon, but it was carnivorous, and it seemed to have grown a set of meat-eating teeth and claws for its new career."

Ian coughed nervously. "It does sound odd. Does she have any ideas?"

"The report I saw mentioned possible radiation poisoning, mutation, and accelerated tissue growth. But so far that's just a bunch of speculation. There's no telling what's going on yet."

"Colonel, I hope you don't mind my saying so, but this sounds like it could be very serious.

"Nothing's been confirmed, I'm telling you. Dr. Jakes has been apprised of the situation, and I'm sure he's checking things out. If there were any danger, I'd be notified immediately."

"It looks like I decided to get involved at exactly the right time," Ian said softly.

Phineas Kemp smiled and stood up from the desk. "You know what's wrong with you, Coopersmith? You have a real hero complex."

"How so?"

Kemp chuckled. "If you don't know, then I couldn't possibly explain it to you. Are you sure you never wanted to be a movie star?"

Ian smiled. "No, not really."

"All right, forget it." Kemp checked the time and picked up his attaché case from the desktop. "I've got to get to that briefing, and you've got to get outfitted for the next shuttle. Are you ready to ship out now?"

"That's what I'm here for."

"Very well. Get downstairs and see Lieutenant Myers. Tell him to book you onto the next shuttle. I'll meet you on Copernicus tomorrow, and we'll ship over to the Dragonstar together.''

Kemp moved to the door, then paused to look back at Ian. "You know, Coopersmith, I guess I owe you an apology, but it's very hard for me to give those things out. I guess it's just in my nature to be this way. Sorry. I really mean that.''

The colonel extended his hand in friendship, and Ian grasped it firmly. He shook his hand and said something innocuous like "Thank you, sir," and suddenly Kemp was gone down the hallway, walking at a brisk, stiff-legged pace. He looked like some kind of goony bird.

Ian shook his head slowly. This guy was one complex of complexes, that was for sure. But despite all his problems with Kemp, Ian had to admit a grudging respect and even admiration for the Chief of Deep Space Operations.

Looking out the window of the small office, he could see a shuttle being prepared for launch, and he knew he'd have to hustle to get on board the next flight.

Time to get on with the next mission, he thought. It's about bloody time, too.

Ten

Mishima had always felt very comfortable around the Saurians.

As he walked slowly from the entrance of the crew quarters toward the residence of Thesaurus, he took the time to absorb the sights and sounds and smells of their primitive culture. Having lived and worked within the confines of the Saurian preserve for so many months now, Mishima tended to take his surroundings for granted. When an environment becomes so familiar that one doesn't even notice its existence, he thought reflectively, it is a very sad occasion.

It had been agreed that "north" inside the cylindrical world would be pointing toward the Saurian/alien end of the ship, and that "south" would be the end that contained the Mesozoic preserve. "East" and "west" would then be to the right and left of that longitudinal axis. Mishima knew it was merely a convention, but he had accepted the terms, and his sense of direction now seemed perfectly natural as he headed south down the steps of the Saurian temple, turning east at the base of the stairs and walking toward a large group of dwellings that had been carved into a rocky promontory—the highest geographic point in the Saurian preserve.

Carved into this rocky jut of land were the residences
of the Saurian priest class—the select group of the race,
who held the keys of power in the reptilian society. The
keys unlocked the vault of knowledge, as was typical in
primitive cultures, and they were retained by ensuring
that the masses did not learn too much.

It was with members of the priest class that the IASA
staff had been able to communicate most effectively and
one of the first had been a gentle old Saurian whom Ian
Coopersmith had ironically named Thesaurus.

Mishima remembered the first time he had met the
old philosopher-priest, soon after he had arrived on
board the Dragonstar as a member of Dr. Jakes's hand-
picked team of experts. It would be the mission of the
research team to discover as much about the physical
makeup and operation of the alien vessel as possible.
Mishima recalled walking into sick bay one afternoon
for some antihistamines and was surprised to see the
supine body of a Saurian in one of the hospital beds.

It was Thesaurus, being treated for the radiation
burns he had received during the battle with the TWC
terrorists. Mishima approached the bed slowly. The
Saurian, who wore a digital translator around his neck,
eyed him warily. Mishima offered a gentle greeting, and
the Saurian responded. A halting, awkward conversation began—the two of them had embarked upon the
road to friendship.

The close relationship Mishima enjoyed with Thesaurus was the exception rather than the rule throughout
the various camps and research facilities inside the
Dragonstar. Mishima and Thesaurus were two of the
loudest supporters of more cooperation and work between the two species, but so far little had been done to
accomplish this. Mishima suspected that Colonel Kemp
was the major stumbling block to this movement but
had no concrete proof.

Mishima had become friendly with Thesaurus, and
they often took walks together among the many gardens
and botanical parks that were spread throughout the
Saurian city of Hakarrh. This morning Mishima had

received a message from Thesaurus that he would like to meet with him.

There was a large set of steps cut into the face of the promontory, filled with switchbacks and landings, which led to the Saurian priest's homes. Naturally, since Thesaurus was one of the older members of the ruling class, his residence was close to the top. Mishima began the long climb up, looking out over the landscape and renewing his sense of wonder about the place.

You could get a good view of things from this height. Due north was the impossible height and expanse of the flat end of the cylinder. A sheer perpendicular plain of infinite size, it rose up into the mist and clouds that gathered up near the Illuminator. Behind the flat end of the cylinder lay the alien control sections—the dioramas, life factories, command quarters, and the small areas the IASA teams had staked out as research centers and laboratories. To the south, Mishima looked down upon the Saurian city. It was a collection of random architecture—minarets, domes, cubes, and large mall-like areas. The streets were all wide boulevards, and there were many parks and gardens. One could also see domesticated dinosaurs serving as beasts of burden and workers throughout the countryside. Outdoor bazaars were a major force in the economy, and their multi-colored tents made the landscape look like a country quilt. Beyond the city to the east and west lay the huge stretches of agricultural land where the agrarian class Saurians raised simple crops.

All this activity was hemmed in by the Barrier, a wall fifteen meters high and ten meters thick made of earth, stone, and wood. A rampart ran along its top edge, punctuated every one hundred meters or so by a watch-tower. The world of the Saurian race consisted of a thirty-kilometer-wide strip of land curved about the interior of a gigantic spinning cylinder—not much of a world, thought Mishima, yet the Saurians had done pretty well for themselves.

Technologically they appeared to be comparable with European civilization at the end of the eighteenth century. They hadn't yet invented many mechanical devices, and steam and electricity were not even a dream among them. Mishima found it interesting that the Saurians used biology and botany as their primary sciences, having learned, albeit primitively, ways to control some of the herbivorous dinosaurs and to attain to fairly efficient agricultural techniques.

Finally Mishima reached the level near the top of the promontory where Thesaurus lived. A device like a wind chime, carved from the hollow bones of a Pteranodon, hung over the door. Takamura sounded it gently.

Presently the door opened to reveal a tall, almost skinny Saurian with parched-looking skin. He had a long neck and a snub-nosed snout. It was a reptilian face, but with stereoscopic vision and a large cranium. He wore a lemon yellow robe that resembled silk, and he looked very old. Around the Saurian's neck hung a small electronic device which encoded and decoded both the Saurian and human languages—a translator that Mishima had helped design based on the early experience of Ian Coopersmith.

"Takamura," said the old Saurian. "Welcome." The Saurian spoke in his own language, and the translator immediateley mimicked the words in English. Their entire conversation would be carried out like this.

"I got your message. You wanted to see me?"

"Yes, Takamura. I have noticed trouble among our people."

A warning bell sounded in Mishima's head. Everybody was smelling problems lately, and he didn't like it. "What kind of trouble, Thesaurus?"

"I do not know. Many of the agrarian class have been having spells of madness. It is like a sickness, and there are signs that it is becoming widespread."

"You mean a disease? Perhaps our biomedics can look into it?"

Thesaurus walked to the single window cut into the residence and looked out onto the expanse of Hakarrh. "No, I don't think it is that kind of sickness. More a sickness of the . . . of the thought center."

"Anything to do with the R-sleep?" Mishima asked, referring to the cyclic periods of reversion to their more primitive state which all Saurians underwent. It was a strange genetic reminder of their reptilian beginnings, which the Saurians called the Dark Fold.

Thesaurus shook his head, a mannerism he had learned from the humans. "No, I don't think so. I have been discussing the whole phenomenon with my elders, my colleagues, and we have questioned some of the victims. This is not connected with the Dark Fold."

Mishima took a seat in an uncomfortable chair that had been designed for the Saurian posterior. "Still, perhaps we should run some tests in our laboratories. Could any of the victims be persuaded to come with me?"

"No. That is impossible."

"Why?"

"It was necessary to kill them."

Mishima wondered at such a necessity, but he knew better than to question it. "When was the last incident?"

The Saurian barked out an ironic chuckle. "Only this morning. Indeed, it may be recurring as we speak."

Mishima nodded. "I heard some of my people talking about a riot this morning at one of the bazaars."

"That is the incident," Thesaurus said. "And I must tell you that I am fearful, Mishima."

"Why?" He pretended to be totally ignorant of any possible implications.

It was difficult to read the thoughts (or emotions, if indeed they had them) of the Saurians by looking at their faces. This was not to say that they did not possess a definite range of expressions, but rather that most humans had not yet learned what the various facial registers meant. With this in mind, Mishima attempted to study the facial expression of Thesaurus. It seemed to be conveying true concern. Compassion and intelligence burned brightly in those large reptilian eyes, like lamps to banish the darkness of fear and ignorance.

"You ask why?" Thesaurus barked out another short

laugh. "Because in all my birth cycles I have never seen this kind of mass hysteria. That is why I termed it a disease."

"Well, is it possible that I might borrow one of the next victims if there is another outbreak? There's a chance we might be able to help."

Thesaurus walked to Mishima's side and placed a three-fingered claw/hand on his shoulder. "My friend," the creature said, "there is talk among my class."

"What kind of talk?"

"Talk that we never had this kind of trouble, this kind of chaos . . . till the humans arrived."

Mishima allowed the words to settle in. This had a familiar ring to it. The British in India, the colonists in America, Cortez in Mexico, Cook's ships in Hawaii, the parallels were endless, and it seemed as though humankind was destined to forever repeat history's ill-learned lessons. He smiled as he looked up at the Saurian. "Did you tell them they are probably correct?"

"You are making a joke?" Thesaurus seemed confused by the smile.

"No, I was being sadly ironic. I forget your word for the gesture, the expression. I tend to agree with your philosophers: we humans have brought you a bunch of problems. Before we came, you thought the whole universe began and ended within the confines of this ship. You had never even seen the stars. Talk about innocence. Milton had *nothing* on you fellows."

"Who is Milton?" Thesaurus asked.

"One of our ancient artists. He wrote about the loss of innocence, and I was thinking that your people are perfect examples of the concept. I mean, look what happened when we arrived: we brought deception and killing and death right away."

"But my people understood. It was not your fault. Our own history is touched with times of conflict and bloodshed. We have had our share of war and destruction."

"Yes, so I've heard," Mishima said. He got up,

walked to the window, and looked down on the Saurian city. "Goddamn it! Why is the road to civilization always such a bitch!"

Thesaurus shook his head. "Perhaps because it would otherwise be so easy to remain primitive?"

"Yeah, maybe . . . maybe the answer is just that simple." Mishima returned to his seat. "At any rate, Thesaurus, I'm glad you've told me about the problems you've been noticing. My people are also seeing some strange things . . . which reminds me, have you ever found any of the dinosaurs out there . . . have you ever found any of them to be *changing*?"

"What do you mean by this?"

Mishima was not sure how much Thesaurus would understand of mutations and evolution, but he pressed on. "I mean, have any of your people ever found dinosaurs that seemed different from others of their kind? As though they might be hatched from normal mothers but themselves are changed in some strange ways?"

Thesaurus nodded slowly, a hissing sound building in his throat. "Yes, I understand you now." The Saurian paused to consider the question. "No, I have not heard of such a thing, but it can be researched through the oral histories and the libraries. Why? Is it important?"

"It might be. I don't know yet." Mishima checked his chronometer and saw that the day was slipping away. There was so much work he wished to get done, and the hours seemed to be against him. Again he stood up, but this time he moved toward the door to the outer landing.

"You must go?"

"Yes, but I thank you again for thinking of me, for wanting to tell me about the riots and the sickness."

The old Saurian nodded. "As I said, I am fearful."

"Then you promise me a victim to study if this happens again?"

"Yes, I am certain we can arrange such a thing."

"Thank you, Thesaurus. Stay in touch with me." Mishima grasped him by the flesh of his shoulder, the usual form of greeting and parting among the priest class. He felt a closeness to this strange creature.

"Goodbye, Mishima. We shall speak again."

Mishima had begun to descend the carved steps when the Saurian called out to him. Mishima turned and looked back at Thesaurus. "Yes?"

"It has just occurred to me to ask, my friend—have you heard from Ian Coopersmith?"

Mishima smiled at the mention of the captain's name. The tactical engineer had become something of a legend among the IASA staff. Just the mention of his name commanded immediate respect.

Mishima shook his head. "No. I never knew him personally. He remains on Earth."

"He will never come back to us?" Thesaurus asked.

"I'm afraid I couldn't answer that."

"That is unfortunate. I am thinking that perhaps we could use a human like him to help us now. Perhaps I could even travel to your Earth someday."

"Really?" Mishima said in surprise, instantly imagining what a carnival the media would have with that kind of stunt.

"Yes. I think that I am missing the company of Captain Coopersmith. He was a very good man."

Mishima nodded. "From everything I've heard, he would be a good man to have around right about now."

"Yes." Captain Coopersmith could help us solve the mystery. There is something very wrong here. Something is happening to all of us."

The Stegosaurus lumbered away from her nest to fetch a drink. Finding her way to a nearby pool was an amazing feat of memory for the beast, for although she had two brains—one in her skull, the other a more primitive knot of ganglia at the base of her spiked tail—she was an extraordinarily dull creature. Despite the extra hundred-plus million years for biological improvement, her species had reached an evolutionary dead end.

She dragged her huge body from her nesting place along a worn path through an outcropping of rock. The light from the Iluminator beat down on her camou-

flaged hide with its usual comforting heat—the heat that
warmed the Stegosaurus's eggs and relieved the beast of
the duty of warming them herself. She remained in the
area of her eggs out of habit, perhaps to guard her
emerging offspring, perhaps merely following deeply
etched atavistic instincts.

And now that she was thirsty, she sought out a familiar pool.

It was a little more than a widening of a stream into a
basin. The pool was a popular watering hole, and many
species could often be seen standing cheek to jowl sharing a cool drink. As the Stegosaurus sauntered down to
the water's edge, she ignored a group of Ankylossaurus
on the opposite bank. She dipped her bullet-shaped
head into the pool.

The stream was fed by an underground system of
pumps and valves and other hidden machinery, and the
creatures who used the pool took no notice of what lay
beneath the sparkling depths. Nudging some reeds and
mosses away from the edge, the Stegosaurus continued
to drink. There was a leisurely pace to her actions
because, although she was ever alert, her plated back
and spiked tail were enough of a defensive system to
make most predators wary of trying an attack.

Her eyes stared ahead with a normal dullness, peering
unwittingly beneath the surface where something began
to glow.

It was a slight flash at first, like the glint of gold in a
prospector's pan, but within moments it grew. One of
the elements of the pumping machinery had started to
glow, irradiated by automatically controlled energies
within the outer hull. The ship was undergoing changes,
and the irradiated machinery was a by-product of that
change.

The pulsing element had a hypnotic effect on the
Stegosaurus, and she stood there, a mouthful of unswal-
lowed water ignored in her mouth. The Ankylosaurus
were equally entranced, peering into the water with
wide-eyed fascination. Radiation emanated from the
depths, penetrating the Stegosaurus's hide, burning its

primitive brain. It stood there transfixed by the light until the water began to boil from the heat of the underwater element. The steamy mist and the bubbling broke the mesmeric trance, and the Stegosaurus blinked.

No longer thirsty, she turned and fought off a feeling of disequilibrium, moving ponderously back toward her nesting area. She had received a staggering dose of radiation, and she stumbled several times along the path. Flies seemed to swarm behind her eyes, and hot flashes raged along her spinal cord.

As she reached the depression that held her nest, she barely noticed the other members of her scattered herd, not even the father of her children, who casually cropped bushes in the distance. The image of her half-buried eggs swam in her vision for a moment, then her forelegs buckled, collapsing her to the ground, where she drifted into unconsciousness.

The Stegosaurus lay comatose for several hours, occasionally examined by her herd but largely ignored.

When she awoke, the first thing she noticed was the oppressive heat. The cooling radiator effect of the plates along her back did not seem to be working, and the creature's body felt aflame. Her tiny brain seemed ablaze as she struggled to an upright position and glared about as though looking for an enemy. Raising her head, she honked out a plaintive cry.

Her tail lashed reflexively, knocking about the surrounding rocks and underbrush. She could think of nothing but her maddening need for a drink. There was a burning pit in the center of her being, and she needed to fill it, to quench it as quickly as possible.

Spinning wildly about, her blurry gaze fell upon the seven off-white domes rising above loosely packed dirt.

Her burning madness and thirst drove her forward, and in a moment she was standing over the eggs. Dipping her beaklike snout, she punctured the leathery shell of one of the eggs. White mucous coated her mouth as she crazily slurped up the albumin and the half-formed fetus in the yolk.

Her thirst was not slaked.

One by one, in a growing rage, she smashed the eggs and drank their contents.

A kind of alarm was sounding in her brain, but she could not stop herself. Lifting her head, she cried out in pain and suffering. Her entire body began to itch, a fiery painful burning, and she thrashed her yolk-smeared snout into the dust to stop the terrible irritation. Her flanks tingled as she clawed at a spot with her hind claws until she opened a sore.

Wandering off in a private madness, away from her devastated nest, the Stegosaurus felt her brain frying away in the heat.

Eleven

Colonel Phineas Kemp prepared to address the people assembled in one of the smaller debriefing rooms of Copernicus Base. It was an intimate, stepped auditorium equipped with VDT screens, a holographic imager, and a light-pointer so that a lecture could be amply backed up by all manner of visual aid. As he stepped up to the miked podium, the buzz of conversation in the hall subsided. Kemp took a moment to scan the audience, searching out the familiar faces of Becky Thalberg, seated next to Ian Coopersmith (Kemp was surprised they were not holding hands like a couple of college kids), Kate Ennis, and of course, "Long Jack" Neville.

The remainder of the audience was comprised of World Media Corporation people, an army of production-crew types—directors, producers, writers, still photographers, electricians, video cameramen, grips, stagehands. Kemp realized that for most of them this was their first trip off Earth, and they were reeling from the experience, having varying degrees of reaction—everything from nausea to transcendental awe.

By sounding an electronic chime on the podium, Kemp brought the assembly to order. Silence descended upon the room, and he could feel the crowd's attention cascading down the bank of seats to wash over him. Once again Kemp commanded a position of authority, and it fit him like an old shoe.

Smiling easily, he began to speak. "Good evening. I realize for most of you, that this is your first trip off-planet, and I apologize for hustling you off to a meeting as soon as we touched down here at Copernicus Base. But there are a few things that I would like to cover before we begin the next stage of this operation."

Phineas paused for an instant to judge the group's reaction to his introduction. Aside from the obvious boredom of the IASA people and Neville's near panic, everyone seemed to be paying respectful attention. Phineas continued, keying in some background holographic projections.

"This is the Dragonstar as seen from space. If this ship were on the surface of the Earth, with one end lying in Baltimore's Inner Harbor, the other end would be in Manhattan's East River. Three hundred twenty kilometers long, and more than sixty-five in diameter."

Kemp paused as the audience murmured among themselves as the impact of the alien ship's sheer size sunk into their minds. He keyed in a new sequence of images of the ship's interior and continued.

"The interior is a marvel of biological and engineering genius. A totally self-contained world, carrying an exact duplicate of the Earth's environment more than one hundred sixty million years ago—a perfect model of the Mesozoic Era."

Kemp watched the audience as they absorbed the images of that ancient era of the Earth, alive once again. The lush green of the undergrowth; the tall redwoods and ginkgoes; the steamy, humid mist rising from the swampy marshlands.

"And of course, what is flora without fauna?" Kemp asked as the placid botanical scene was shattered by the emergence of an Allosaurus from the thick folds of the jungle growth. In sharp contrast to the muted shades of green, this large carnivore was striped in bright orange and browns. He moved with surprising agility, running, leaping, and pirouetting like a dancer across an open meadow as it descended upon a grazing herd of Ankylosaurus.

The audience emitted a collective gasp as the predator capered wildly behind Colonel Kemp, watching with horrid fascination as it attacked and feasted on one of the smaller armored dinosaurs. The Allosaurus flipped its prey onto its back with a deft flick of its powerful tail, then sank its snout of kitchen-knife teeth into the exposed soft underbelly. In triumph, the Allosaurus raised its bloody snout from the feast and stared coolly into the lens of the intruding camera, pausing for a terrible instant before returning to its meal.

Kemp keyed in a new sequence of shots, the interior as shot from an ornithopter traveling along the longitudinal axis of the cylindrical ship. "I need not tell you that the interior of the Mesozoic preserve is a dangerous place to be—even with adequate protection. When your documentary crews are shooting in the preserve, there will be very strict rules that must be obeyed. The IASA can protect you out there, but only if you follow the rules. This is very important. I don't want any of you playing the idiot or the hero by wandering off on your own. The creatures in this self-contained world have hearty appetites."

Kemp smiled, and a round of nervous laughter filled the small auditorium. He glanced down at Neville, seated between Kate Ennis and his nurse. The writer of more than four hundred books looked as though he was about to have a seizure. The man weaved back and forth slightly, and his face was very, very pale. His nurse was checking his portable LM equipment, making an attempt to be very discreet. No one else noticed, however, because of the constantly changing array of images from the holographic projector behind Colonel Kemp.

The aerial view of the Dragonstar's interior revealed the varied geography of the Mesozoic world—its swamplands and rivers, lakes and plateaus, volcanic mountains overlooking lush jungle basins. The ornithopter-borne camera moved slowly toward the north end of the cylinder until the Barrier and the agrarian squares of land beyond were visible.

"Incredible as all this is, the spectacle is capped by the existence of the race of beings we call the Saurians. Centuries ago, their ancestors built their equivalent of the Great Wall of China, and you can see it in these shots, encircling the entire end of the cylinder. This wall, which they call the Barrier, keeps them separated from their low-life cousins."

There was another ripple of laughter in the room as Kemp went on. "You will be spending a lot of time among the Saurians, and we have prepared a pamphlet on what we have discovered about their physiology and culture, which may help you to get along inside their lands. Please pick up one of the booklets on your way out—they're on a stand by the exits."

Kemp turned off the projectors. "That's about it for now. We will be spending the next thirty-six hours here on Copernicus Base, then we will be shipping off to the Dragonstar itself. I have arranged for special tours of Copernicus Base and some lunar surface excursions for those of you who would like to take advantage of being up here on the Moon. Before we wrap this up, are there any questions?"

Phineas hated to add this to his presentation, but it was *de rigueur* in these kinds of situations. He knew the crowd would not let him escape easily. And so he was not surprised to see a forest of hands rising up out of the assembly.

"Yes, over in the corner, back row."

A middle-aged man wearing a set of coveralls stood up. "You mentioned it being dangerous out in the Mesozoic Preserve. Just how safe are we out there?"

A murmur passed through the crowd. Kemp raised his hands for silence. "Very safe. Believe me, there's nothing to worry about. You will be escorted everywhere by armed details who have logged long hours in the preserve."

A young woman rose to her feet. "What's this we heard about one of your armed guards being killed up there recently?"

Kemp was taken aback by the question. How did these people know about that already? He smiled slowly. "And where did you get that story from, might I ask?"

The young woman chuckled. "Colonel, I work for World Media Corporation. Stories are our business, remember?"

The group chuckled nervously.

He cleared his throat, retaining his composure. "A report did reach me while I was on Earth about such an incident. During a routine paleontological survey one of our guards got careless and paid the price. Let me remind you that this incident marks the first such accident since the research teams have been aboard the vessel."

He paused for a moment as a chorus of reaction ran through the crowd, then pointed to another questioner. "Yes?"

A man in his thirties remained seated as he spoke. "I work for World Media too, Colonel. That was not an official press release she was talking about. It was a leak, as you probably know. My question is this: Was there any reason to keep that information classified?"

Kemp cleared his throat again. Damn these reporter types. He'd never had them on his base before, and now, though he'd invited them, he felt as though his territory had been invaded by a strange kind of enemy. He smiled at the question and tried to remain as cool as possible. "Of course there was a reason." He paused to laugh easily. "It was to keep all you people from getting too scared and backing out. After all, I want this picture made, don't I?"

Practically everyone laughed at the tension-breaking attempt at a joke, and Kemp was thankful. Other hands shot up, but he ignored them by waving off everybody. "All right, I have an appointment with the Joint Chiefs coming up, so I'm going to have to cut this short. Captain David Lowen, my liaison officer, is standing by to take over. He's that handsome young blond guy in the corner. Dave, why don't you come up here and wrap this thing up."

As his liaison man approached the podium, Kemp looked out at the crowd and smiled his best media smile. "Thank you all for your attention. I'd like to wish you all good luck up there. Let's make the world a film they'll never forget."

There was a burst of applause as Kemp waved and departed the podium. He gestured to his people in the first row to leave with him. Becky and Ian responded to the signal and got up from their seats.

Once the trio had exited the room and were out in the relative privacy of the corridor, Becky gave Phineas a playful punch on the shoulder. "Still as smooth as ever, aren't you?"

"What are you talking about?" he asked.

"For a minute there, I thought those news sharks were going to get you, but you greased right out of that one. I feel sorry for Dave Lowen, though."

"He can't tell them anything he doesn't know," Ian said. "And I have a feeling Phineas picked his liaison officer very carefully."

They all laughed as they walked along.

"I wasn't kidding about the Joint Chiefs meeting, though," Phineas said. "I've got to be there in a few minutes."

"Are we invited?" Becky asked.

"Wish you were. It would certainly make it a bit more interesting. But I'm afraid not. Seems I missed the list meeting with the people from Management and Budget, and my ass'll be in a crack if I don't show up for this one."

"Fudging around with a bunch of bureaucrats is the last thing I want to be doing right about now," Coopersmith said. "I don't know how you do it, Phineas."

Kemp smiled at the two of them. "I'm afraid it comes with the territory. Well, I really must get on with it. See you at zero six hundred tomorrow in the launch briefing room."

Becky and Ian nodded and said their good evenings to Kemp.

*   *   *

After the Colonel had disappeared down the long corridor, Ian looked at Becky and smiled. " 'It comes with the territory,' indeed."

Becky made a mock frown. "He was veddy serious, I assure you."

They both laughed for a moment, then looked at each other. Neither one spoke, and as the silence became longer and more awkward, Becky felt an urge to say something. Looking at her chronometer, she smiled engagingly.

"Got any plans for the rest of the evening?"

Ian's expression was inscrutable. He appeared to be thinking over all the implications of her question. After a pause he replied, "Well, no, I don't really. But I know that I need to talk to you . . . sooner or later."

"I was hoping you'd say that." She was encouraged by his candor.

"Good. There are a lot of things that need to be said, Becky. I guess now's as good a time as any to get them out."

"Sounds like serious business," she said, trying to lighten the mood of the conversation. "Why don't we go down to the Village Pub and have a drink or two while we do all this heavy talking?"

"All right." Ian's expression now readable: he was smiling.

Not long after Becky Thalberg and Ian Coopersmith headed for the Copernicus Base watering hole, Captain Dave Lowen finished handling the documentary crew's questions and dismissed the assembly. During the mad rush for the exits, amidst a rising drone of excited conversation, Dave Lowen searched out the panicky face of John T. Neville and his traveling nurse, Ms. Wilkins. He had been assigned by Kemp to play watchdog on the old guy until they shipped him up to the Dragonstar, and Dave wasn't looking forward to the duty. Even though he hadn't gotten much of a chance to talk to Neville, the writer seemed like fruit farm material.

As the crowd thinned out, Neville's nurse helped him to his feet, carrying the portable LM units in her free hand. The odd couple approached Dave as he stood by the podium gathering up his notes and briefing sheets. Neville appeared to be exhibiting a combination of claustrophobia, anger, and general panic.

"Ah, here we go, sir," he said brightly as Neville drew up next to him. "Sorry to bundle you off to this lecture as soon as you set foot on the Moon, but it was the colonel's orders. Priorities, you know."

"Fuck his priorities," Neville said. "He didn't tell us anything that isn't contained in his silly fact sheets."

"Mr. Neville, please," his nurse whispered.

Man, this guy was going to be a character, Dave Lowen thought as he reached out and took the old gent's arm. "I realize you may have been inconvenienced, sir, and Colonel Kemp foresaw the problem too. That's why he prepared a special treat for you."

Neville's wild-eyed look seemed to soften a bit. "A special treat? For me?"

Lowen smiled. "That's right. Won't you please follow me down to the shuttle deck?"

"But we just came from there. We're not going back into *space* again, are we? Right now, I mean?"

Lowen laughed easily. "Oh no, sir, you'll see." Dave recalled how out of shape Neville had been during the shuttle flight from Vandenberg. For a guy who'd been writing about this stuff all his life, he wasn't very prepared to accept the reality of spaceflight. He was the first guy Lowen had ever seen who tried to puke his way to the Moon.

Dave exited the briefing room and walked toward the elevators, with Neville and his nurse slightly behind him. They entered the lift and headed up toward the shuttle deck.

"You know," Neville said with a nervous edge in his voice, "they say that we SF writers were never in the prediction business, but that's a lot of bullshit."

"Really?" Dave said, trying to stifle a yawn.

"Bet your ass, sonny! Whenever I wrote a book, I crammed as much hard science as I could into it. And I hoped that everything I dreamed up would come true. Make me look like a genius, right?"

The elevator doors opened and they stepped out into the reception lounge by the pressurized doors. There was a crowd of people already there—news crew members armed with cameras and lights. Kathleen Ennis was standing by the double doors with a microphone in her hand. Her fashionably cut raven-black hair shone brilliantly in the hot lights; her dark eyes were like polished stones.

"What's going on here?" Neville asked as he spied the NBC media crew.

Kate Ennis moved to the old man's side quickly and smoothly. One smile totally disarmed him. She was a very attractive woman—tall, lean, long legs. "Hello, Dr. Neville. I'm Kate Ennis from NBC Satellite News. It's a pleasure to meet you, sir."

Neville smiled broadly and leaned forward to kiss Kate wetly on the lips. He attempted to pull her close to him, but she expertly pulled away just in time. "It's always a pleasure to meet a woman as beautiful as you, Ms. Ennis. To what do I owe this occasion—other than the fact that I am a famous old fart that everybody likes to interview?"

"This is the surprise I was talking about, Dr. Neville," Dave Lowen said. "When the shuttle docked and everyone was hustled off to the assembly, Colonel Kemp realized that we were missing out on a historic event—the first trip to the Moon by America's foremost science fiction writer."

"And so," Kate Ennis continued, "the colonel arranged for us to . . . ah, restage your arrival on the Moon. That's what all this crew is for."

"Yes," said Captain Lowen. "I'll escort you through the double doors in the airlock corridor as though we were just arriving, and Kate Ennis will conduct a small interview, recording the historic event."

Neville nodded appreciatively, smiling and leering at Kate Ennis. "A great idea. Absolutely inspired."

A man in headphones, connected to a portable control console, signaled to Kate. "Okay, Ms. Ennis. Ready when you are."

Lowen keyed open the double doors and moved inside with Neville. They waited for another signal, and then reentered the shuttle deck reception area, where the lights were trained upon them. Kate Ennis, standing in front of the cameras, was already talking.

". . . and the Earth shuttle *Campbell* has just touched down in the hangar, ladies and gentlemen. Any moment now, honored author, scientist, and elder statesman Dr. John T. Neville will be stepping down to the lunar surface and coming through these doors directly behind me."

The doors whooshed open as Kate continued, "And here he is. Dr. John T. Neville."

Neville did a good imitation of being surprised to see the media crew. He quickly recovered and smiled into the lens of the closest camera. He was a longtime veteran of interviews and media coverage, that much was clear.

"Dr. Neville, I am Kate Ennis from NBC Satellite News, and I would like to congratulate you for making your first trip to the Moon. After all these years of writing about space travel, I'm sure it must be quite a thrill to have your dream come true."

"You bet it is, honey." Neville turned and looked into the camera. "And I'd like to tell everyone around the world watching this broadcast that I could have made the trip thirty years ago if I had wanted to. It's just that I didn't have any real reason to be here until now."

"How would you describe flight up from the Earth?" Kate asked, smiling smoothly and professionally.

"You know, I'm glad you asked me that question," Neville said. "I was sitting in my seat on the shuttle, watching the Earth drop away, and I was thinking how it reminded me of my novel *The Secret of the Moon Marauders*. Strange as it may seem, way back in 1951, I envisioned a shuttle almost exactly like the one I was riding on."

"Was the experience of being in outer space itself in any way like you imagined it?"

Dave Lowen was listening to the whole load of bullshit off camera, trying to keep from laughing out loud.

He kept recalling Neville's green, panic-stricken face on the video monitor during the shuttle flight. He didn't look like he was noticing anything except the condition of his stomach.

"Katie," said Neville. "Let me tell you—I had always imagined that space travel would be an arduous task, a real challenge to the mind and body, but I have to admit that at least in this instance my instincts and my predictive abilities were way off base."

"In what way, Dr. Neville?"

"Our technology has made space travel such a painless, almost effortless endeavor that, I'll tell you, I hardly noticed the flight."

Kate smiled. She felt that the interview was going badly but had no idea how to improve her subject's responses. "I was wondering, Dr. Neville, since you are a man of words, if you said anything of significance when the ship first touched down on the lunar surface or when you first stepped out of the ship?"

"You mean if I said anything like the old 'One small step for man' business?"

Kate cleared her throat and smiled weakly. "Yes, something like that."

Neville looked directly into the camera, and an expression of total seriousness clouded his doughy features. "You know, Katie, I'm going to tell you something—I was so glad to be out of that ship that I think the first thing I said when I stepped down was 'Christ, am I glad *that's* fucking over with!'" And with that, Dr. Neville threw back his head and laughed long and loud. It was a braying, hyenalike laugh that became infectious, and without warning everyone on the set, including Kate Ennis herself, erupted into laughter.

It seemed the more people laughed, the worse it became, and Kate had to force herself to address the camera to conclude the interview. "Well, there you have it, ladies and gentlemen—the historic first visit of the world's most famous living science fiction writer, Dr. John T. Neville, to IASA Copernicus Base on the Moon. We now take you back to our studios in New York."

Kate dropped her microphone and leaned back against a bulkhead as she again burst into laughter, which set off another round among her crew.

Neville looked around and joined in the laughter. When it died down he looked about innocently and muttered, "Was it something I said?"

And the crew again erupted into laughter.

It was a very old wall. And it was in constant need of maintenance.

Xick knew that his job would never end, that the Barrier would always be there, slowly disintegrating. He was the supervisor of a group of young Saurian males—fresh from the nurseries and as yet untrained or selected for their serving classes. All young males were employed as laborers until they were selected for training in one of the society's castes.

Being a warrior, Xick was always watching out for good military prospects, but he had little to do with the selection process. He used his squad of fighters to keep the laborers in line and to protect them as they worked on a crumbling section of the Barrier.

The Saurian stood upon a rickety-looking scaffold on the outside of the Barrier where the laborers worked quickly. They were surrounded by the watchful eyes of the warriors who guarded the area from any curious predators.

Work on this particular section had been going slowly. It had been discovered that a large colony of burrowing lizards had been infiltrating this part of the Barrier, lacing it with tunnels and holes. This had weakened the structural elements to a great degree, and now this entire section of the Barrier cried out for replacement. Xick had decided to do the outside work first to be done with it and not have to anticipate dangerous work later.

His crew had just finished flushing out and poisoning the colony of burrowers, and they were now beginning the actual repairs. But he felt there was something wrong with this particular crew. Although they wore the tunics signifying they were in rational states of mind and thereby not eligible for the Dark Fold, they seemed quite irritable and not finely attuned to their duties.

Xick had heard about the violence and near riot in the mercantile center, and he hoped his laborers were not drifting into a similar situation. He watched the young males below him struggle with a glazing pot full of mortar, and he wondered why so many things seemed to be going wrong now, more than ever before—before the humans had come with their strange machines and their quick-death weapons. He could not help thinking that the humans had brought many new problems to his world. He didn't trust the humans, and no amount of lecturing by the priests would ever change his mind.

Feeling paranoid and skittish, he barked at his charges, urging them to work more quickly, with more energy. Some of them looked up with listless expressions; others hissed openly at him. He had never known such defiance from males fresh from the nurseries. He would show them not to speak to a warrior like that!

Just as Xick stepped forward, planning to strike the most defiant of the young males, a fight broke out in their ranks. One of the workers was shoved into a pot of mortar, and the melee was suddenly on. At least a dozen of the laborers began striking each other with tools. Xick signaled to the warriors who had been guarding the area to intervene, and immediately most of his squad began climbing down into the scaffolding to bash some heads. The supervisor had never experienced such troubles, and it was most embarrassing—he hoped none of the other squad leaders got wind of this incident.

The warriors were quick and efficient, doing what they were trained to do, but in the confusion; they did not notice the Stegosaurus until it was almost upon the scaffolding. It must have rambled out of the edge of the forest and crossed the intervening clearing to the Barrier with surprising speed.

The Stegosaurus was honking, bleating as though in great pain. Xick looked down in shock to see it charging toward the base of the temporary ramparts. In that moment he could see that this was no normal herbivore. Its eyes were rimmed in blood, and foam bubbled from its twisted mouth. Its plates were skewed at odd angles, and its flanks were ravaged by oozing sores.

Shouting out a warning that was too late, Xick jumped up the scaffolding. He reached the edge of the Barrier railing and pulled himself up, but many of the others were not so fortunate.

At full charge, with amazing speed, the Stegosaurus careened into the supports of the scaffolding, its five tons of bulk breaking everything like so many matchsticks. The sound of snapping beams and groaning wood filled the air, mixing in with the terrible cries of the laborers who plummeted down from their perches.

The maddened Stegosaurus did not stop until it had smashed into the base of the Barrier, crushing many of the Saurians against the wood and stone like pieces of overripe fruit. It recoiled from the neck-snapping collision, lashing its spiked tail about. Debris rained down upon it, crushing its tiny head, and yet its hind legs still danced and struggled, not yet receiving the message that it was dead. It staggered back, away from the Barrier, finally falling into the dust, twitching and spasming.

Xick stood atop the Barrier, stunned by the sudden destruction.

His scaffolding was gone, many of his workers and guards had been killed or injured, and the Barrier had been damaged further. He could see a large crack in the outer mortar, radiating up from a red splotch on the wall where the Stegosaurus had crashed. Worse yet, there was a bloody carcass down there. Scavengers would make it impossible to resume the repair work until the bones were picked clean.

Later that evening, Ian Coopersmith escorted Rebecca Thalberg back to her quarters in the biomedical wing of Copernicus Base. They had spent a few hours in the Village Pub, not reminiscing over old times but getting their feelings out on the table, sharing the anxieties both had experienced since the end of the "Dragonstar war," and making an honest attempt to map out what the future might hold for the both of them.

It hadn't been the most pleasant of conversations, Ian

thought, but at least the liquor had loosened them up and let the honesty start flowing. He had told her about his problems at home, and his feelings about her (no, he wasn't in love with her, but he damned well felt *something* for her, and it didn't feel like mere friendship), and how his wife and family would always be first in his mind, but how he had discovered that he couldn't be with them twenty-four hours a day (they just didn't share the same interests or see life as a series of challenges to be overcome, as he did).

Becky too had wanted to get the record straight, and although her sentences came slowly, at times awkwardly, she also succeeded in making herself clear. It was true, she had said, that she'd never met a man like Coopersmith, but it was also true that he was not the man for her (not because of him, but because of her). Her feelings for Phineas had been changing and changing and then changing once again, and she doubted whether her sojourn with Ian in the preserve had really influenced much of anything as far as Colonel Kemp was concerned.

They both agreed that Phineas was a man to be respected, admired even, but a damned hard man to like once you got to know him. It wasn't just that he was so serious all the time but that he took himself so seriously. He always seemed preoccupied with what everyone was thinking of him, and he forgot to think about those around him.

That was how their conversation went, and when it started to degenerate into a psychoanalytic session, Ian suggested they both retire for the evening. Becky had had enough to drink to slyly signal that Ian would be welcome to spend the night, but he declined more out of fear than out of respect. It was too early in the game to get reinvolved with her—it was that simple. He had left Earth to get his thoughts, his priorities, and his career back on the proper paths, and diving into an affair right away would only cloud up the waters.

And so he found himself walking down the empty corridors of Copernicus Base, away from the biomedical wing. He wasn't sleepy; he was still wired up from the shuttle flight and his confrontations with Phineas and Becky. There had been a lot of excess emotional baggage that needed unloading, and he was feeling better that it had finally been done.

Taking an elevator up to Level One, he walked quickly to an observation bay and looked out across the expanse of the lunar surface. The superstructures of some of the docks, the observatory, and the mass loaders were visible in the dusty silence. There were a few vehicles moving about, kicking up rooster tails of volcanic ash, but it was basically calm and desolate out there. Ian looked up and sought out the floating bulk of the Dragonstar, distant but clearly visible due to its great size.

There was something about the alien ship that wouldn't let him go. He had always known he would have to return to its mysteries and its essential challenge.

All right now, he thought. I've come back, you big bugger.

Twelve

The plan for the documentary was mapped out by Phineas Kemp and his staff of production advisors far in advance of the actual shooting. He had imagined that a good plan, based upon IASA protocols, would help to avoid many of the usual snafus that accompany film-making. A chronological unfolding was decided to be the optimum approach to telling the entire story, and so the early footage, which was shot at Copernicus Base and in space at close proximity to the Dragonstar, went off without much of a hitch.

Phineas was pleased with his crew and the way all the IASA staff were cooperating with what proved to be a massive undertaking. Once the crews had been shipped up to the Dragonstar itself the problems began to make themselves clear.

For all the shots in the Mesozoic preserve, a special film base camp had to be established with a force-field perimeter and a full complement of guards and equipment. Originally planned as a small installation, the film base camp soon grew to rival Mikaela Lindstrom's paleontological survey camp—the largest IASA installation within the Mesozoic preserve.

Kemp sat in his temporary office in the film base camp, carefully going over the shooting schedule on a portable monitor. If there were no glitches, all the major holography should be finished by the end of the next twenty-four hour period. Editing and postproduction work would not require a large amount of time, and then they would be ready for the live broadcast and the historic meeting of John T. Neville with the Saurians. Kemp was still excited by the project.

His intercom buzzed, and he slapped at the keypad absently. "Yes, Colonel Kemp here."

"Phineas, this Bob Jakes."

"Bob! I've been meaning to get in touch. Did you get my memo on the film crew?"

"Yes, I got it. In fact they're already here, setting up in the main lab."

"Great. Great. Everything's going okay, I assume?"

"Yes, the crew's fine, but that's not what I called about. Something else has come up that you should look into."

Kemp sank back in his chair. Christ, more bureaucratic stuff to deal with. Becoming an administrator certainly had its drawbacks. "What is it, Bob?"

"You never got back to me on that report Mishima Takamura forwarded to your office—the one on the radiation detection and the schizophrenic phenomenon in the Saurian population."

Phineas was getting lost quickly. "What report are you talking about?"

"You mean you never read it?" Jakes's voice was a bit strident.

"To tell you the truth, I remember seeing it come in, but with this frigging documentary to finish, I guess I just haven't gotten around to reading it yet."

"That report was flagged 'Eyes Only.' It was a Level One Priority, and you 'didn't get around to reading it'? Are you kidding me, Phineas?"

Jakes sounded very upset, and Phineas didn't want to hear this kind of crap. He'd better cut things off quickly and get to the heart of things. "Listen, Bob, let's just say I've been very busy. Now, if you update me on the report we can get down to cases. What did the report have to say, and what does it have to do with your call at this point?"

Jakes summarized the report as quickly as possible, emphasizing the fears of Thesaurus and the growing suspicions of Mishima Takamura, concluding that he felt the Joint Chiefs should be alerted to the subtle changes being recorded within the Dragonstar's interior. He also tied in the incident with Lindstrom's survey team, implying that the film crew might be in danger if there were other mutated species running loose in the preserve.

"We've been down here for three days now and have had no problems whatsoever," Kemp assured him. "Now, what's the new data?"

"There's been another incident in the Saurian preserve," Jakes said.

"What kind of incident?"

"Some sort of mass hysteria thing. Three warrior-class fellows went berserk and killed ten others. It took some time to subdue them."

"Christ! What happened?"

"The Saurians had them executed, except for one, whom they turned over to us for some tests." Jakes paused to clear his throat. "We've just finished the tests. That's why I'm calling."

"Go on, I'm listening," Kemp said. He was indeed listening, but he did not want to be. The last thing he needed at this point was more problems. He just wanted to get this documentary finished, and then he could deal with anything else the Fates cared to throw his way.

"All right," Jakes said. "Listen to this. We ran a series of neuroscans on our subject and found that his brain is riddled with tumors."

"What kind of tumors?"

"Radiological carcinomas," Jakes said. "There's evidence that the subject has been exposed to some heavy radiation dosages. This is the same kind of thing Mikaela Lindstrom found with that accelerated growth mutant she encountered.''

Kemp harrumphed loudly. "Look, Bob, I'm no scientist. What the hell does this stuff mean?''

"We're not sure. We've been testing other Saurians, and of course ourselves, and finding no trace of this cell change. Whatever's going on seems to be a very random kind of activity.''

"Any ideas on what might be causing it?''

"Yes, there are quite a few theories, but none of them sound too good. Takamura's report mentions the ones that have the highest possibility.''

"Goddamn it, Bob, I didn't read the frigging report! What do you want me to do, flagellate myself? Now, what the hell do you guys think is going on?''

Jakes paused for a moment, then continued. "I think we're in the middle of something that the aliens—the ones who made this ship—built into the works.''

"What does that mean?'' Kemp didn't like the almost reverential tone in Jakes's voice.

"I mean that things seem to be following some sort of pattern, as though a specific procedure were being followed. Nothing major yet, but lots of little things indicate a change in the status of this ship. And of course there's the energy burst we detected several weeks back which could have been a response to the signal we triggered when we originally entered this ship.''

Kemp cursed himself for not taking the time to keep up with the day-to-day business aboard the Dragonstar and began to wonder if perhaps he had become a bit too preoccupied with the World Media documentary project.

"Colonel, are you there?''

"Yes, Bob. Sorry, I was just giving this whole thing some thought. Do you have any suggestions?''

"Takamura and I have been talking it over, and we think it might be a good idea to conduct a general evacuation.''

"What? What did you say?"

"Until we can get to the bottom of some of these new events, we were thinking that it might be a good idea to get most of the staff off-ship. We've got more than two hundred people on board, and I don't have to tell you that we're responsible for their safety."

"You just did," Kemp said dryly.

"I'm sorry, Colonel, but this whole thing is very important to me."

"I appreciate your getting in touch, Bob. But I'm afraid you don't understand the position I'm in. Evacuating this ship right now would be impossible. The IASA has a contract with World Media for this project, and they've been hyping the shit out of it down on Earth. More than two billion people are expecting to see the whole story of the Dragonstar on their holies right in their own homes. We can't back out of it now. It's just impossible."

"Well, I'd like to go on record as not agreeing with your decision, Colonel. I'm sorry, but that's the way I feel."

"It's your prerogative, Bob. I understand, and I want to thank you for your concern. Look, we're going to have the whole project wrapped up in another day or so, and when the broadcast is over, we can all get together and decide on the best course of action. I'll notify the Joint Chiefs about what your findings have been, and we'll take it from there."

"You mean you're not going to inform the Joint Chiefs now?"

"That's right," Kemp said firmly.

"I think that's a big mistake, Phineas."

"Why don't you let me worry about that one, Bob." He paused to clear his throat. "Now look, I've got a few more things to take care of here. Good luck with the production crew. I'll be in touch within twenty-four hours. See you then."

Phineas signed off before he heard any reply from Dr. Jakes. There were simply too many things going on at once, and he had to take one step at a time. He did feel bad about not keeping on top of the memos that were piling up in his office, and Jakes did have some valid things to say, but it was all going to have to wait until the documentary was completed.

Phineas had detected an emotional strain in Jakes's voice, and he knew that would hamper any real decision-making that might be necessary from the chief science officer. There was no room for emotional response to critical situations. That had always been the problem with Becky and himself—too much damned emotional garbage getting in the way. He grinned easily. Despite what the women were saying about equal this and equal that, they were still the more emotionally dependent members of the species, of that Kemp was certain. And that made them less competent in a crisis—he was equally convinced of that.

Well, there would be plenty of time for social philosophizing later. He had a film project to complete. He whipped through the remainder of the schedule on his monitor and checked out the various assignments—making sure that everyone and every contingency had been carefully planned for. Kemp was pleased with the orderly geometry of the schedule. It was one of his usual meticulous creations, and he could always admire a job well done.

His intercom buzzed again. "Kemp here."

"Yes, Colonel, this is Lasky. We're just about ready here . . ."

It was the director of the second production unit, and Kemp was pleased to hear that the crew was ready to shoot the sequences in the Mesozoic preserve. "All right, Les, I'll be right out. I'm anxious to get this thing rolling."

The second unit crew had been packed into a caravan of Omni Terrain Vehicles. It was time to go out into the hostile environment of the preserve and recreate the survival trek of Rebecca Thalberg and Ian Coopersmith.

Becky and Ian were riding in the second vehicle, having agreed to be filmed in the preserve during their interviews.

Mikaela Lindstrom rode in the lead vehicle with Phineas Kemp, a driver, and two armed escorts as they left the base camp and began a short journey through the lush green jungle of the preserve. The OTVs moved well through the thick undergrowth and into a marshy swampland. In the distance, bordering the Jurassic bog, rose a majestic forest of redwoods, shrouded in a steamy mist. To Mikaela it was a magical landscape that never lost its special dreamlike qualities. To others it was the stuff of nightmares, a land of fear and terrible death.

"How far are we going, Dr. Lindstrom?" the driver called.

"Out to the Mordor Plateau," Mikaela said. "There's plenty of room for the crew to set up their equipment, and the scenery will give them a good variety of shots."

The driver nodded. Mikaela looked over at Phineas, who seemed lost in thought. She smiled and decided to needle him a bit.

"Such a furrowed brow, my colonel. Do you sense trouble brewing?"

"What?" Kemp asked absently. "Oh, no, I was just thinking over a few things."

"Like what?"

"Sorry, Mikaela, but these things are classified for the moment."

She feigned insult, then smiled coquettishly at him. "Why, Colonel, does that mean you don't trust me?"

"Now look," he said, missing the humorous jibe. "We've been through this sort of thing before. I just can't go on talking about everything that crosses my desk and my mind. You know it's the responsibility of the position that—"

"Phineas, be still, I was only *joking*, for God's sake. I swear, sometimes you can be such a stick in the mud."

"Sorry, Mikaela, but I have a lot on my mind these days." He looked into her deep, electric blue eyes, then out through the side viewing port of the primitive scenery.

"I was wondering, Phineas, have you had any weird feelings about shooting the sequence coming up?"

He looked at her with an expression of true bewilderment. "Whatever are you talking about?"

"Well, with Becky and Ian riding in the car behind us, getting ready to go out there and recreate their Tarzan and Jane thing, I was wondering if it might be getting to you at all."

Phineas smiled. "Mikaela, I can assure you that it's not getting to me in the least. In fact, I recently had a long talk with Coopersmith back on Earth, when he was arranging to return, and we were able to get everything aired out. Whatever went down is behind us now. We've all got a job to do."

"That's so very noble of you, Phineas." Mikaela chuckled lightly. "What about Becky? Did you have a long talk with her, too?"

Phineas continued looking out the viewing port, and Mikaela began to wonder if maybe she had inadvertently touched upon a still tender spot. "Well, not really," Phineas said after an awkward pause. "But I think we understand each other now."

"You think you 'understand' each other now?" Mikaela laughed again. "Why, Phineas, is that a euphemism for saying that you two had one last fling in the sack?"

Phineas became visibly rigid in his seat, and he refused to look away from the port. Bad signs, thought Mikaela, as she decided to press her advantage. "Phineas, I'm talking to you. Is there anything wrong?"

He finally looked up at her, appearing for an instant like a small boy who had been caught doing a terrible thing. "Yes, I heard you. I was just thinking how uncannily perceptive you paleontologists can be with such a paltry amount of physical evidence.''

Mikaela laughed at his little irony, instantly wondering if he had indeed fallen into Rebecca Thalberg's bed while they had been on Earth together. It wouldn't bother her if he had. She was happily above such petty jealousies, feeling secure enough in her own person to know that most people got what they deserved in terms of treatment from others. If Phineas felt the need to check out Becky one last time, then there had to have been a good reason for it. Whatever it was, Mikaela felt she could deal with it.

She was about to tell him this, in so many words, when the driver interrupted with a message.

"Colonel, there's something up ahead."

The OTV had just cleared the swampland and was trundling up a long slope peppered with ginkgoes and thick protoferns. Something had emerged from the vegetation and was blocking the path of the lead vehicle. Even from a distance, the creature looked large and imposing.

"Slow down. Signal the others," Kemp said. Then, turning to Mikaela: "What is that thing?"

She climbed into the gunnery bubble and studied the beast through the telescopic sight. It was a theropod, but not one she could readily identify. The carnivore stood on two powerful hind legs, balanced by a thick tail. Its large head with its half-open mouth and sharp teeth signaled the potential danger it represented.

"Take it a little closer," Mikaela said. "Let me get a better look at this guy."

The OTV moved on at a cautious pace. The dinosaur in its path showed no signs of bolting, as they often did in the presence of machinery. Mikaela was surprised by the beast's outlandish coloring—thick bright yellow and orange stripes, accented by black speckling. The beast's hide seemed out of synch with the rest of the subdued forest colors. As the OTV drew clower, Mikaela could see that the creature was four to five meters in height and appeared to be a cousin of the Allosaurus family.

There was a pronounced sagittal crest running from its snout to the back of its head—a skull formation she had not seen previously. There was something about the look of the creature that she didn't like. She had a feeling of intense déjà vu, and her first impulse was to implore Phineas to turn them around and get them out of there.

"Well, what is it?" he was asking.

Mikaela shook her head. "I don't know. Some kind of predator, but I don't recognize it. We're still running across secondary species. This is probably one of them."

"He doesn't seem to want to get out of the way, sir," the driver said.

Kemp motioned to one of the armed guards. "Rhoades, get up there in the bubble and be ready to give him a few bursts."

Mikaela climbed down from her perch to allow the guard to replace her as Phineas leaned forward into the control cabin and tapped the driver on the shoulder. "All right, let's just go around him and see what he does. Give him enough room to run if he wants to. If he attacks, we'll have to cut him down."

Mikaela touched his arm. "Phineas, you know I don't like to do that."

"Neither do I," he said coolly. "But if it comes down to it, I don't have any choice."

The driver accelerated, and they trundled quickly toward the brightly colored carnivore, who stood his ground like a war memorial statue. As the OTV grew closer, Mikaela could see that the speckled markings on the beast's hide were not natural colorations, as she had assumed from the greater distance, but running sores.

There was a deadly familiarity to the cancerous wounds that made her heart leap into her breast.

Maneuvering smartly, the driver whipped the OTV to the left of the creature, who stood watching the beetle-like vehicle lumber past. The beast tilted its great head, staring at them with a large, flat yellow eye. It seemed to be searching the clear blisters for signs of life. As the lead vehicle moved past, it began to advance on the second one in line.

Before the beast had moved very far, the guard fired off a warning burst of slugs, which ripped up the dark loamy earth at the dinosaur's hind claws. It reared back, snapped its head in the lead vehicle's direction, then, apparently thinking the better of it, leaped off into the deep folds of the forest. It disappeared within an eyeblink, and Mikaela marveled at how quickly the large creature had been able to move.

"Looks like we scared it off, Colonel," said the guard in the turret.

"Keep an eye out for it, just the same. I don't want him coming back in the middle of our party."

The guard nodded and smiled as Phineas looked back at Mikaela. "There now, we didn't hurt the fellow, did we?"

"Phineas, that was a mutant . . . like the one that attacked me and Penovich."

"What? How can you be sure?"

She explained to him the significance of the open cancers on its hide.

"Then we should be extra watchful once we get out and get set up," he said flatly.

Mikaela was a bit stunned by his stony reaction. "You mean you're still going to let them go through with the shoot?"

Phineas shrugged. "Why not? This is the last full day of shooting. I don't want to muck up the schedule now. Besides, I've got a fully armed platoon out here. Nothing's going to happen that we can't deal with. They're just a bunch of big dumb beasts."

"Well, at least let's put some distance between us and that last one," Mikaela said. "Tell the driver to take us up to the farthest quadrant on the plateau, all right?"

"If it will make you feel better, fine."

Riding in the third OTV, along with an armed guard and

several members of the film crew, were Neville and his nurse, Ms. Wilkins. With each lurch of the Omni Terrain Vehicle, Neville's stomach threatened to let go of its moorings and come heaving up his throat. God, he hated this mess.

The OTV pitched violently from side to side as it negotiated a ravine, then began climbing forcefully up a long sloping grade that opened onto a great plateau. Where in hell were they going to stop? How much more churning and shaking was necessary for this silly movie? His LM equipment jostled about in the knapsack at his side, and he managed only a weak smile at Ms. Wilkins who (damn her!) seemed to be having the time of her life.

Neville hated the whole ordeal. He had found spaceflight a physically and mentally straining experience, lacking all of the excitement and flair that he had so often imagined. Riding up to the Moon in one of those claustrophobic ships possessed the thrill of being accidently locked in a steam bath. And if that wasn't enough, they then packed him off to this terrarium in the sky, which was absolutely teeming with the most vicious, insidiously ugly, disgusting, and vile beasts to ever walk the Earth.

Watching the holograms had been bad enough, but when that constipated colonel invited him to join the shoot in the Mesozoic preserve, how could he have turned down such a once-in-a-lifetime opportunity. (How? Very easily—if he'd had any balls at all.) But then he would have had to deal with the image problems of such a stance. How would it look for a writer of his stature to tell everybody how much he loathed all this gosh-gee-wow crap?

Not very good.

And so good old Long Jack had smiled and jumped up and told the colonel that he couldn't wait to get a look at those wonderful dinosaurs firsthand.

And they had just seen their first one.

Ole Long Jack wasn't so senile that he hadn't noticed

the lead vehicle swinging around to avoid a big meateater, then take a few potshots at the hideous son of a
bitch. Christ, those things gave him the creeps. Just the
thought of being picked up in those strong, purposeful
little forelimbs, being scrutinized by one of its dumb
saucery eyes, and then being popped whole, a light
snack, into the stinking, fetid maw . . .

It was enough to make him want to vomit.

"Are you all right, Dr. Neville?" asked his nurse,
who was monitoring his LM readouts.

"What? Of course I'm not all right. We're riding
through the most hostile environment the Earth has ever
seen, and you're asking me such a question. Why
couldn't I just slip into a nice, comfortable, schizophrenic episode, be totally oblivious to this whole horrible trip."

Ms. Wilkins chuckled. "Oh, Doctor. I think you've
got the wrong spirit of the whole thing. Try thinking of
it as a trip to an amusement park or something like
that."

"There's nothing amusing about this whole mess. If I
didn't have this stupid image to uphold, I would never
have consented to such a thing. Oh, if old John Campbell could see me now! He'd choke on one of those
cigarettes of his."

His nurse laughed as he forced himself to look back
out the viewing port. The yellow and orange striped
bastard had vanished after they'd taken a few shots at
it, but old Long Jack didn't trust the foul-smelling
suckers—no way. It was probably skulking along in the
bushes right next to their caravan, just waiting until they
stopped so it could jump out and scarf somebody for
lunch. Jesus, they were disgusting.

He watched for any sign of it, but nothing appeared
as the caravan crested the rise and fanned out across a
high, wide plateau. Rocks and primitive trees dotted the
landscape like small oases in the middle of a desert, but
there was no sign of the party crasher in the striped suit.
Old Long Jack would continue to keep an eye peeled, to
remain as paranoid as possible, yessir.

*   *   *

Mikaela touched his arm, indicating that the caravan had reached an ideal spot for the shoot, and Kemp signaled his driver to halt. The rest of the OTVs parked in a formation reminiscent of the wagon trains of the American Old West, and the crews started jumping out and setting up their gear.

"All right," Phineas said, looking at Mikaela. "Let's get this over with. You're going to be in the first scene with Williamson, aren't you?"

She smiled and climbed up to the entrance hatch, then flashed her beautiful eyes upon him. "Why, Phineas, can't you tell? When was the last time I went out into the jungle with my makeup on?"

He just smiled as he watched her leave the vehicle and join the members of the film crew who were assembling around director Les Lasky and his narrator/interviewer for the project, the famous British stage actor Alistair Williamson.

Jumping down, Phineas sought out Neville. He wanted to keep the old guy by his side, and therefore out of harm's immediate way. He was eager to hear the famous writer's impressions of the magnificent alien ship and its interior world.

"Jacobs," he said to the closest guard. "Get the perimeter-watch set up and have somebody bring Dr. Neville up here."

The IASA soldier saluted and moved off. Phineas watched the production get rolling. Lasky was quick and efficient, and he knew what he wanted from all his people. He was easy to understand, and he was sure to have everyone prepared before he started the cameras rolling. He was a consummate pro, and the documentary was going to have a very polished, very crisp feel to it.

"Colonel," a voice crackled in Phineas's helmet mike, "this is Martino. I've got a blip coming this way. Land based, pretty good sized. Might be our friend from before. Whatever it is, it just cleared the rise."

"All right, Sergeant, I copy that. Keep me posted."

Kemp directed a team of marksmen to fan out beyond
the perimeter watch and head off whatever it was that
was homing in on them. Overhead, a squadron of
Pterodactyls glided about, watching the strange ac-
tivities below, staying in the area like a flight of vultures
waiting for a kill.

"Okay, Colonel, we have a visual . . . it's the same
guy we ran into before. Coming this way."

Phineas flipped on the PA in the OTV and alerted the
film crew, who had already begun filming Alistair
Williamson interviewing Becky and Ian. Instantly their
cameras swung around and picked up the IASA forces
fanning out against the approaching carnivore. Kemp
knew this was going to make great footage for the
broadcast, full of danger and immediacy. Ian Coopersmith, true to his reputation, cast off the role of film
star in an instant, reaching for an automatic weapon
and joining in the deployment of troops. Becky, also a
veteran of the Mesozoic way of life and death, decided
to move off with the film crew behind the OTVs.

Looking across the expanse of the plateau, Kemp
could see the creature closing in. It jogged along with a
long-legged stride, a fearless advance punctuated by
much swinging of its large head and a vicious snapping
of its jaws.

Neville closed in on Phineas with a look of abject
panic on his face. He moved with surprising agility, despite the extra baggage of dangling LM tubes and wires.
His nurse scrambled behind, carrying his porta-pak, in a
desperate effort to catch up with her charge.

"Don't you think you should be shooting that son of
a bitch?" Neville asked.

Phineas reached out to give the old writer support as
he practically collapsed into his arms. The alarm
beepers on the porta-pak LM were all clamoring for attention, joining together in a weird, atonal, medical/
musical composition. "Take it easy, Dr. Neville. It's
going to be all right. My men have got everything under
control."

"Disgusting creature," Neville muttered.

"Dr. Neville," his nurse said between gasps. "Please, you shouldn't get yourself so excited."

"Vile beast!" Neville was beginning to exhibit flecks of foam at the corners of his mouth.

"Please, Doctor," Nurse Wilkins cried. "If you don't calm down, you're going to kill yourself."

"Me kill myself? What about that thirty-ton monster? He looks like he could do a very nice job, thank you."

In spite of the imminent danger, Phineas could barely keep from smiling at the old man. He tried to nod sternly and directed his attention toward the perimeter. Mikaela had moved alongside him and put her hand on his shoulder.

The marksmen waited until the predator had drawn close enough to be caught in a lethal cross fire. In order to employ this tactic they had allowed the beast to push dangerously close to the line of OTVs that formed a wagon-train barrier around the film crew, several of whom had clambered up on the vehicles to record the advance of the beast.

It moved with a crazed urgency, jaws snapping and slavering in anticipation of its imagined meal. Its large hind claws tore great divots of earth from beneath it, marking its trail toward the human position. Overhead, as though sensing the coming carnage, Pterodactyls wheeled and waited.

When the marksmen opened fire, their hollow-point and jellied-nitro-filled rounds ripped into the bright flesh of the dinosaur, rippling the folds of scaly skin like water in the wind. The first volley of shells staggered the creature, stopping it in mid-stride and causing it to stumble off to the left. Only an instinctive slash of its heavy tail kept it from falling to the earth. Reeling and weaving like a wounded prizefighter, the animal struggled to regain its balance.

Finally, as both splayed, three-toed claws gained equal purchase in the hard earth, it threw back its head and let loose a high-pitched cry of pain and unrestrained fury. Opening its yellow eyes even wider, it selected the closest OTV as its prey and forced itself foward, lumbering ahead on drunken legs.

The marksmen unleashed a second volley, more violent than the first. A locust-swarm of slugs assaulted the beast, shredding its neck into ribbons, exploding its skull, turning its primitive nervous system into useless jelly. The beast recoiled from this vicious attack, standing perfectly upright, rigid as though at attention, overwhelmed by the systematic, death-dealing shock of the attack.

It opened its mouth to cry one final time, but only a feeble squeaking sound emerged as the great bellow-lungs collapsed. It hung motionless for a moment before toppling, with unbelievable slowness, to the hard-packed dirt of the plateau. Great clouds of dust and dirt rose up around the carcass, and almost immediately insects materialized out of the air to begin their ritual buzzing about the bleeding hulk of meat.

"Good Christ!" whispered Neville in a soft, hoarse voice. He looked at the corpse of the beast, which convulsed one more time. The old writer appeared ready to vomit. He moved several feet from the group and retched.

Kemp fingered his helmet mike and cleared his throat. "Good shooting, Martino. Nice work."

Mikaela looked up at him with an expression of urgency creasing her sensuously angled face. "Phineas, I hate to spoil your fun, but we'd better get out of here right away."

He knew she was referring to the instant response of the environment to the smell of blood and death. Within minutes scavengers of all shapes and sizes would be flocking to their position—all whipped into a feeding frenzy.

"You're right. Quietly inform Lasky and his crew. I'll get my men moving right away." Phineas barked orders into his helmet mike, and everyone started scrambling back into the safety of the OTVs. Even as they moved, clouds of dust could be seen across the plateau—creatures running quickly across the hard, dry earth.

Mikaela helped Nurse Wilkins with Dr. Neville, whose LM porta-pak was playing a veritable symphony of warning bells and alarm beepers. The old man was walking with a pronounced wobble as he headed back to his vehicle.

"Shoot that bastard," he cried out. "Watch out, you bugger!"

Mikaela helped him into his vehicle and rushed back to where Phineas stood watching the rest of the crew. Coopersmith, standing several vehicles down the line, was supervising the rapid evacuation, and Phineas knew that everything was well in hand. "Let's move out," he said grimly, and helped her aboard.

As the caravan scurried away, the hordes of scavengers descended on the still warm flesh of the dead dinosaur. Mikaela watched the action from the viewing port until it dwindled from view.

"It's a hell of a way to live, isn't it?" Phineas joked.

"That's not funny," Mikaela said.

"I was just trying to relieve some tension. Sorry."

"That was another one of the mutants, Phineas. I don't know if anyone else noticed, but I saw the sores. If we'd been able to cut him open, we would have found him laced through with tumors."

"As soon as we finish this project, we'll get onto the problem with a full-scale program," Phineas said.

"I just hope you're not too late."

"I've already had this conversation with Bob Jakes," Phineas said. "I am quite aware of the consequences."

"Well, that's pretty interesting, because I don't think any of the rest of us are."

"Hey, take it easy. You know what I mean?"

Mikaela looked at him warily. "No, I'm not sure I do, Phineas. I know that you usually do what you want, that you normally get your own way, but I'm not sure you realize what your way might mean this time around.''

"The documentary will be finished tomorrow," he said. "That is, assuming that you can find us a suitable replacement location for today's shots instead of trying to pick an argument with me.''

Mikaela sighed audibly. "All right, but I'm not finished with you yet." Mikaela called up a map on the console screen and scrolled through some coordinates in a quick search for locations.

"My dear," Phineas said, running his hand down the small of her back to fondle her buttocks, "I hope you're never finished with me.''

Thirteen

Gregor Kolenkhov, a member of the Joint Chiefs of Staff at Copernicus Base, was seated in the communications bridge of the IASA lunar installation. Banks of monitors and screens displayed information of every conceivable type, but the screen that the portly Russian watched was a simple, portable holovision. The HV was tuned to World Media's sat-channel 80 and the last round of preliminary commercials before the initial segment of the grossly hyped documentary on the Dragonstar began.

"Just about ready?" asked Kolenkhov's staff communications officer, Major Peter Altermann.

"Yes," Gregor said. "After a veritable barrage of advertisements, however."

The two men watched as the projection dimmed to gray, then burst forth with colorful computer-generated three-dimensional images. Letters from the swirling chaos of a spiral galaxy, spelling out the program title:

THE DAY OF THE DRAGONSTAR

A great orchestral sound track enhanced the majesty and importance of the event everyone was about to see. Over this, the familiar voice of World Media's most popular narrator, Alistair Williamson, boomed the introduction:

"Humankind, having taken the first precarious steps away from the safety of its home world, has encountered what may arguably be called the most important discovery in the history of the human race—the alien vessel known as the Dragonstar.

Tonight you will discover for yourselves the wonder and the awe of what has been called "the largest artificially constructed device in the known universe." Its dimensions are . . ."

Major Altermann turned and winced at his superior. "Geez, Dr. Kolenkhov, looks like they're going to milk this for all it's worth."

"Yes, well, it is a fantastic event in our history, but I sincerely hope that the crass, insensitive minds of free enterprise do not cheapen its glory too much." Gregor laughed heartily and fumbled one of his dark, rich Turkish cigarettes from his pack.

"Well, this is really Colonel Kemp's baby, from what I hear," the major said, his East Texas accent curling and twanging every word.

"Most certainly," Gregor said, lighting his cigarette with his customary flourish. "It was a labor of love, as I understand it. We didn't see much of him around here while they were filming it, that was for sure."

"Yeah," the major said. "Well, they've been promising one hell of a show. I guess we'll just have to wait and see, huh?"

"Aren't you coming down to watch the live segment?" A voice intruded upon the thoughts of Mishima Takamura, and he turned to find the round, wrinkled face and gray eyes of Dr. Robert Jakes looking at him.

Mishima shook his head slowly as he looked up from his desk. A portable HV blared out the World Media documentary from a shelf behind him. He had been watching it with only half his attention while he continued to work over some calculations on a terminal.

"No, I don't think so," he said wearily. "I'm just too tired, Bob."

"You work too hard, Mishima. What's the hurry?"

"I don't know. Just a funny feeling I have. I didn't like the projections we were getting on that last batch of tests."

"Well, they'll wait till morning for me," Jakes said. "I think I'll go down to the live set and watch the broadcast. Then I'm calling it a night."

"See you later, Bob." Mishima smiled and waved at his superior as he disappeared out the door and down the long corridor. He liked Dr. Jakes immensely, and respected the man's ability to see all the facets of a problem before offering a solution. But he knew that Jakes's age and poor health were catching up with him. Sooner or later he was going to have to retire, and that would be a real loss to the agency.

Mishima allowed his attention to drift back to "The Day of the Dragonstar," conceding that the production was indeed a first-class job. World Media had spared no expense to present comprehensive coverage of the entire story. The documentary was full of drama, tension, information, and style. It was everything they had promised it would be, and despite his ill feelings toward Phineas Kemp, he was forced to admit that the man had done a very good job.

But none of it was going to matter very much if the radiation levels continued to rise.

Hakarrh, the capital city of the Saurian preserve: wide avenues and colorful tents; minarets and towers looming above the rows of tiny shops and stalls; large botanical gardens and parks, breaking up the patterned monotony of civilization. It was a strange kind of city. Its dirt roads and mud-brick and stone architecture appeared both primitive and alien, but its heart beat with a recognizable vitality. To be honest, though, Phineas had never actually liked being in the Saurian preserve.

He had always felt the place to be besieged by the most noisome odors—a melange of smells that conjured up images of strangely cooked foods, alien exhalations and excrements, and rampant disease. Even though he had been assured by the microbiologists on Jakes's team that the bacterial makeup of the Dragonstar's interior was an exact match of the Earth's, and that there was no cause for alarm, he still had odd feelings about remaining too long in close quarters with the Saurians and their environment.

On this particular evening—the evening of the World Media broadcast—the Saurian city was ablaze with the lights, sounds, and music of a grand celebration. A platform had been built, and the Saurians had prepared a program of entertainment for the cameras to be presented after the historic meeting of John T. Neville and a band of selected Saurians who represented the various class levels of their society. Neville had met one or two Saurians already, but the World Media people were staging things to look like a first-time event.

Phineas sat in the front row of the grandstands, which had been built in the center of Hakarrh's largest botanical garden. A massive crowd encircled the stands, which had been reserved for dignitaries, officers, diplomats, and members of the elite classes of the Saurians. The throng, mainly comprised of Saurians, also held perhaps a hundred of the IASA staff permanently assigned to the Dragonstar on the various research teams. There was a festive atmosphere to the occasion as the time ticked away, bringing them all that much closer to the moment of the live broadcast.

"This is all so exciting," Kate Ennis said, impulsively reaching out and taking Phineas's hand.

He was surprised by her action, and relieved that Mikaela had not yet joined him. She was aboard the ornithopter that would land in the center of the grandstand and bring Neville to his historic meeting with the Saurians. Phineas had arranged it so that Mikaela would perform the formal introductions. She had been so pleased and honored; Phineas was glad to have made her so happy. He did love her—it was just that he had a difficult time letting her know often enough. Oh well, there were lots of people like that. At least he wasn't alone with his problem.

He looked over at Kate, who looked stunning in a clinging gown, and patted her hand. "Yes, it is, isn't it?" he said, wondering if this beautiful woman was making a pass at him. He was terrible at noticing such things.

After all, he hadn't realized that Mikaela Lindstrom was attracted to him until she had almost been forced to spell things out. Some men were very attuned to women and some were not. Phineas simply belonged to the latter group. Taking the time to think things out, he decided to test the possibilities—so he took Kate's hand firmly in his own, waiting to see if she would withdraw it.

She did not.

Over the grandstand and the platform hung a large screen that displayed a two-dimensional image of the World Media broadcast to the assembled crowd. The massive screen afforded all the Saurians an excellent view of the whole story of their discovery and involvement with the humans. Phineas found it amusing to watch the reactions of the Saurians during various parts of the broadcast. They hissed loudly and harshly whenever a carnivorous dinosaur appeared in the footage; they clapped and roared whenever their own likeness appeared; and they seemed to begin a curious, chantlike humming when they watched outer space scenes.

"What are they doing?" Kate asked.

"I couldn't tell you. I'm no expert on the lizards."

"Do you always call them that? It sounds so slangy, so derogatory."

Phineas shrugged. "I suppose it does. I never really thought about it."

"Don't you like them? The Saurians, I mean."

"I don't know if 'like' is the right word." He tried to choose his words carefully. "I think 'trust' is more accurate."

"But they helped you defeat the TWC terrorists."

"Well, that could be interpreted to be their defending themselves as much as actually helping us." Phineas shook his head slowly. "I don't know, Kate. They're

just so different from us. There's still a lot we don't
understand about them. I just think we should be
wary."

"And yet you staged this whole thing for the project." She looked at him with bright eyes. "You can't be
too worried."

"Don't misunderstand me," he said quickly. "I
didn't say I thought they were dangerous per se, just
that they are so different from us that we really can't
claim to know them all that well. Do you see what I'm
trying to say?".

"I think so," Kate said, her eyes drifting up to the big
screen and then down to her chronometer. "Look, it's
getting down to the last scene. It's almost time for the
live segment."

As the preedited footage of "Day of the Dragonstar"
wrapped up, Phineas heard the first muted sounds of an
ornithopter engine cutting through the moist, humid air
of the interior. The orchestral score and production
credits were now rolling across the giant screen, and
Phineas knew that they would be live as soon as the next
raft of commercials had been hurled across electromagnetic heaven.

"Here they come," Kate cried, pointing up toward an
aircraft that seemed to lope easily across the sky. It was
a combination bird and helicopter, incorporating the
movements of both. The ornithopter had proved to be
the aircraft most easily controlled within the confines
of the giant spinning cylinder. Air currents and wind
vortices made airfoils unreliable, but the ornithopter
handled them with relatively few problems.

When the last commercial had faded into gray obliv-
ion, the screen phosphored and flashed, reforming with
the image of Alistair Williamson. Phineas looked at the
narrator as he appeared on the screen, then down to the
platform directly in front of the reviewing stand to
observe him live.

"And thus concludes Part One of our broadcast of
'The Day of the Dragonstar,' " Williamson said. "We
are now speaking to you live from the city of Hakarrh in
the Saurian preserve inside the Dragonstar. I am sur-

rounded by citizens of the city and a majority of the IASA staff permanently assigned to this great vessel.

"The sound you hear in the background is the approach of an IASA ornithopter, which will momentarily touch down before me. On board the aircraft is Dr. Mikaela Lindstrom and the most famous living science fiction writer in the world, Dr. John T. Neville. The ornithopter is bringing Dr. Neville to the city of the Saurians for a special live event, a veritable piece of history in the making, which World Media Corporation and the International Aeronautics and Space Agency invite you, the audience of the world, to witness."

The sound of the approaching ornithopter became louder, and Alistair Williamson moved to the side of the landing area while the camera panned across the large crowd and the colors and textures of the Saurian city and finally zoomed in on the aircraft that hovered easily above the panorama. As Williamson took a new position to the left of the grandstand, the cameras again picked him up.

"Having spent much of his life speculating on the adventures and discoveries of humankind's future, Dr. John T. Neville will soon become part of his own future history. The 'first contact' story—that which examines the experience of humankind meeting with an alien race —is one of the true classics of science fiction literature, and Dr. Neville penned one of the best back in 1940 when he wrote 'Down Among the Ynglings.'

"Who would have imagined that someday he would find himself in a situation very similar to that of his space-faring heroes in pulp magazine fantasy? And yet it brings to mind the classic question of art imitating life versus life imitating art."

The ornithopter was now directly overhead the platform, and a hush settled over the crowd as it began to make its final landing approach. There was only the whispering *whoomp-whoomp* of the engines and the rotor wings beating against the heavy tropical air. Even Alistair Williamson had paused in his monologue to admire the graceful landing of the ornithopter.

As the engines wheezed into silence, Williamson

moved back into the camera's range, with the aircraft in the background. "And now, the historic meeting is about to occur. To my right, in the first row of the reviewing stands, is a delegation of Saurians, who are now preparing to greet the occupants of the ornithopter, Dr. Neville in particular."

The camera pulled back to reveal several things happening simultaneously. The crew hatch of the ornithopter popped open and a set of steps was lowered to the platform. First off was an IASA staff member in the familiar powder-blue coveralls, then Dr. Mikaela Lindstrom stepped down. She looked back and held out her hand to offer assistance to a wizened, white-haired old man, Dr. Neville, who descended the steps with a seemingly cavalier attitude. In the grandstands, a small group of Saurians stood up and assembled in formation. All of the creatures wore the robes and regalia of their particular caste within the biologically structured society.

Alistair Williamson continued his narration, admirably filling in the moments leading up the climactic event with ever increasing hyperbole and false drama.

"Well, Phineas, your dream is about to come true," Kate said, watching as Dr. Neville walked forward along a red carpet to a halfway point where he would meet the advancing Saurian delegation.

"Yes, it certainly is. I can't believe it."

Phineas Kemp smiled broadly. It was an especially satisfying feeling to see something that had previously existed only in your mind take form and substance and become reality, assisted by the efforts of many others who have paid heed to your dreaming. It was a feeling of accomplishment, a sensation of power being subtly wielded.

He watched as the Saurians approached, each one wearing the translating devices that would allow them to communicate with Dr. Neville. There were several IASA aides-de-camp accompanying the entourage as they moved forward in their multicolored robes. There was a quality to the event almost like a pageant or other formalized ceremony, which pleased Phineas very much. It was almost exactly as he had imagined it.

As Alistair Williamson continued to describe the events, much like a sports commentator might whisper over a golfer lining up his tournament-winning putt, the Saurians came face to face with Neville. Dr. Mikaela Lindstrom and the IASA aides stepped back so that the cameras would have a full view of the action.

The first of the Saurian group, a member of the priest class who wore a lemon-yellow robe, approached the old science fiction writer and extended a forelimb in greeting. Dr. Neville grasped the reptilian hand/claw with a certain reluctance, and the smile on his face seemed somewhat wooden, but things appeared to be going well in general.

Several of the other Saurians, dressed as agrarians, merchants, and warriors, all crowded about Neville. There was much hand/claw grasping, pats on the shoulder, and even pecks on cheeks. At the climactic moment, the sounds of a triumphant symphonic march boomed from the loudspeakers and a barrage of fireworks went whistling into the air above the platform.

Kemp thought everything was going beautifully. It was a perfect crowning effort to the enormously successful documentary broadcast. As the first volley of fireworks burst over the reviewing stand, however, something happened.

As Neville confronted the group of Saurians, he thought to himself, My God, what an ugly bunch. Am I really going to have to touch one of those things?

The trip had been absolutely nothing like he had envisioned it—this would be his sole moment of glory. Ah, but what a moment! Pictures of this would be in every history book from here to doomsday. Billions of people were watching even now, most never having heard of John T. Neville.

Goddamnn, would he ever sell some books now! Maybe it was time for Neville Base Gamma.

Oh, well, might as well get this over with.

It was with these thoughts that the famous science fiction writer hobbled toward the reptiles to shake their leaders' hands.

They smelled funny, and he sure as hell didn't trust them, but by God it was a privilege and a duty after writing so many books about aliens to actually meet some real live ones. Of course, never in a million years had he ever envisioned this kind of contact being so brazenly ceremonial. Now, Long Jack Neville was as proud as any man to wave his entire flag—but this all seemed so traditional.

The Saurian in the yellow robe seemed to be having about as much fun as he was, Neville noted as the beast walked over to shake hands. No doubt it had been Kemp who had instructed the creature in hand shaking. These things probably twined tails or something.

With his best PR smile Neville extended his own hand, took the Saurian's leathery hand, and pumped.

"Hey. Name's Neville. Long Jack Neville, and I know you don't know me but I'm quite famous among my people and I've been writing about this kind of thing for a long time and it's a real privilege to finally put my hand where my words have been, if you know what I mean."

The Saurian extending the greeting did not respond. Its face betrayed no emotion. But the creatures about it seemed quite nervous and agitated, and Neville could not tell why.

"Well, aren't you going to say anything, friend?" Neville said. "I mean, you might as well make use of these boxes they've got strapped on to translate. We could have a real fine conversation. I must say, you all are a sight friendlier than some of the fellows I've conjured up from this old bean."

The first fireworks went off. Normally, Neville loved fireworks. He would set a bunch off in his backyard everytime he published a book—he made a party of it, inviting friends. But now, in the middle of all this, they somehow seemed, well, crass.

Besides, they seemed to unnerve the natives, too.

The group of Saurians surrounding Neville tensed visibly as the sounds of the explosions ripped through the air, punctuating the boisterous phrases of the orchestral music. The warrior lizard standing closest to the old man suddenly swung about violently and rapped the agrarian class member up against the side of his large serpentlike head.

The Saurian shaking Neville's hand dropped his hold.

"Hey, wait a minute friend!" Neville said. He stepped forward and raised his hand. "Here, let's finish this properly."

The Saurian swung his attention back to Neville.

The writer shuddered at the look in the thing's eye. Certainly not human, and certainly not civilized.

The Saurian opened its mouth, stepped forward a pace, and bit off Dr. John T. Neville's hand.

Neville wrenched away, his forearm pulsing blood.

Immediately, his maintenance equipment began to howl, which set off the Saurians even more.

"This," Neville said, "this only happens in . . ."

Before he could finish the sentence, he found himself screaming and trying to stagger away from the place. But a Saurian claw detained him.

The Saurians converged on him, nostrils quivering at the scent of the blood pumping from Neville's arm.

"You'll hear from my agent!" Neville cried in total panic.

Several of the delegated Saurians threw back their heads and emitted long, sorrowful cries. The sounds were a mixture of pain and anger, rage and madness.

Then the group fell upon Long Jack Neville and, in full view of the cameras, tore the old man apart, piece by grisly piece.

And began to devour him.

Before the stunned Dr. Lindstrom and the two IASA aides, the science fiction writer was dismembered and decapitated by the frenzied attack of the Saurians. There was an explosion of pink mist in their midst, a sudden pooling of blood on the platform, and the collective screams of both Saurians and humans alike.

"My God!" Phineas yelped as he watched the slaughter take place. He forced himself to his feet and drew out his sidearm, ready to fire into the pack. "Get those people out of there," he screamed, pushing past

Kate Ennis and a cameraman who was suicidally trying
to record Dr. Neville's death.

The grandstands began to empty as panic overtook
the crowd. Humans and Saurians alike swarmed away
from the scene of the attack. The IASA aides with
Mikaela had grabbed her, pulling her back aboard the
ornithopter, and then fired a few rounds into the group
of suddenly crazed Saurians. To make matters worse,
the Saurians had fallen upon Neville's remains and
begun a feeding frenzy to rival anything to be found in
the Mesozoic preserve.

Kemp stood firmly in the fleeing crowd and fired into
the Saurian mob, felling one of the merchants. One of
the others looked up from its bloody repast, its snout
smeared with bits of flesh, and roared angrily. Phineas
placed a magnum slug in the center of its skull, throwing
it back into the midst of the others, who fell upon him
and began dismembering him also.

The ornithopter lifted off, hovering above the chaos,
spraying the platform with automatic fire. The slugs
stitched a pattern of death among the Saurians' thick
hides, and they danced a momentary dance of dying, a
reptilian Grand Guignol, and then fell into a bloody
heap.

The music and the fireworks continued to erupt in
the background as the remainder of the IASA staff
gathered together in an armed pack, surrounding all of
their kind in a protective circle. Beyond them, the
massive throng of Saurian spectators milled about
aimlessly, barking and hissing, obviously on the edge of
total panic and mass hysteria.

Once Phineas could see that Mikaela had escaped immediate danger and was hovering above the scene in the
'thopter, he tried to arrange his thoughts, to calm down
enough to take command. Reaching out for Kate, he
pulled her into the center of the circle of IASA staffers.
"All right, back to your vehicles! All of you that can,
get out of here on the double! Everyone else stay together until we can get some backup."

"Oh God, Phineas, what's happening? Oh my god!"
Kate Ennis was on the edge of complete panic herself,

and he shook her with one hand to steady her. The last
thing he needed was for somebody to go crackers on
him right now.

Looking through the crowd, he signaled at a communications specialist. The man pushed his way through
the crowd as quickly as he could.

"Key up the tactical base HQ. Get us some cargo
'thopters on the fly. We've got to get these people out of
here ASAP."

The comm specialist went to work as Phineas looked
up at the ornithopter still hovering above the crowd, offering weapons fire cover if it proved necessary. By
chance or by design, the group of one hundred or so
humans had migrated to the center of the platform,
surrounded by the now bare scaffolding of the grandstands. Below, on ground level, the great crowd of
Saurians still flowed and mixed like confluent currents
of water. There was obvious confusion and panic in the
air as the Saurians continued to surround the area.
Phineas could not tell if the reptilian horde would attack
or not, but he was determined to get everyone out
before there was any more bloodshed.

Turning cautiously and surveying the entire scene,
Kemp was horrified to see two camera people up in a
corner of the grandstands, their equipment still recording every detail of the debacle. *My God, they weren't
still sending this down to Earth?*

Kemp hustled up two guards and ordered them after
the camera crews. As the sound of an approaching formation of cargo 'thopters could be heard in the sky
above them, Kemp was trying to imagine what the world
audience must be thinking after seeing this total disaster.

Totally unbelievable. Incredible.

These were the thoughts of Mishima Takamura as he
watched the carnage on his portable HV. At first, as
many other witnesses would later attest, he was not sure
what he had seen. Suddenly the Saurians were on the old
man, tearing him limb from limb, and there was a
bloodbath.

He had sat there, stunned into silence and total disbelief, thinking that perhaps the entire thing could have been avoided if he had gone over Kemp's head and contacted the Joint Chiefs of Staff. But as he watched the portable HV, amazed that the cameras were still rolling, he knew that hindsight was always the best, and that the world of "if" and "should have" was a place where nobody really lived.

But God, what a circus of horrors. The cameras recorded the aftermath with a vicious clarity: the assembly of IASA people huddled together on the platform like a giant rugby scrum, cargo 'thopters dropping down to absorb large pieces of the mob, while the Saurians swarmed about the platform in a state of shock, seized by paranoia and fear and the elements of mass hysteria.

Voiced-over the broadcast were the patched-in voices of two of World Media's most popular commentators, describing the action with a somber, detached tone, which Mishima assumed was supposed to add a touch of dignity to the ghoulish production. If good taste or decorum had anything to do with it, instead of ratings, the producers would have cut back to Earthside studios long ago. But no, thought Mishima, they were going to hang around just in case the "Sauries" decided to chow down on any more of their friends.

Turning the HV off, Takamura left the lab and headed for the communications room. The one thing he kept thinking as he hurried off was that he wouldn't like to be in Colonel Kemp's shoes right about now.

Fourteen

Gregor Kolenkhov had seen enough.

The warning lights on Major Altermann's consoles were flashing for attention, and there was a cacophony of bleeps and bells signaling all classes of communication trying to get through the board. The major was hard-pressed to validate everything that was coming through.

"Get me Alvarez," Kolenkhov said. "Level One priority . . ."

Altermann punched him through immediately, and a central screen on Gregor's console snapped and flashed, abruptly conjuring up the harried image of Christopher Alvarez, Chairman of the Joint Chiefs.

"I was wondering how long it would take you," Alvarez said. He was a vigorous-looking man in his sixties, but his face appeared drawn and pale.

"I still can't believe it," Kolenkhov said. "I can't believe what we sent out on a worldwide broadcast."

"I've already spoken to Bertholde and Rheinhardt," Alvarez said. "We're meeting in the Staff Room in ten minutes."

"I'll be there," said Kolenkhov. "Fuck your mother! What a mess!"

Alvarez nodded grimly. "I've told Rheinhardt to put a lid on things as best he can. He wants to send a few shuttles up there with some armed commandos—just in case the Saurians give them any more trouble. I told him to go ahead."

Kolenkhov nodded. "All right, I'll meet you in a few minutes."

Christopher Alvarez signed off, and Kolenkhov slowly stood up from his chair, stretching and yawning. "Try to take care of this thing, Major, and watch the security codes. Rheinhardt's put a cover on all our operations concerning Dragonstar till further notice."

"I'll catch them as they come in, sir."

"Good luck, Major." Kolenkhov headed for the door, thinking that the damned alien ship had been nothing but trouble since they found it. Maybe the best thing to do would be to give the big tin can a kick toward the Sun and let nature take its course.

Captain Ian Coopersmith had barely had a chance to ac-climate himself to his new command as director of the tactical base for the Dragonstar project. Located within the Mesozoic preserve on the Smithsonian Prairie, the force-field-protected base afforded IASA's tactical arm with a central point of operations that offered quick ac-cess to almost any part of the giant cylinder.

He had been watching the documentary broadcast from his command post when the Saurians went beserk, and stared in disbelief and abject horror at what had followed. He had sent out the two cargo 'thopters im-mediately when he saw what was happening, almost a minute before his base had received the panicky trans-mission from one of Kemp's aides. Mikaela had called in from the ornithopter that continued to provide aerial cover for the IASA people. She had been very upset (to put it mildly), but she managed to keep her head enough to give Ian a full accounting.

Thank god Becky had decided against attending the proceedings, he thought. She had not been terribly enamored of the eccentric Dr. Neville after he had attempted to grab her ass during their initial meeting on Copernicus. Ian wished Becky was with him now.

Unfortunately, she had stationed herself at the PSC, the paleontological survey camp, to supervise a series of medical tests that Lindstrom and her people had recently designed.

"Captain, I've got a Mayday coming through on the priority channel," said Sergeant Kinsey, his communications officer. "You want me to patch you in?"

Ian's comm unit crackled with background noise as a voice came on-line: "This is Barkham in Cargo Two, Captain."

"Yes, Lieutenant, I copy. Go ahead."

"Captain, I've got a maximum load, on a home-base heading, but I'm having some engine trouble."

Ian keyed several pads on his console and checked a scanner screen. "Okay, Lieutenant, I've got you on the scope. Can you make it back here?"

"Hard to say. I took her up as high as I could so that I could increase the glide path in case I lose total power. My RO says I still have about sixty klicks to go."

Ian swallowed hard. He had a 'thopter pilot and fifteen passengers over the Mesozoic preserve and threatening to get dumped in the middle of the jungle. On the other side of the Barrier, he was looking at another one hundred plus people who still needed cover and evacuation.

Nothing like a little excitement on your first day back on the job.

After checking Cargo Two's position, he spoke clearly and calmly into the mike. "Okay, Barkham, how's it holding on?"

"Negative, Captain. I'm down eighty percent and fading fast. I've got a glide factor of about forty percent, so I'm not going to be getting too far."

"Okay, Lieutenant, you're going to have to ditch her."

"Doesn't sound like my idea of a good time," said

the pilot. "Any suggestions?"

"Only one. You should be approaching the old Saurian ruins, about twelve degrees east of your present position. Your best shot is to try to touch down within the stone walls of the ruins. Try to get everybody up on one of the ziggurats, and you'll all be reasonably safe till I can get some people in there to get you out. Do you copy that?"

"I've got you, Captain. Been looking for a visual on the ruins, but nothing yet." The pilot's voice was beginning to show signs of strain. "Losing power and altitude fast."

"You should be almost above it," Coopersmith said. "It probably looks very overgrown from the air. Look for the peaks of gray stone."

There was no immediate response from the speaker—only a *whomp-whomp* of background noise.

"I see it. Man, we almost went right past it. Okay, Captain, I'm going to take her in. Wish me luck."

"You'll make it. Just be cool, Barkham."

The lieutenant provided Ian with a running commentary as he lowered the cargo 'thopter closer and closer to the jungle of the Mesozoic preserve. The ruins of the old Saurian city were not a large target, but there should be ample room to make a crash landing, and the stone temples would provide better than adequate protection from most of the carnivores.

Watching his screens closely, Ian followed the descent of the crippled aircraft as he listened to the narration of Lieutenant Barkham. "Two hundred meters and closing. I can see the stone wall. Almost down now. Okay, we're going to make it. Hang on."

The speakers crackled with the sounds of mayhem for a few very long moments, then Barkham's voice penetrated the chaos. "Captain, I did it. This thing won't be flying again very soon, but we're down. Inside the walls, I think."

"All right, Lieutenant, nice job," Ian said, thinking quickly. "Take stock of your passengers, get back to me with a report, then try to get everybody up to some high ground, up in one of the pyramids. Okay?"

"Affirmative, Captain. I'll be back on channel ASAP. Barkham out."

Ian keyed off the channel and checked the HV screens that had been carrying the documentary broadcast. Mercifully, the live transmission had been stopped, replaced by a studio shot. IASA brass must have finally cut the damned thing off. Talk about embarrassing. He wouldn't be in Kemp's place right now for anything.

Turning back to Kinsey, he wiped his forehead with his sleeve. Perspiring like a son of a bitch already, and the fun had just begun. "What's the latest from Hakarrh?"

"Not too good, Captain."

Phineas had almost fallen into the false hope that the Saurians who milled about the stage in stunned confusion would eventually disperse. When the huge throng finally erupted into violence, he truly believed he was going to die.

He was not certain how the riot had started, but suddenly there was a chorus of screaming and yelling, and there was automatic gunfire spraying into the crowd from both the armed guards and the hovering ornithopter.

It was a nightmare. An outdoor slaughterhouse. The Saurians, teetering on the edge of panic and primordial terror and violence, had finally slipped over the brink. They had begun by attacking each other, ripping and slashing into their own ranks with a mindless rage. It was a pitched battle with no defined sides, no structure or rationale. And it was only a matter of time before the Saurians began to flow upward and crash over the edge of the grandstands and platform like cresting waves in a storm. Despite the small-arms fire of the IASA guards and the cover from the ornithopter, the Saurians continued to advance upon them, and Phineas had no choice but to assume command.

Gaining the attention of those around him, he began to lead the pack down the back of the platform. His only hope was that they could make a run for the temple boulevard, and make their way back into the alien crew section of the Dragonstar. It was either that or remain in their present position until they ran out of ammo, whereupon they would be slaughtered like cattle.

As the mass of people began to work their way off and away from the platform, the seething, frenzied pack of the Saurians surged up and over the scaffolding, collapsing platform and grandstands. Looking back, Phineas could see that some of his charges were being caught in the crumbling debris, but he rallied them, urging them forward down the boulevard toward the temple.

The ornithopter carrying Mikaela continued to supply air cover with automatic weapons fire but was now forced to be cautious because of the proximity of the Saurians to the IASA crowd. Phineas looked up to see the second cargo 'thopter returning to the platform. Signaling to the aircraft, Phineas directed some of the crowd who were closest to climb aboard as soon as possible.

Before he realized what had happened, Phineas saw that the crowd had panicked and swarmed over the 'thopter like frenzied insects. They battled each other, everyone trying to be the first through the open cargo bay. Jamming and pushing, clawing at one another, the crowd surged forward into the 'thopter. The excess weight and disequilibrium caused the aircraft to tip dangerously close to the platform, its lightly beating airfoils smacking into the heads of some of the crowd.

"Get back!" Phineas cried, even though he knew no one could hear him in the din of the crowd and the engine whine. "Get some of those people out of the way!"

Seeing that it was useless to stop the panic, Phineas grabbed Kate Ennis's hand and pulled her violently away from the 'thopter. They threaded their way through the mob. Phineas moved quickly, dodging bodies like an expert footballer, looking back to see that the mob had totally overwhelmed the aircraft, stuffing it with bodies so that it would never lift the weight. The 'thopter listed badly to one side, and it was obvious that it wasn't going anywhere.

To make things worse, the Saurians had stormed the scaffolding of the platform and were converging quickly on the ornithopter.

"Let's go!" Phineas cried. "We've got to get out of here!"

Kate started running with him as they broke free of the main body of the crowd. There were others around them who followed their lead, but the majority of the panicked mass remained about the cargo 'thopter in the crazy hope that it could save them all. Because of their wild attack, the aircraft would rescue none of them.

As they reached the temple boulevard and began running unhampered, Phineas could see the steps of the temple in the distance. He started to believe that maybe they were going to make it, that maybe they wouldn't die after all. Where the hell was the small 'thopter, the one carrying Mikaela?

Kemp looked back as they ran, scanning the sky, but he saw no trace of the aircraft.

"What's the matter?" Kate asked as they ran. "What're you looking for?"

"The other 'thopter. It's gone!"

"The little one?" Kate sounded confused as she pushed herself to keep running.

"Yes. It must have been running low on fuel. Looks like we're on our own now. Come on. Got to keep up the pace now."

They ran toward the large stone staircase, putting some distance between themselves and the main body of the fray. As they ascended slowly, each riser taking more breath and effort, Phineas looked back and down to see the carnage they had narrowly escaped. The cargo 'thopter was on its side now, literally being torn apart

by the crazed Saurians and the heaving mass of bodies
that eddied about the wreckage like oily water. Kemp
wondered how many would survive this fiasco.

Kate Ennis seemed to have gained her second wind,
and she was taking steps with more agility than before.
Phineas looked up to the top of the massive set of steps
as they reached the halfway point.

Had he seen movement up there?

If there were more Saurians waiting for them at the
top, they were finished. Below, there were other stragglers from the grandstands, and beyond them, the moving pack of the Saurians.

"Look!" Kate cried, pointing up.

Phineas could see them too. Standing at the edge,
weapons in their hands, people in IASA coveralls motioned Phineas upward. He recognized them as Bob
Jakes's people, and Phineas was never in his life so glad
to see a scientist smiling at him.

"It's okay, Kate, we're almost there. Just a little bit
farther now."

Kate Ennis chuckled as she looked over at him.
"You're the one that's turning blue, Colonel. I'm doing
fine."

Nearing the top of the steps, Phineas could see more
of the people from Jakes's research team. It appeared as
if the entire staff of laboratory workers had come down
to offer any help they could. Phineas saw Mishima
Takamura standing off to the side issuing orders with a
bullhorn, and he smiled. Takamura was a young,
dynamic kind of guy, and he was certainly the type to
organize a bunch of scientists into a SWAT team.

"Colonel Kemp, are you all right, sir?" One of the
research staffers was standing over him, offering a hand
up and over the final step.

"I'm fine," Phineas said, taking the man's hand. It
was a terrible lie—his knees and ankles were crying out
for mercy, and the muscles in the small of his back were
cramping up like knotted clumps of wet rope.

Turning, he and the scientist helped Kate to the top of

the steps. Beyond their position the stone facade of the Saurian priests' temple rose up against the polished metal of the cylinder wall. Kate looked at the ancient structure with awe and fascination. She had seen holographs of this part of the ship but had not actually been so close to the artifacts.

"Feeling all right, Ms. Ennis?" Phineas asked, taking her hand.

"This beats hell out of jogging, I can tell you that." She forced a smile. "Look, here come some more."

Looking down the steps, Phineas could see others who had managed to escape the Saurians and the cargo 'thopter disaster. Of the original crowd, it appeared as if perhaps fifty survivors would make it to safety. Kemp studied the faces of those who clambered up the temple steps, wondering who was going to make it and who was not.

Mishima Takamura apparently spotted Phineas, because he had dropped the bullhorn to his side and was trotting over toward him. Takamura was a young man in his thirties, with dark eyes and hair, of medium height and a little on the lean side. He had always impressed Phineas as an intense, serious, and very intelligent man. There was a fire burning behind his eyes that you couldn't miss, and he always spoke in a direct, solemn tone of voice.

"Colonel Kemp, are you all right?" Takamura asked.

"Yes, I think so. It was a real mess down there."

"I know, I was watching it on the HV." Takamura looked embarrassed.

"Christ! How much of it went out on the network?" In the pitch of the excitement, Phineas had forgotten that the event was being beamed back to Earth.

Takamura shook his head. "Plenty, I'm afraid. It was still being broadcast right up until the grandstands collapsed. That's when I headed down here with my staff."

"This is looking worse all the time," Phineas said, thinking aloud.

"Here come some more," someone cried.

"Oh, Phineas, look!" Kate pointed down toward the bottom of the steps.

A large group of survivors on the lower third of the steps were being pursued by a smaller pack of warrior-class Saurians. They were carrying their crossbowlike weapons and quivers of biological squaves—kind of living arrows which burrowed into you once they struck.

"Give them some cover," Takamura cried, raising his rifle and taking aim on the Saurian pack.

The group of scientists in white coveralls began firing simultaneously, releasing a volley of shells into the first rank of the warriors, who had just gained the bottom steps. The bullets ripped through their tough hides, throwing them back into their brothers, who seemed to become more enraged by the counterattack. Some of the Saurians, succumbing to the scent and sight of blood, quit the chase, falling upon the carcasses of their fallen comrades, but others filled the ranks and continued up the steps after the fleeing humans. Takamura's men fired almost continuously into the pack, bringing them down with surprising accuracy and efficiency.

"Come on, Colonel," Kate Ennis cried, breaking Phineas out of his trancelike admiration of the IASA scientists. "I need your help."

Looking down, he saw Kate on the steps, helping some of the survivors up to the sanctuary of the landing. Phineas stepped into action and started helping the exhausted, terror-filled staffers up the final steps. Below them he could see the temple steps dotted with many pockets of survivors, all scrambling as fast as they could up to the point of relative safety. He was glad to see that so many had followed his course and were going to make it. He estimated perhaps seventy-five people were now on the steps.

As Phineas began helping people up to the top, Mishima Takamura moved to his side. "Have you seen Dr. Jakes?" he cried above the growing noise.

"No, wasn't he here with your people?" Phineas was shocked to think that Jakes might not be safe.

"He went down to the grandstands to see the show. Damn!" Takamura said. "Where the hell is he?"

Phineas moved back up to the top with Mishima. "Do you have a man with a radio down here?"

Takamura nodded. "Back by the entrance to the temple. Dr. Horton is carrying it."

Taking Kate Ennis by the hand, Phineas guided her up and across the temple landing toward the entrance to the large stone edifice. He saw an older woman in a faded, pale blue jumpsuit crouched down by the temple entrance. She held a small comm unit.

"Excuse me—Dr. Horton?" Phineas said. "I'm Colonel Kemp."

"I know who you are, Colonel," the woman said sharply. "You're the one responsible for this spectacle, isn't that right?"

A bolt of anger flashed through him, but he knew that this was not the time or place to get into a pitched verbal battle. The bitch had a lot of nerve, though. He had to give her that.

"I'm sorry you feel that way, Doctor, but I've got a job to do right now. I'm going to need to use that comm unit." Phineas expected a wise-ass remark, but the woman merely handed him the communications gear and looked away.

Flipping through the channels, Kemp signaled tactical base headquarters.

"Tactical base. Come in, please," said an unfamiliar voice.

"This is Colonel Kemp. Is Coopersmith there?"

"Just a second, Colonel."

There was a very short pause until Ian's voice shot crisply from the tiny speaker grid. "Phineas, is that you? Are you all right? Where are you?"

Kemp reported his position and the state of affairs. Even as he spoke, more survivors were being pulled over the last step. ". . . But we need some help. What happened to your 'thopters? Have you heard from Mikaela? Is she okay?"

"Mikaela's back at the PSC. She's a little shaky, but

she's all right. I've ordered the 'thopter back here for refueling and some sharpshooters. It should be off the ground in another minute or two."

"What about the other 'thopter? I saw what happened to the last one down below." Phineas swallowed hard, trying to listen to Ian's voice above the growing noise.

"Bad luck with that one, too," said Coopersmith, who detailed the plight of the cargo 'thopter that had crashed in the Saurian ruins.

"We're going to have to send some people out there to get them," Phineas said.

"First things first, Colonel. I've only got one aircraft left, and I was figuring to get it back to Hakarrh ASAP."

"What about Copernicus? Have you heard anything from them?"

Ian chuckled. "Are you joking? Christ, Phineas, they're hopping bloody mad."

"I don't give a shit if they're mad," cried Phineas. "I just want to know if they're sending us any fucking help."

"Affirmative, Colonel. Two shuttles full of troops are on the way to the main docking bay. ETA within the next ten minutes."

"Any word from Becky?" Kemp asked the question reluctantly, considering to whom he was forced to ask it. But it was information he wanted to know.

"Yes, she's at the PSC. No problems. That 'paley' camp seems like the best place to be right about now, I'd say."

"Did you get a passenger list from the first cargo 'thopter?" Kemp asked.

"Which one? The one that made it back here once, or the one that put down in the ruins?"

"Both, actually," Phineas said. "I'm looking for Bob Jakes."

There was a short pause. "Okay, here we go. I've got it on the screen now. Let's see. Okay, Jakes was on

Cargo Two, which is now on a sightseeing mission in the ruins.''

"Did he make it? Is he all right?"

"As far as I know," Ian said. "They've got some minor injuries up there, but nothing life-threatening."

Phineas exhaled slowly. It was good to know that the old bastard was okay. "How safe is that bunch in the ruins, Ian?"

"Reasonably so. I've radioed them some basic survival information, and I think they'll be all right till we can get to them."

"Good. We're getting things under control down here at the temple, and we should be going into the crew section fairly soon. I'd like to coordinate the rescue operations once I get up to the lab's comm room. We've got some real messes to clean up."

Coopersmith chuckled ironically. "Yes, I'd say so. Let's hope we can patch things up with the Saurians. What the hell set them off?"

"I haven't the foggiest," said Phineas. "Damndest thing I ever saw. Poor Neville. A bad way to go, eh?"

Ian chuckled again, with some bitterness, this time. "Are there any good ones?"

"All right," Phineas said. "I'm going to be stationing myself in the alien crew section. In the lab. I should be there shortly, so keep me posted with any new developments. Kemp out."

"Tactical base out."

Switching off the comm unit, Phineas gave it back to Dr. Horton, who accepted it without a word or a second glance. He turned to Kate and motioned her to accompany him.

Phineas caught Takamura's attention and drew close to him.

"Yes, Colonel?"

"Dr. Jakes is all right," he said, explaining the emergency landing of the cargo 'thopter.

Takamura seemed relieved. "I am so glad, Colonel. Bob Jakes is like a father to me."

"Yes, I know. Grand old men have a habit of being like that, don't they?" Phineas smiled and tapped Mishima on the shoulder. He had expected the young scientist to smile at his little joke, but the man continued to look at him rather stonily.

"Is there something wrong, Doctor?" Phineas wanted to know what the problem might be.

"Oh no, of course not, Colonel. Everything's just fine, can't you tell?" Takamura grimaced.

"If I insulted you or Jakes, I'm sorry, Doctor. I assure you I wasn't trying to be flippant."

Takamura shook his head slowly, as though surprised at Kemp's naiveté. "Colonel, it's like this—it's been a long day, and I'm tired. I really don't feel like getting into it right now. Maybe some other time, all right?"

Takamura turned to walk away, and Kemp grabbed his arm, turning him back in a hurry. "Wait a second! I'd like to know what's going on right *now*, Doctor."

Takamura looked at him with a sly grin. He nodded calmly and with confidence. "It's pretty simple, really, Colonel. I just think this whole mess could have been avoided if you'd read those reports I prepared, or if you'd listened to Dr. Jakes."

"You don't understand," Phineas said. "There were other factors to be considered."

"Yeah, I know. Real big ones, like money and ego, right, Colonel?"

The words stung Phineas like a slap in the face. He felt doubly embarrassed because Kate Ennis was witness to the ugly scene. It was better to cut things off here, before they grew even worse.

"That was uncalled for, Doctor. I think we'd better take this up at another time."

Takamura performed a mock bow of deference. "Very well, Colonel, although I'm certain that time will not serve to mitigate the truth."

Phineas turned away from the man and headed for the entrance to the alien crew section. The majority of the survivors had been pulled over the last step, and the pursuing mob of Saurians had been successfully held off. The rescue operation was just about over. There were other pockets of survivors already crowding through the temple entrance, and Phineas felt comfort in the anonymity of the large group.

"Don't pay attention to that," Kate said. "He doesn't know what he's talking about."

"Don't be so sure about that." Phineas was unable to look her in the eye.

"I think you're jumping to conclusions just because of one person's emotional outburst."

Kemp laughed lightly. "Takamura didn't sound very emotional to me." He forced a smile to his lips. "Besides, I thought you women were such champions of the emotional outburst."

"Oh, that's very clever, Colonel. I thought I was on your side."

Phineas sighed. "You are, Kate, and I'm sorry." He led her down several metallic corridors to a set of elevators, reaching to key in the correct alien codes on a touchpad. "And the way things are shaping up, it looks like I'm going to need all the help I can get."

Fifteen

Lieutenant Commander Svetlana Muranova took the lunar shuttlecraft *Georgian* out of autopilot mode. Through the front viewing port, she could see the expanse of the Dragonstar ahead of her position like a small planet. Every time she drew close to the alien vessel, she was again reminded of how damnably gigantic it really was. She mentioned this to her co-pilot, Lieutenant Sergei Andruschenko as they prepared for close approach.

"It is incredible," said Sergei, a small-boned, pale-skinned man who looked more like a poet than a shuttle pilot. "I'd love to see what is going on in there right now."

"Have you ever been inside?" Svetlana asked, pushing a strand of dirty-blond hair away from her ice-blue eyes.

"Me?" Sergei laughed. "Why would they let a simple pilot like me inside? No, but I would give anything to see those dinosaurs firsthand, wouldn't you?"

She shrugged. "I don't know. After seeing what happened to that old man, I'm not sure about exactly what I'd like to do."

Sergei grinned knowingly. "True, my comrade. So very true. I hear that Kemp's ass will be in a crack for this one."

"And we should be surprised? I mean, look at the mess, Sasha. On worldwide holo yet."

Svetlana's headphones beeped, and she keyed in the incoming call. "*Georgian*, we copy."

"Greetings, Lana, this your backyard cowboy aboard the *San Diego*." The voice with the Oklahoma drawl boomed in her ears, and she smiled in spite of the break in protocol.

"I copy, Lieutenant Jack Colter," Svetlana said, conjuring up an image of Lieutenant Colter in his command cabin wearing his cowboy hat. Colter was probably the most flamboyant shuttle pilot in her wing, and probably the most popular, too. Everyone seemed to like his easygoing, carefree manner. "I assume you are ready to discuss close-approach coordinates?"

"You betcha, honey! Shall I race you to the dockin' bay, or do you want to do this in a more orderly fashion?" Colter laughed heartily.

There was another series of beeps in Svetlana's headphones as Copernicus Base intervened. "*San Diego*, this Dr. Kolenkhov at Copernicus. Since we are in the middle of a very serious operation, I would suggest that you remove the bullshit from your communications."

Jack Colter cleared his throat. "Dr. Kolenkhov, nice to hear from you, sir. I didn't know you were patched in."

"That was obvious, Lieutenant. Now carry on, please. Copernicus standing by."

"Affirmative, Copernicus," Colter said. "Request CA coordinates from *Georgian*, ASAP. Do you copy, Lieutenant Muranovich?"

Aboard the *Georgian*, Svetlana and Sergei were having a good, silent laugh as she keyed in her mike. "We copy, Jack. Navigation computer is ready to send you our specs. Sending . . . now." She keyed in a command sequence that linked up both shuttle's computers, setting up a docking sequence that allowed the *San Diego* to enter the docking bay first, followed quickly by the *Georgian*.

Looking out the viewing port, she could see *San Diego* on the starboard side, following a parallel path with her own ship. Ahead of their position lay the immensity of the alien ship, now so close that it had lost its cylindrical appearance—instead it had become a vast plain with edges that curved downward.

"Attention, *Copernicus*," Colter said. "This is *San Diego*. We are on a go path for the docking bay. Ten kilometers and closing. Stand by, please."

Svetlana Muranova had slipped into a holding pattern beyond the docking bay. She and Sergei Andruschenko watched their instruments and confirmed with visuals through the viewing port. The *San Diego* coasted down below their position toward the orange-lit square of the docking bay, looking like a fat mosquito preparing to alight.

"*San Diego* closing on path. Five kilometers. Stand by, please."

Svetlana was checking a readout when Sergei's voice cut through the cabin. "Wait. What is this thing?"

Looking up, Svetlana saw that her co-pilot was pointing through the viewing port straight down toward the surface of the Dragonstar. There was a strange light beginning to emanate from the surface metal of the alien ship. From their distance, it appeared to be a formation hovering like a phosphorescent fog or aura within five hundred meters of the hull. It glowed with a fierce greenish light. She had never seen anything like it before.

"Sasha, what is it?" she asked softly.

Andruschenko shrugged. "I have never seen any such thing."

Her headphones burned in her ears. "Whoa, *Copernicus*. This is Jack Colter on *San Diego*. We got an unidentified formation up ahead. Do you copy?"

"Affirmative, *San Diego*. We also copy down here," said the voice of Kolenkhov. "Approach with caution."

"Caution? What the hell does that mean?" Colter

said. "Affirmative, Copernicus. We are closing to within two kilometers. I'm getting a VLF radiation reading —probably caused by the formation on the surface. Looks like a stasis field, Copernicus."

"We copy, *San Diego*. Whatever it is, it's spreading over the whole ship and growing larger and more dense. Suggest that you reverse course, *San Diego*—immediately."

"I think that's a great idea, Copernicus," Colter said. "Stand by. We're getting out of here."

Svetlana listened and watched as the other shuttle, piloted by the crazy cowboy, slowed to a stop within one klick of the docking bay. She wished there had been some personnel stationed at the bay itself—perhaps then they could have received a close-up report as to what was happening. But since it was totally automated, there was little that could be done.

The *San Diego* had cut off its forward thrusters, coming to a complete stop before reorienting for a reverse trajectory. Svetlana was watching as the green-glowing energy field gained depth and configuration. It was expanding and becoming more powerful.

"Oh-oh," she said to Sergei. "Something's happening down there." Keying in her mike, she cried out, "Jack, get out of there!"

Before she could receive a reply, it happened.

Like an arm reaching up out of a mist-covered lake, a column of green energy snaked out of the stasis field to envelop the *San Diego*. At the same time, an explosion of static filled Svetlana's headphones. Suddenly the other shuttle became transparent, and within an eye-flash it was gone.

"Oh no!" Svetlana said. "Oh no." She had the feeling that she was part of a crazy dream, that it couldn't possibly be real.

"Copernicus, this the *Georgian*," Sergei cried. "We just lost *San Diego*."

"We copy, Lieutenant," said Gregor Kolenkhov. "She is gone from our scanners. Get out of there immediately."

"Stand by, Copernicus." Sergei turned to his pilot and saw that she was staring into space with a dazed expression. Hesitantly, he smacked her lightly across the cheek. She was half a head taller than he, and probably had about thirty kilograms on him too.

But the light blow seemed to be what had been needed. Svetlana slowly turned to face her co-pilot, choosing not to recognize the necessary smack in the face. How embarrassing! How totally unlike her to give in to the pressure she had been trained to face.

"Yes, Sasha?" She must regain her composure quickly.

"Cancel the CA coordinates. We must evacuate the area right away." Sergei's voice had an odd quality to it, a tone she had never heard before.

"Thrusters on full," she said, keying in the touchpad. Outside the viewing port, the expanse of the Dragonstar suddenly slid off to starboard as the shuttle reoriented itself. "Prepare for hi-gee acceleration."

Sergei checked his screens as he monitored the radiation field that danced across the hull of the alien vessel. A piece of the stasis field was reaching slowly up toward them. Oddly, Sergei remained calm as the green death ascended. He thought the formation reminded him of the tentacle of a giant squid reaching out for its prey. Svetlana keyed in the main thrusters and the ship accelerated, but it was not quick enough. Suddenly the cabin was filled with a ghostly green light, and for an instant the scene was frozen, etched on the retinas of the two pilots like tintype photographs. This was followed by a surge of intense heat as the molecular bonding of the ship started to break down. The headphones crackled with a warning from Copernicus Base, but Svetlana Muranova and Sergei Andruschenko never heard it.

The stasis field had reached their hull.

"Fuck your mother!" cried Dr. Gregor Kolenkhov as he turned away from the telescopic view on his monitor. He had just watched the second of his two shuttles get zapped by the stasis field that had come up around the hull of the Dragonstar. Four pilots and forty troops, all gone in a flash. Damnable shit!

He pounded his meaty fist against the console top, unable to release the feelings of frustration. He could feel the gaze of Major Altermann upon his back, and the awkward silence in the room was almost a palpable thing in itself. Slowly he turned back to his communications officer and wiped his mouth with the back of his hand. It was a nervous, meaningless gesture, but it somehow made him feel more at ease.

"What the hell is going on here?" he asked the major rhetorically. "What else could go wrong?"

"I don't think you really want to know, do you?" the major asked. "Oh-oh, there's a Level One coming in for you."

"Put it through," Gregor said, flicking on his throat mike. "Kolenkhov here."

"Gregor, this is Rheinhardt. We're in deep shit, son."

"I know. I've been watching. Forty-four people gone just like snapping your fingers."

"It's not getting any better. I've pulled back all craft from the area, but I'm getting reports that the docking bay has been jettisoned from the hull, and the outrigger impulse engines have also been cut loose."

"What? By who?"

Oscar Rheinhardt snorted indignantly. "That's the rub, man. By nobody. From what we've been able to observe, it's being done without any human intervention. We can't even get close to the hull of that big son of a bitch now."

"But what about everybody inside? What's happening in there?"

"That's the worst part," Oscar said sadly. "We don't know."

Something very strange was going on, thought Ian Coopersmith as he tried to coordinate everything at the tactical base headquarters.

Just a moment after breaking the connection with

Colonel Kemp, there had been an immense power surge that had caused all the equipment to crackle, brighten, pulse, scream, or vibrate—depending on the nature of the beast. His instruments indicated that this had been caused by an unidentified EMP—an electromagnetic pulse—of tremendous power. Only because of the heavy shielding at his installation did the pulse not knock down all base functions.

"Are we still on line, Sergeant?" Ian asked his aide quickly.

Kinsey checked several banks of readouts, then nodded. "Affirmative, Captain. What the hell was that?"

"I don't know, but I plan to find out." Ian paused, considering his options. He turned back to Sergeant Kinsey. "Has that ornithopter left yet?"

"Which one, sir?"

Ian chuckled without humor. "The only one we have intact, for God's sake. Wake up, Sergeant."

"Oh, right, Captain. Let me check." Kinsey patched in a line to the landing pad, and a monitor showed the birdlike craft huddling down while robot-controlled refueling lines were retracting from its tanks. "She's just about ready to go, Captain."

Keying in his throat mike, Ian called the 'thopter pilot. "Zabriskie, this is Captain Coopersmith, do you copy?"

"I read you, Captain," said the pleasant female voice. "What can I do for you?"

"You can stay right where you are until I get there. I'm coming with you."

The speakers cracked with some interference. "Change of plans, Captain?"

"Yes, you could say that. Hang on, Zabriskie, I'll be right over."

"Okay, Captain. Zabriskie out."

As Ian stepped toward the door, another Priority One call came through. Sergeant Kinsey patch him in. "Coopersmith here."

"Captain, this is Dr. Mishima Takamura. I'm at the

research team lab." The man's voice seemed strained and tinged with fear.

"I copy, Doctor. What's up?"

"We've got some big problems here, Captain. We were bringing in all the survivors from the Saurian riot when everything started happening. We just had a serious EMP phenomenon."

"So did we," Ian said. "But our shielding seemed to have handled it. What about you?"

Takamura cleared his throat. "I'm not sure. Our instruments seem to be operating, but our systems are getting overridden by some other command systems. It's as though something is taking control of our equipment. What's worse is that the original alien equipment—the stuff that's been dead since we've been here—is starting to come to life."

"What?" Ian said, feeling a lump form in his throat.

"That's right. Some of the other sections down here in the alien end are sealing themselves off. Colonel Kemp is ordering us to evacuate the lab and the alien crew section altogether. In fact, he's the one who wanted me to contact you."

"Where's Kemp now?"

"Down at the temple entrance. He's trying to set up some kind of barricades and defenses in case the Saurians decide to come up the steps. We're also trying to salvage as much equipment as possible, but we need some help. There's no telling how long we have before we lose control completely."

"All right, Doctor, tell the Colonel I'm on my way." Ian paused for a moment. "And if you ask me, I think you should all get out of the alien end of this thing ASAP. It sounds like this ship has a mind of its own, wouldn't you say?"

"I hate to agree with you, but my answer is yes."

"Well, I don't know about you, but I'd rather take my chances with the Saurians and the dinosaurs than the alien technology. I think Kemp has the right idea."

"We'll be waiting for you, Captain."

"That's a roger. Coopersmith out."

Flipping off his throat mike, Ian turned back to Sergeant Kinsey. "What's the word from Copernicus? Have you been able to get through yet?"

"Negative, Captain. Whatever's going on, we've lost all ship-to-ship status. We're blind and deaf now. Totally isolated."

"All right, Kinsey. Keep trying to raise somebody. I sure would like to find out what happened to those shuttles they were sending."

"Maybe they couldn't make it, sir. Maybe whatever it is that's keeping signals from getting out is keeping their ships from getting in."

"I know. I've been thinking along those lines myself. Well, carry on, Kinsey."

"Totally isolated" sounded very ominous. Something crazy was going on. And it was obvious that this damn ship never had been dead, but only sleeping. Just waiting for the right dummies like us to blunder inside.

Ian grinned ironically as he signaled to Kinsey and left the communications bunker. Walking across the open area between the geodesic domes, he had the thought that somebody had finally built a better mousetrap.

"I'm all right, damn it. How many times do I have to tell you people that?"

Mikaela Lindstrom didn't like to raise her voice, much less scream and rant and rave, but it seemed like the only way she was going to get any attention.

When the ornithopter brought her back to the survey camp, she was admittedly shaken up, and the crowd of assistants that swarmed all over her when she was carried down from the aircraft seemed to make her return even more dramatic than necessary. Before she could say anything, she had been overwhelmed by a chorus of voices offering advice and help and badgering her with ridiculous questions.

Suddenly, Rebecca Thalberg appeared on the scene and directed the mob to swoosh Mikaela off to sick bay.

And although Mikaela appreciated the attention she was getting from her staff and from Becky herself, she kept telling everybody that she really didn't need to be sedated, that she really didn't need to be stretched out in a bed. And when things had finally gotten to be too much, she had started screaming at all the would-be do-gooders.

Now they all stood there staring at her in shock and disbelief—Dr. Penovich and all their assistants, and of course Becky Thalberg herself.

"I think we get the message, Mikaela," Becky said with a tentative smile on her face.

"All right." Mikaela licked her lips nervously. "I'm sorry for yelling like that, but I just didn't want everyone making such a fuss over me. I'm a big girl now, right?"

"Everybody was just worried, that's all," said Dr. Penovich.

"I understand that," she said, sliding off the hospital bed and facing the small assembly. "But I assure you I'm okay. Now, why don't you all get back to your posts. I'm sure we're going to be needed to help out in some way."

As everyone started reluctantly filing from the standard white room, Becky remained, waiting until everyone had left before speaking. "I'm sorry, too," she said. "I guess I overreacted. But I'll tell you, when they hauled you out of that 'thopter, you looked *terrible*."

They both laughed, relieving some of the tension. Mikaela was anxious to know what had been going on since she'd been confined to sick bay. Becky briefly recounted what little they had been able to discover by keeping in touch with Ian Coopersmith at the tactical base headquarters.

"I'm so glad so many were able to get to safety," Mikaela said. "God, it was so horrible to be just hovering over that mess and not be able to do anything."

"You were able to give them some air cover," Becky said.

"That was thanks to Ginny Zabriskie. She's a fine pilot, I'll tell you. And to be honest, I was doing my best to just stay on the radio." Mikaela paused to lick her lips again. She was getting extremely thirsty and moved to the sink to get a cup of water. "I keep seeing that crazy old man getting torn to pieces—that's the worst part of it. I can't get it out of my head."

"You and two billion other people," Becky said. "I never liked Neville, but I wouldn't wish that on anybody."

"Phineas simply adored old Neville. He must be extremely upset."

Becky smiled. "I thought you'd have noticed by now that Phineas doesn't get very upset about anything."

Mikaela wondered: Did she detect some hostility beneath Becky's warm tone of voice? It was possible that the woman still felt some real attachment to Phineas. Well, she thought, now was not the time to start trying to analyze her man's ex-lover. Talk about doing crazy things . . .

"Maybe you're right, Becky." She tried to ease out of the conversation.

That's when the lights went out.

"Oh-oh," Becky said. "What's going on?"

"I don't know. Come on." Knowing the contours of the base as well as anyone, Mikaela reached out and took Becky's hand. It was surprising how absolutely dark it was within the geodesic dome, even though perhaps another hour of daylight still remained outside.

With Becky trailing along, she worked their way out of sick bay and down a connecting tube that led to the main laboratory. As they drew closer, Mikaela could hear the excited voices of her staff. "How could this happen?" she asked her companion as they moved along.

"I don't know. You're asking the wrong person about technical stuff. I wish Ian were here. He could tell you in a second."

When they reached the main lab, Mikaela could see that several inventive assistants had fired up bunsen burners to provide a kind of eerie gaslight atmosphere to the lab.

"I think we should all make our way outside,"

Mikaela said, "and see if we can get this straightened out."

Without a word of protest, the small assemblage of scientists headed toward the outer door, which opened into a small courtyard flanked on all four sides by fairly large buildings, which the staff had come to call the quad. Opposite the main lab, across the quad, lay the physical plant, which housed the communications hut, and the generators for all their electrical needs. As Mikaela reached the quad, she could see two IASA staffers running toward them. She recognized the taller man as Chris George, the communications officer. The shorter one, a woman named Donna Sprinkle, was a member of the tactical unit assigned to protect the survey camp. Corporal Sprinkle was carrying an automatic rifle.

"What's the problem, Corporal?" Mikaela asked as the pair stopped in front of them.

"I don't know, Dr. Lindstrom. Power's just gone."

Suddenly Mikaela understood. Why hadn't she realized it till now? "Oh no," she said softly, in an almost fearful whisper. "The force field."

"That's right," the tactical soldier said. "And without it, we're sitting ducks."

Mikaela looked up at the darkening Illuminator and the growing dusk that saturated the vegetation with lush shades of green.

Darkness was feeding time.

Sixteen

The ornithopter lifted off its pad with a rocking, awkward, goony-bird kind of motion, which was typical of all aircraft of its type. Despite his inertia harness, Ian Coopersmith was tossed about in the shotgun seat like a sack of potatoes. He had never grown accustomed to being a passenger in a 'thopter, much preferring to pilot the aircraft himself, even though rank let him off the hook. He was a good pilot, and he trusted his own instincts better than anyone's in the weird wind currents that existed within the closed cylinder of the Dragonstar.

Because of temperature gradients in the atmosphere of the sealed environment, and because the entire cylinder was rotating on its longitudinal axis, some very bizarre weather conditions were observed. It was not uncommon to encounter thermal pockets and wind vortices of such violent nature that conventional aircraft would be ripped apart by the turbulence.

It was discovered very quickly when exploring the Dragonstar that the birdlike ornithopter was the only aircraft that could safely maneuver within the immense, spinning environment. Knowing all this, however, did not make Ian feel any better about the flight. Zabriskie was constantly wrestling with the cybernetic controls, but she seemed to be an expert at it.

Looking down, Ian studied the terrain of the Mesozoic preserve, remembering what it had been like when he and Becky had been so rudely thrust into its Darwinian realities. It seemed so long ago, and yet it hadn't been very long at all. The 'thopter passed over a swampy section that gradually filled a flood plain and formed a small lake. Long-necked Brontosaurus waded in water that only covered them halfway up their flanks. They were such ponderous beasts, such easy prey for carnivores, that they had learned to spend much of their time in the water, feeding on bulbous water plants and tubers that grew in the muddy bottoms.

It was odd, thought Ian, that the meat eaters shied away from the water as they did. If those boys had ever learned to swim, everybody else would have had some real problems on their hands—or should he say claws?

The lake passed beneath them, giving way to a vast plain that had been given the name of the Mordor Plateau. It was a fairly flat region with sparser vegetation and some unusual rock formations. The plateau rose gradually above sea level, giving way to a range of small but spectacularly sculpted mountains. It was incredible to think that the entire environment had been artificially created by a race of beings whose technology must be light-years beyond humankind's understanding. To build an artificial world like the interior of the Dragonstar was a mind-boggling conception. To actually see it, and realize what had been accomplished, was a numbing experience—the mind refused to comprehend what the eyes recorded; it refused to accept that such artifice could be possible.

No, thought Ian, the hard truth of the Dragonstar only came to be accepted very gradually—in small, subtle ways, until there came the day when you fully understood the enormity of the project that was the Dragonstar. It was only then, thought Ian, that a person could truly understand humility.

As the 'thopter churned and dipped violently, it oc-

curred to Ian that perhaps he had hit upon Phineas
Kemp's biggest problem: the man had never allowed
himself to come to grips with the reality of the alien
vessel. Kemp had never taken the time to perceive the
Dragonstar for what it was—a technological and biological masterpiece which so far dwarfed the dreams
and accomplishments of the human race that it was only
laughable.

No, to Phineas Kemp the Dragonstar was just
another bloody obstacle in his quest for recognition.
The ship was just one more thing in Kemp's life for him
to master or conquer.

How sad. How bloody, fucking sad that Kemp had
never been able to rise above that way of seeing things.
A popular journalist had recently written an article
about Kemp and "his" Dragonstar, making many
grand allusions to Ahab and Moby Dick, and Ian had
always felt there was something wrong with that writer's
perceptions, but until now he had not been able to pin it
down.

No. Despite his problems, at least Captain Ahab had
recognized the magnificence of the great white whale.
At least he had been touched by the mystical power and
significance of the mighty creature. Colonel Kemp, on
the other hand, had never learned to respect the
Dragonstar, by far his most formidable "opponent."

As with many proud figures of tragedy, Phineas
Kemp had come to the magic pool of power and failed
to look any deeper than the surface that reflected his
own proud image.

Jeez, that was good! thought Ian. He would have to
try to remember to write that one down. Funny to find
himself bordering on the profound when he should be
preparing himself for battle. But Ian Coopersmith was a
funny kind of man, wasn't he?

Looking down, he could see that they had passed the
small mountain range and were heading toward an impossibly thick stretch of primordial forest: giant redwoods penciling into the air like monuments to the
majesty of all trees, riotous fronds and ferns growing

out of control, and a never-ending network of vines and tangling tubers. He shuddered as he recalled crawling and sliming through that world, and of the horrors that capered boldly within its shadows. The Illuminator was growing perceptibly dimmer, and he knew that darkness would be filtering down upon the land very soon. Hopefully he would reach the Hakarrh temple before nightfall.

"Mayday! Mayday!" an unfamiliar voice sounded in his helmet phones. "All channels. Level One . . . come in please!"

Reaching out, Ian keyed in his radio. "This is Ian Coopersmith aboard tactical base 'thopter one-one-seven . . . we copy."

"Captain Coopersmith, this is Bonnie Kerin at the paleo survey camp. We've just had a total power loss. Our force field is out, and we're going to need some help fast."

"We copy that, Kerin. Please stand by." Ian keyed out the radio mike and asked his pilot to give them their position relative to the survey camp.

After a quick check of her instruments, Zabriskie gave him a fix and an ETA.

"All right," Ian said, returning to his transmission. "We're about ten minutes from you. Please hang on and we'll try to provide you with some assistance. What is your total population right now?"

"Twenty-six, counting the guards."

"How many OTVs available?"

The transmission faded for an instant, then came back strong. "Let's see, we have three vehicles in camp right now."

"Try to squeeze as many of you into those things as possible," Ian said. "Should be able to get six or seven into each one. That will give you some protection in case a hungry chap happens to wander in. Then have everybody else get down underneath the tread wheels, okay?"

"We copy, Captain. Anything else we should know?"

"Not that I can think of. But you can tell me, how are Dr. Lindstrom and Dr. Thalberg?"

"They're both okay, sir. Dr. Lindstrom is trying to get everybody organized. That's why she had me call."

"Glad to hear it. All right, hang on. We're on our way. Coopersmith out."

"Thank you, Captain. PSC standing by, and out."

Coopersmith looked over at Zabriskie. "Well, you heard the lady: 'Follow that cab.' "

Zabriskie forced herself to smile. She was a tall, big-boned redhead who looked like she could arm-wrestle any man in the pub, but she had a warm smile that Ian found disarming. "What do you think caused the power loss?" she asked.

"Not sure. We've been registering some unidentified radiation pulses since the trouble started. Got some big EMP readings a little while ago—it must have knocked them out. They didn't have the kind of shielding on their gear our tactical stuff has."

Zabriski nodded. "Thank God for agency regulations and specifications."

"For once, I would have to agree with a statement like that. Chalk one up for the bureaucrats."

His pilot chuckled as she began decelerating a bit, wrestling the controls through a thermal pocket. Ian keyed in the research lab's frequency trying to hail Takamura's people. There was a lot of interference, but it was possible to hear someone responding. Fiddling with the controls, Ian was able to pull them in.

"Research lab here, come in."

"Takamura, is that you? This is Captain Coopersmith."

"Yes, Captain, we've been expecting you."

"I'm going to be delayed." Ian gave the scientist a quick rundown on the problems at the paleo survey camp. "What's your status there?"

"The lab and quarters have been evacuated. Everybody is down by the temple entrance. We've got more than a hundred people building some hasty barricades."

"How about the Saurians?"

"Can't tell," Takamura said. "We stopped the bunch of warriors who were trying to storm the steps. We can see big crowds of them milling around in the streets, but they don't seem to be organized into doing anything. This must be very confusing and disorienting to most of them."

"I would say so, Doctor." Ian paused. "Listen, there was one of them I got to know quite well, named Thesaurus. You wouldn't happen to know him, would you? He was one of their big names."

"Oh, yes." Takamura said. "I know him quite well. But I couldn't tell you what became of him. Too much going on, you know."

Ian swallowed hard, hoping that the old Saurian had somehow escaped all the mayhem. "Okay, thanks, Doctor. Try to hold your position as long as possible, and tell Colonel Kemp why we're not going to make it for a while yet. Coopersmith out."

Takamura signed off. Ian could see that they were approaching the large meadow that housed the survey camp. Nearby was a hatch and corridor system that led to an airlock and the outer hull. It was very near where Ian and Becky and the first exploratory mission had entered the Dragonstar.

So much had happened since then. Everyone's lives had changed so drastically.

"Okay, Captain, here we are," Zabriskie announced.

"Take it down slowly," Ian said. He radioed his two sharpshooters in the underbelly of the 'thopter, telling them to keep their eyes open for any hungry beasties, and unholstered his own sidearm, flipping off the safety.

Three Omni Terrain Vehicles were arranged in a vaguely triangular configuration almost directly below them. The twilight had grown very thick, and it seemed to be growing darker the closer they drew to the ground.

"Searchlamps," Ian ordered.

Zabriskie touched a pad, and the OTVs were washed in blue-white harshness. The 'thopter kited about, touching down very close to them.

Jumping down from the cab, Ian told his pilot to be ready to lift off at an instant, and directed his two sharpshooters to flank the area as best they could. Looking to the OTVs, he could see the crowd of faces behind the bubble domes staring out at him. One of the vehicles hatches swung open, and Becky Thalberg appeared. She came running toward him and threw her arms around him.

"Oh, Ian! You don't know how glad I am to see you. I can't believe you're here."

Ian was amazed to realize how good she felt in his arms. Despite the humid air of the preserve, the warmth of her body pressed against his was a welcome sensation. Automatically he rooted through her long dark hair and kissed her neck. She smelled enticing, exciting.

"I'm glad to see you too, Becky."

She drew back from him, a bit embarrassed. "Yes, I can see that."

Mikaela Lindstrom and Dr. Penovich appeared by Ian's side, and the fleeting moment was lost. "Good to see you, Captain Coopersmith," Mikaela said. "Let me fill you in on what's happening. We've got six people in each of the OTVs. It's tight, but we can make it."

"Make it to where?" Ian asked.

Mikaela looked at him with a startled expression. "I don't know," she said. "I hadn't thought of that."

"Neither had I," Ian said. "But I think it's time we did."

Briefly, Ian explained to them the position of the survivors at the Hakarrh temple, and also the people in the downed cargo 'thopter who were stranded in the Saurian ruins.

"It seems to me that the people in the ruins are the safest," Becky said. "I should know, I've been there."

"I was thinking the same thing," Ian said. "I think we should concentrate on getting your party out of this unprotected area and then work on Colonel Kemp's people. The big problem is that I don't have room for more than two passengers at a time, and even then it's a tight squeeze in the belly compartment."

Becky considered the problem for a moment. "Why don't we take the OTVs overland to the ruins? We could be safe there, and you could use the 'thopter to transport the rest of us two or three at a time."

"You're right," Ian said. "There's no way we could get the OTVs across the mountain range and back to tactical base HQ—even though their power wasn't affected by the EMP phenomena."

"And the ruins are more strategically located for the group at the Hakarrh temple. It's much closer than trying to evacuate everybody to a spot farther into the preserve," Becky said.

"I think she's got it," Mikaela said. "I can take the three OTVs overland to the ruins. It will be slow going, but we can make it."

Ian considered his options and realized he had none at all. What Becky said made sense. For the time being, setting up a temporary base of operations in the Saurian ruins would probably be their best tactic—at least until Copernicus Base could get some help in to them. "All right, that sounds reasonable. Let's get straight on who's going now and who will be waiting around for cab rides," he said.

Several minutes passed as the assignments were worked out. Mikaela climbed into the lead OTV and headed toward the ruins with seventeen others. That left eight behind, including Becky (who had insisted on remaining with Ian), plus Ian and his two sharpshooters.

Zabriskie took two paleontologists into the equipment bay of the 'thopter along with one of the survey camp guards at shotgun. Ian reminded her to contact Sergeant Kinsey at the tactical base headquarters and tell him of the change in plans. It was always a good idea to keep everybody abreast of what was happening. The 'thopter lifted off clumsily and smudged out into the pitch-black artificial night. That left Ian, Becky, his two gunners, and four scientists. They would have to tough it out until the 'thopter could get back for the next run . . . and the next.

As the whine and whoomp of the 'thopter echoed

away and were swallowed up by the dense foliage of the
surrounding jungle, Ian became of aware of how
deathly still it had suddenly become. With a rush of
memory, he was brought back to his last tour on board
the Dragonstar, and the same sickening feeling of being
cut off in the darkness of the Mesozoic heartland now
enfolded him like the leathery wings of a great Pteranodon.

"All right," he said, unhooking an electric torch
from his belt and flicking it on. "Let's take what cover
we can in the domes. Murphy, you and Jalecki set up
some flanking cover, and I'll cover the third point.
Come on, let's get moving."

Everyone closed ranks and moved toward the closest
geodesic dome, which had been used as a maintenance
hangar for the OTVs. As the biologists filed inside and
the sharpshooters took up positions on each side of the
structure, Becky stopped and held on to Ian's arm.

"I'd like to stay out here with you, if you don't
mind."

Ian's first impulse was to say something authoritarian
and protective, but something deeper inside cut off that
almost automatic response. He recalled vividly how this
woman had trekked through this hellish place with him
and never batted an eye. There was no way he could pull
that bullshit on her now. Besides, he could certainly use
the company.

"All right," he said. "That would be nice."

As he whispered the words, there was a fierce rustling
in the underbrush beyond the perimeter of the camp,
and a plaintive, bestial cry rose up to crack the sky.

Mishima Takamura moved quickly from the elevator
that opened onto the temple access corridor. He was the
last to leave the research lab in the alien crew section,
and his paranoia quotient was high. During the entire
descent, he kept imagining that the device would suddenly halt in its shaft and trap him in its stifling small-
ness. He had never been a big fan of tight spaces, but he
had forced himself to conquer his fears for his once-in-

a-lifetime chance to go into space.

But the reason for his paranoia went far beyond a case of claustrophobia.

The alien ship was definitely coming to life. While he carried some vital instruments out of the lab, placing them on the power cart he now guided down the empty corridor, he could not help but notice how different things were in the alien section. Displays, consoles and devices that had been dark, silent, and dormant since their arrival were suddenly being activated.

But what was worse, what was more bizarre, was the way it was all happening with a total disregard for the humans on board. The ship seemed to be going about its preordained tasks as though there were no intruders present.

What did it mean? What was happening on board the Dragonstar? Mishima was convinced that all the strange events were connected, that everything pointed toward some larger event. He had his own ideas as to what might be going on but just the thought of it made him uneasy, and in a most unscientific manner he forced himself not to think about it.

The final threshhold, beyond which lay the Saurian temple, yawned ahead of him, and Mishima quickened his pace. The sooner he was free of the restrictive corridors and the automated alien machinery, the better he would feel. The cart glided along silently ahead of him as he cleared the doorway. He paused to take a breath, then moved through the temple to the outside.

Using whatever debris and materials they could find, the survivors had thrown up barricades along the top of the steps leading to the temple. It reminded Mishima of the Saurians building their great wall. There was an irony there somewhere, but he was too tired to search for it.

He could see Phineas Kemp walking along the front line of defense, the pretty young journalist in tow, pausing to talk to some of the IASA staffers now and then, but primarily playing up the role of a field marshal inspecting his troops.

The scene was almost laughable, and it demonstrated to Mishima what a complete asshole the colonel was. There was something about Kemp that Mishima didn't like. He hadn't respected the man from the first moment they'd met.

Pushing the cart of equipment over to a group of his assistants, he helped them unload and connect up the gear. The auxiliary generators would always be useful, but right now they would get the monitoring equipment running. He had not gotten far along in the setup when he was interrupted by none other than Kemp himself.

"What's going on here, Doctor?" the colonel asked in a noncommittal tone of voice.

Mishima looked up at Kemp and made an effort to be cordial. There was no sense in causing a scene in front of everyone. "We were able to get out some of our monitoring equipment, and I'd like to know why we haven't been contacted by Copernicus Base."

Kemp smiled ingenuously. "So would I, Doctor. How do you propose to find out?"

"I'm going to try to activate it using short wave equipment. We had an EMP effect that wiped out the portable gear, but this stuff from the lab was apparently shielded by being in the alien crew section." Mishima didn't feel like explaining himself and his techniques to a man like Kemp. He considered ways to end the conversation as quickly as possible.

One of his assistants came to his side. "Doctor, I've got something on the screen."

Without another word, Mishima turned away, following the woman to a portable monitor that had been set up near the end of the barricade where it reached the temple wall. "What is it?" Mishima asked, looking at a blurry image on the screen.

"It's a view of the hull from one of the cameras near the docking bay. It's attached to a piece of the hull's superstructure," the lab technician said. "We were able to activate it with the short-wave application. But there's something causing an almost impossible level of interference outside on the hull."

"Any idea what's causing it?" asked Mishima.

"Not really."

Phineas Kemp, who had followed Mishima, looked at the screen with an intense expression on his face. "Wait a minute. If that's the docking bay, then where the hell is it?"

"What?" Mishima asked, looking more closely at the screen. "What do you mean?"

"I mean the docking bay's *not there*. It's gone." Kemp said. "And where're all the ships we had out there? Weren't there two lunar shuttles on their way out? Where the hell are they?"

The colonel had a good point, Mishima admitted. He looked pointedly at his assistant. "Are you sure you have the right camera input?"

"No question about it, Doctor."

Something was definitely wrong out there. The docking bay had been a specially constructed rig built so that IASA ships could arrive and depart the Dragonstar with a minimum of difficulty. It had been attached by powerful electromagnets that would have prevented the docking assembly from being blown off the hull even by high explosives.

And now it seemed as though the docking bay had simply vanished.

"It looks to me like we're cut off from the outside of the ship," Kemp said. "And we've received more bad news from the tactical command."

Briefly, Kemp explained to Mishima and his assistants the problems and rescue operations at the survey camp and the Saurian ruins. "It seems to me," he said, "that we basically have two options, especially if we can expect no immediate help from the outside. One, we can stay here and fight a war of attrition with the Saurians if they choose to attack us. Or two, we can take off through the Mesozoic preserve and join up with everyone else in the ruins."

There was a heavy silence for a time as everyone considered Kemp's words. Finally Mishima spoke. "Perhaps there is a third option, Colonel."

Kemp seemed surprised but not upset that Mishima would challenge him so diplomatically. "Really? And what might that be?"

"Well, isn't it possible that we could send down some emissaries to the Saurians and get this thing resolved? I mean, maybe we don't need to fight our way out—maybe they would just let us leave."

This comment stirred up a bit of discussion among the assembled staffers and scientists who had been listening in on the dialogue. Mishima welcomed the additional input,. but he was certain that Colonel Kemp loathed policymaking by committee. He couldn't stifle a sly smile as he regarded the colonel, who remained passive as he scanned the reactions of the small assembly.

"That's interesting," Kemp said after the discussion had died down. "And you're right—it is a distinct option. I guess I hadn't thought of it. But I feel it's also the most dangerous one. Wouldn't you agree, Dr. Takamura?"

Mishima nodded. "Probably. There's no doubt in my mind that the Saurians have been severely affected by the radiation levels we've been detecting—there's no other explanation for what we've just been through. And although it appears to be affecting the warrior-class and agrarian-class individuals primarily, I wouldn't bet on us being able to hash this thing out with the priests—they might be very pissed off at us."

There was a murmur of laughter in the crowd as he continued. "But it is a possibility that we should at least consider. I was at one time quite friendly with Thesaurus, one of their philosopher-priests."

Kemp nodded slowly. "Well, it's certainly worth trying, especially if we can get some volunteers who wouldn't mind walking into the arms of the Saurians."

"Or maybe their jaws," someone cracked.

There was a sharp round of laughter, followed by some anxious silence. Mishima knew they were waiting for some fool to volunteer.

"I guess I'm the one to do it," he said with a touch of exhaustion.

Everyone looked at him with some surprise.

"I mean," he continued, "it was my crazy idea, right? So why shouldn't I be the guy to try it out, right?"

"I'm not sure that would be a good idea, Doctor," Kemp said.

"And why not?" Mishima was feeling suddenly defensive. Did Kemp always feel so threatened by any outside authority or show of courage?

"It's simple, really. With Dr. Jakes stranded in the ruins, that leaves you in charge of the research division. Correct me if I'm wrong on that."

"No, that's right. I am the chief project assistant." Mishima could already see what the colonel was leading up to, and he was probably right.

"Well," Kemp said, "I don't think it's a good idea to risk the head of an operation to a mission that may be this risky, that's all."

"He's right," one of Mishima's assistants said. "We wouldn't want to lose you, Mishima."

Mishima nodded appreciatively. It was gratifying to know that his people liked him and respected him enough to want him to stick around.

"All right," he said. "I can see your point, Colonel, but I don't see anybody else volunteering for the job. Does that mean that we just forget about it?"

Kemp grinned wryly and shrugged. "Good point, Doctor. I really don't know what it means. I'm all for trying anything that might make our situation a little easier, but I think this one is strictly a volunteer proposition, don't you?"

Mishima nodded and looked about at the faces of those who were standing close by. He could easily see the fear and apprehension in their expressions. It hadn't been that long ago that they'd seen what an angry, hungry Saurian could do to a human being.

"I'd like to try it." A small voice suddenly punctured the awkward silence.

Mishima stared down at diminutive Kate Ennis, the NBC journalist who had been standing by Kemp's side, quietly recording the entire scene.

"Kate, you can't be serious," Kemp said.

"Are you sure you know what you're taking on, Ms. Ennis?" Mishima asked.

Kate Ennis stepped forward, nervously straightening her soiled jumper. Her exquisitely sculpted face reflected her anxiety and the pressure she, and all of them, were under. But beneath that exterior Mishima could detect a fiercely burning spirit, a strength that was coming quickly to the surface.

"Of course I know," she said. "And I think I'm qualified for the job."

"Kate, I won't hear of this," Kemp said in a patronizing voice. "This is ridiculous."

That seemed to anger her, but she kept her emotions in check as she turned to stare at the colonel. "Phineas, listen to me. I've been a journalist for thirteen years. I've interviewed every conceivable type of person in thousands of foreign locations. I've been confronted with foreign languages and customs from every part of the world, and I've done my job—which is to talk to them, damn it! It seems to me that this assignment is pretty much the same thing."

At first glance Ennis seemed fragile and delicate, but after hearing her impassioned little speech, Mishima knew she could do the job.

Colonel Kemp was smiling and nodding his head. "How can I argue with that kind of logic, Kate? Although I think you'll find these chaps a bit different from any of your previous subjects."

"And I don't think you should be going by yourself," said a young corporal wearing a tactical insignia on the shoulder of his coveralls. He turned to face and salute Kemp. "Corporal David Potlack, sir. I couldn't help overhear the conversation, sir, and I figure if the lady here isn't afraid to check out the lizards, then neither am I, sir."

Kemp smiled at the young man and shook his hand. "All right, then, I guess we have a mission to plan. Ms. Ennis, meet your escort, Corporal Potlack. Now let's sit down here and see what would be the best way to go about this."

*   *   *

Christ-on-a-crutch, he never thought he'd be in a situation like this!

Dr. Robert Jakes lay sprawled on a slab of stone about two hundred meters above the jungle floor. He'd been carried there by several of the passengers from the cargo 'thopter because he'd banged up his ankle when they first touched down. He laughed at the thought. "Touched down" isn't exactly how he'd have described the way the 'thopter had thrashed through the tree tops and flung itself over the stone wall into the courtyard of the ruins. If it hadn't been for the thick tangle of vines and underbrush that were slowly reclaiming the stone buildings, and which had served as a marvelous cushioning pad, the 'thopter would have had a worse time of it.

As it was, there were some cuts and bruises and a few sprains, but that was all.

Darkness had wrapped them all up more than a hour ago, and everyone was huddled about a utility lamp that Lieutenent Barkham had brought up from the 'thopter. The scene reminded Jakes of a pack of early hominids bunched about a simple campfire, listening to the horrors of the night, which seemed to caper boldly just beyond the light's perimeter. And they represented an interesting mix of people, thought Jakes as he looked about the assembled group. Barkham and a couple of IASA staffers, two executives from World Media Corporation, several scientists from the research team, and a handful of the documentary crew.

Most of us not very well cut out for this kind of survival game, Jakes thought. A bunch of softies, he thought with a smile. Myself included. Even Lieutenant Barkham, whom everybody was kind of looking up to for advice because he represented the authority figure, the captain of the ship, and all that jazz, was not too skilled at getting by in the wilderness.

Granted, he had just gotten word that some help was on the way, but Jakes was shocked to hear that things were going so bad everywhere that everybody else was planning to come here.

He tested his ankle tentatively, twisting it slowly and finally putting some pressure on it. Felt better, no more shooting pains, just a dull throbbing. He would probably be able to get around on it by the next day, although there wasn't much of anywhere to go when you were perched halfway up a stone ziggurat.

It was funny how the conversation would come in waves or flurries. It seemed to hit them in cycles. Everybody would be talking for a while, and then suddenly it would kind of peter out and there would be nothing but silence.

Things were in a silent phase right now, and everybody seemed to be tuned in to the symphony of night sounds that could be heard cutting through the darkness like sharp knives, or maybe sharp teeth. Jakes had spent very little time in the Mesozoic preserve, and this whole experience was starting to get to him. He had, of course, gone through the usual love affair with dinosaurs as a kid, but now that he was out among the damned things, he would just as soon not ever see one. About the closest he had come to any of them was from the air, just passing over, thank you—but now there was the chance that he might be meeting one of the boys close up.

His group was not terribly well armed—two automatic rifles and three sidearms—and Jakes had no idea what was needed to bring down the average predator. Every once in a while there would be some kind of hellacious scream or growl that would jump out of the forest below them, and it would seem so damned close that Jakes would swear the creatures were lurking right next to them. It was amazing how much louder everything sounded at night. It was probably the mind and the imagination up to their usual tricks, but Jakes didn't care much about that.

A vicious snarling tore open the silence, and everybody looked at each other. Whatever had made that noise had sounded damned close and damned big.

"I wonder if they can smell us up here?" asked one of the young guys from the documentary crew.

"Not unless you're bleedin'," said someone else. "You gotta be bleedin'."

"I thought that was just for sharks. These are dinosaurs, right?"

"Hey, who cares," one of the women said. "I mean, do we really want to know if those things can smell us from down there?"

Everyone chuckled nervously and settled back into an uneasy silence. They all seemed to be studying the steady glow of the electric lantern as though it were about to dispense some important bit of information instead of just light. Then there came a new sound, which made everyone become visibly more tense.

A scrabbling, scratching sound.

Sharp claws on rough stone, furiously churning and scritching, growing louder and more frenzied as it continued, accompanied by ravenous snarling—a slavering, bubbling sound of hunger and insanity.

It was easily the most terrifying sound Bob Jakes had ever heard in his life.

Shit! Is it getting louder because it's getting more frantic or because it's getting closer? He kept the question to himself for two reason: one, he didn't want to alarm the others, and two, he didn't really want to know the answer.

Barkham and two of the tactical men moved out of the group toward the sloping edge of the pyramidal structure. One of them shone a flashlight down into the darkness.

"There he is," Jakes heard one of them say softly.

"Jesus, he's a pretty big one!" the other whispered, albeit loud enough for everyone to hear. "You think he could make it up here?"

"I don't think so," Barkham said.

"Well," said the younger of the two troopers, taking aim with his automatic rifle, "I'm going to pop him one."

"No!" Barkham said. "Even if you kill him, all you'd do is draw a bunch of other ones to the spot. The scent of blood draws 'em out of the fucking woodwork."

Dropping his rifle, the trooper nodded while the other kept the light trained down toward the beast. Its crazy scratching was getting less rapid, and the message that it was too hard a climb finally starting to get to its dull, tiny brain. Good thing, too, thought Jakes. Between the noise and the trigger-happy staffers, Jakes didn't know if he could stand this kind of tension all night long.

If he could sincerely believe they were safe up on the ruins, it wouldn't be so bad on the nerves, but the jury was still out on that particular deal.

No one spoke for he didn't know how long, then just as abruptly as the scrabbling had started, it ended.

"Finally gave up," said the trooper with the flashlight. "There he goes."

That seemed to be the signal for everyone to start talking, because suddenly there was a low murmur of conversation which gradually became louder until it seemed as if Jakes was the only one not talking. It went on like that until the earthquake started.

At least it seemed like an earthquake, and that's what everybody started yelling when the ground shook and the very foundations of the massive stone ruins began to vibrate and tremble. People started screaming and moving closer together, away from the edge of the edifice, where pieces of cut stone were starting to flake off and fall into the darkness.

Jakes had to admit that it sure as hell felt like an earthquake, but he knew that was impossible. He also knew that there was only one thing that could cause the entire encapsulated world to vibrate and shake like tectonic plates being scraped so roughly together.

Engines starting.

Seventeen

They had requested that she change clothes before going down into the city of Hakarrh, and Kate Ennis had to admit it wasn't a bad idea. The fashionable gown she had worn to the live broadcast had long ago been ruined. So now she stepped from the temple wearing a set of IASA standard-issue coveralls that were at least two sizes too large. She looked like a mechanic in a turn-of-the-century garage.

"Not as flattering," Phineas Kemp said when he saw her emerge. "But at least you won't have to worry about it snagging on anything."

"Very funny," Kate said.

"Here, Ms. Ennis," said Dr. Takamura, who handed her a small pendant device. "This is a digital translator. It's been encoded for the Saurian language and English. You've seen how they operate, I assume."

"Yes," she said with a nervous smile. "I can just wear it around my neck, right?"

"That's right," Kemp said. "But remember that you have to wait after speaking for it to broadcast your message. Then you have to wait for it to translate whatever the Saurians say back to you."

"It just makes the whole process of communicating a little slower, a bit more awkward, perhaps," said Takamura. "But equally effective—as long as you choose the proper words."

Kate looked at the young physicist. His oriental features were complemented by his dark eyes and thick dark hair. He was a handsome man with more dash and verve then she usually associated with scientists. He seemed to have more than his share of self-confidence and social graces, which many academic types seemed never to have learned.

She smiled at him, then cleared her throat dramatically. "Yes, Doctor, choosing the proper words has been a problem for us humans for a long time, hasn't it?"

"Well put," Takamura said. He performed a little mock bow, and Kate wondered if he might be making a pass at her in an offhand kind of way. He certainly could be a charmer when he wanted to be.

Just then Corporal Potlack joined them and announced that he was as ready as he'd ever be. He carried an automatic rifle with extra ammo clips hanging from his belt. His helmet visor was flipped up, revealing his lean bearded face. Despite the man's small build and height, he appeared quite formidable. Implanted headphones and a throat mike were also visible, and Kate wondered if she would have to wear similar gear.

"All right," Kemp said. "Remember to stay close together and head straight for the 'condos.' "

Kate smiled at the slang reference to the dwellings of the priest class, which had been cut, pueblo-style, into the face of the promontory above Hakarrh. They figured that that would be the safest place to attempt contact with the Saurians, since the lower castes were never allowed in the condos and the priest class didn't seem to be as affected by the radiation madness that had raced through the other classes like a plague.

"Don't worry, Colonel," Corporal Potlack said, smacking his weapon affectionately. "I won't let anything happen to us."

"Okay, I guess that's it," Phineas said as he reached out and took Kate's hand in both his own. "This is a courageous thing you're doing, Kate. Good luck."

"I'm not sure how courageous I feel," she said softly. "I just want to do something to help."

Kemp smiled apprehensively. "You're doing more than anyone would ever ask of you." Turning to Corporal Potlack, he gave the man a crisp salute.

Following the trooper's lead, Kate walked past the barricades and began to descend the steps. Everyone on the first line of defense began to clap, and the applause was mixed with cheers. Kate felt a swelling in her chest and tears in her eyes.

They had covered perhaps one quarter of the distance down toward the boulevard when the applause died out. For a moment there was only silence. Kate scanned the area below and was pleased to see that it appeared to be deserted.

Corporal Potlack stopped abruptly. "What's that? You feel it?"

At first Kate didn't know what he was talking about, then she too felt a tingle of vibration in the massive stone steps. As she stood perfectly still, the vibration increased rapidly. Suddenly it was no longer a tingling in her boots but a full-fledged tremor. The immense set of steps seemed to be shifting and dipping away from her feet.

Corporal Potlack yelled something and reached out for her as she toppled outward. His hand locked upon her wrist and pulled her back as they both fell across the sharp edges of the steps. By now the stone foundation was actually heaving and shaking. All around them the air crackled with a high-pitched keening sound that continued to grow in intensity and power.

"What's happening?" Kate cried out as the noise grew almost unbearably loud.

"I don't know," said the trooper, "but we'd better try to get back up."

"What?" Kate was confused and terrified. The steps were heaving so violently now that it seemed as if they would shake themselves to pieces at any instant.

"C'mon!" Potlack screamed, pulling her back up the steps with surprising strength. She could feel her legs moving, even though she had lost all control and coordination.

"Watch out!" Potlack yelled again as he yanked her from the path of a falling rock that was tumbling down the stairs at a high, rollicking speed. There was a terrible crunching sound as a great fracture appeared in the stone steps to their left. A huge fissure opened up like a jagged mouth and raced along a fault line in the stone. Potlack moved even more quickly now, and suddenly Kate was surrounded by other people as a crowd descended on them and carried them the rest of the way to the top.

The keening had changed pitch and was now a great roaring sound. With a sudden, inertial pull, as though she were tied to the end of rope, she was pulled off her feet with the rest of the crowd, and everyone fell in a tangled mass of arms and legs. Something cataclysmic was happening, but she hadn't the slightest idea what it might be—she only knew that it was very bad, and that she was probably going to die.

She rolled over and tried to get to her feet, but the tremors were so powerful now that this was impossible. Behind her, the stone colums of the Saurian temple had begun to fracture and split. Despite the chaos going on around her, she watched the massive supports flake and crumble as the temple came crashing down. As the huge pieces of stone impacted, many of them exploded, sending out smaller, deadly missiles which laced through the crowd like grapeshot. Someone grabbed her and threw her to the ground on her belly as the first volley of lethal flying debris ripped over her head.

She was shot through with pain from a hundred different cuts and bruises, but she was alive. Someone had saved her life, and she struggled to roll over against the weight of whoever was holding her down. Summoning up all her strength, she pushed up and to the left, heaving the dead weight of a body off her own. Looking at the person who had pulled her down, she recognized the face of Corporal Potlack, his open eyes already glazing over, a large sliver of stone embedded in his chest like an assassin's knife.

* * *

The only thing he could see in the flashing light of Murphy's flashlight was the cold, flat look of death in its eye. The carnivore had stumbled upon them quite by accident as it came crashing headlong through the forest chasing a smaller unseen prey.

Jalecki had been the one unlucky enough to be stationed closest to its point of entry into the survey camp. It had been incredibly quick and agile for its five meters of height and seven thousand-plus kilograms. Although Ian had not gotten a good look at it, it was a typical theropod predator—huge, pile-driving hindlegs; thick, powerful tail; absurdly small fore claws on a tapering body that expanded into an oversized head that was three-quarters jaws and the rest eyes.

Jalecki had managed to get off a single burst, a warning shot at best, before the monster's tail lashed out and flicked him like a fly at the end of a snapping bath towel. The man was thrown headlong into the thick trunk of a ginkgo, striking it with bone-crushing impact.

In an instant, the dinosaur leaped to the base of the tree and snapped up Jalecki's broken body in its jaws. The only consolation was that he was already dead.

By this time Murphy was firing at its thick hide, at the same time trying to get a light on it. Ian could see that this one had more subdued markings than some of the others—muted grays and greens—which tended to make the beast less visible, especially at night.

Becky had picked up a flashlight and was shining it into the bastard's big yellow eye, hoping to keep it blinded, even for a few moments. Ian had ripped a clip of slugs through its neck, and Murphy had come up from the rear and filled its flanks with dumdums. As it thrashed about on the edge of the forest, Ian could see glimpses of dark, syrupy blood glistening on its hide, and he knew that it was a goner.

It was just a question of how long it would take to die.

The carnivore emitted one last screeching, wailing song of pain and agony. It belched up gobbets of undigested flesh, mixed with a bubbling froth of its own blood, and tottered forward. When it fell, it barely missed the geodesic OTV hangar.

"Son of a bitch!" yelled Murphy, who was running on all cylinders, fired by a maximum shot of adrenaline. "Jesus, did you see that bastard. Oh, John, John."

"Coopersmith moved over to the trooper and put a hand on the man's shoulder. "I know how you feel, Murphy, but we've got to get out of here. Our shots and the blood are going to draw a crowd fast."

Murphy looked up and forced a panicky smile to his face. "I know, I know. But John was my buddy."

"He was dead as soon as he hit the tree," Ian said. "Now let's put a move on."

Becky had already alerted the four scientists in the hangar, and everyone was ready.

"We've got to change positions fast," Ian said. "I suggest we move to the building that's farthest away from this point."

"That would be the physical plant," said one of the paleontologists. "This way. Hurry!"

As they followed him through the darkness, Ian could already hear the sounds of approaching scavengers and other predators. The foliage seemed alive with rustling motion as the hungry creatures careened in toward the camp. A chorus of screeching and roaring was building to a feverish level. What a place to raise a family, thought Ian. I'm sure glad I'm no dinosaur.

Reaching the physical plant dome, Ian directed the four civilians inside, instructing them to take cover behind the heaviest machinery they could find. He gave John Jalecki's automatic rifle to Becky and positioned her and Murphy at points equidistant around the dome.

"That 'thopter should be back soon," Becky said.

"Yes, but I hope it doesn't come down at the wrong moment."

Beyond them, back where the first attack had come, Ian could hear the first sounds of the scavengers' feast. Low-pitched growling. The ripping and sucking of a carcass being pulled apart.

"I don't like this," Becky said. "I feel like we're too vulnerable."

"We can't leave the camp," Ian said. "The 'thopter would never find us in the dark. We've got to stay here."

"Maybe we should get into some trees," she suggested.

"Only if we could get everyone high enough," Ian said. "Somehow, I can't imagine our scientists being too good at shinnying up a ginkgo."

It was only a matter of time before another big predator was attracted by the scent of freshly killed meat. A young and feisty Tyrannosaurus lumbered into the camp clearing like the king that he was, calmly surveying his domain. Thankfully, it was a very young rex —only about half its eventual adult size—because a really big one could take a lot of slugs before you could bring him down.

Even though the rex was closest to Ian and wasn't acting like he was taking much notice of them, Murphy let go with a wild burst from his automatic rifle. He must have had it cranked up to the maximum, because four hundred rounds screamed from the barrel in two and a half seconds, missing the beast entirely but managing to neatly saw down a nearby redwood sapling about two meters from the earth.

Even a beast with so dim a brain as the rex could not help but take notice of such a disturbance, and slowly its awareness and attention were shifted away from the pack of scavengers. It turned its ugly head like a gun turret and tilted down a cold, moonish eye at Murphy.

Ian could hear his gunner fumbling for a new clip from his belt pack, and he wondered if Murphy wasn't already too panicked to be any more good.

"Ian, he's coming this way," Becky said.

Looking up, Ian watched the rex flare his nostrils and get a good scent on them. It moved forward several steps, leaping from foot to foot with great ease and strength. The creature was apparently confused by the mixture of fresh raw meat and the strange, enticing smell of human flesh, because it suddenly stopped and raised its snout to get a second sniff.

"Get 'im, Captain," Murphy said. "My clip's jammed."

"Take it easy, man." ian was trying to remain cool. The heavy, humid air was filled with the night cries of feeding and small skirmishes. The rex listened for another moment as it seemed to be watching Murphy, then it leapt forward with astonishing quickness.

Ian had set his weapon on its slowest delivery so he could better lay in a volley of shots without having to stop to reclip. "Aim for the eyes!" he yelled to Becky as he himself drew a bead on the beast's neck. A well-placed stream of slugs would sever the spinal cord, and that would be the end of the game.

But just as he raised the gun sight to his eye, the earth heaved violently, almost dropping him to his knees. The entire forest seemed to be resonating like a struck tuning fork, and the Tyrannosaurus rocked back and forth as the earth vibrated beneath its splayed claws. It paused and looked dumbly about for the cause of the new disturbance.

"Ian, what's happening?" Becky ran to his side.

The people in the geodesic dome came running to the entrance to see what was going on, and Ian waved them back inside. He was still watching the rex, which was beginning to lumber forward again, despite the tremors that were rocking the entire ship.

"Ian!" cried Becky.

"I don't know for sure," he shouted. "It sounds like the bloody engines."

"That's impossible," Becky shouted.

"Watch out, Captain, here he comes!" Murphy ducked and ran behind the physical plant dome as the carnivore closed in.

Ian tried to take aim and unleashed a volley at the beast's neck. The slugs ripped into its belly and stitched a line up the side of its neck, staggering the creature, causing it to wobble and stumble backward. At the same instant, a tremendous burst of inertial motion ripped

Ian and the others off their feet. It caused the ginkgoes to sway violently, and snapped some of the taller redwoods.

Looking up, Ian was just able to see the Tyrannosaurus be ripped off its hindlegs and fall upon the naked, snapped-off trunk of one of the redwood trees. The trunk impaled the great beast like a pin through a butterfly, and although it struggled for an instant, bellowing out its final cries of agony, it was dead almost immediately.

But the howling, roaring sound now seemed louder, and the scavenging creatures had panicked, running off into the forest in all directions. As Murphy and Becky moved closer to him, Ian could feel the great cylinder resonating under a steadily increasing acceleration.

"What is it?" Murphy asked, trying to catch his breath.

Ian looked at him as he climbed to his feet. "I'd say it was the sound of rocket motors."

"Oh my God, Ian!" Becky said. "It can't be . . . *can* it?"

Ian nodded slowly. "I'm afraid we're being taken for a ride."

His ieg was bleeding slowly as he walked through the rubble. It was relatively quiet, and he had a moment to think about what had happened.

In terms of actual time passing, the violent tremors and quakelike vibrations of the Dragonstar's engines kicking in had not taken very long. Upon reflection, Colonel Phineas Kemp realized this. It only seemed to take an eternity for Becky and Corporal Potlack to race back up the temple steps; it only seemed as though it had taken forever for the masonry to fracture and the walls to come crashing down.

As he stood there, dazed, the reality of everything that had happened began to sink in. In the relative calm of the moment, he found himself thinking of Mikaela, and more than anything in the world he wanted to be able to talk to her and know that she was all right, to hold her in his arms and bury his face in her sweet-smelling hair, to let his hands race over her firm body. He wanted to pull her close to him and forget about everything else in his crazy life.

That was an unusual response for Phineas, he knew. But things were getting away from him, out of control, and although he was not accustomed to situations like this, he felt he could cope with it by withdrawing for a while. Just fall back, regroup, and then he could move forward again.

He told himself he would attempt to locate Mikaela as soon as he had his leg looked at. And thinking of Mikaela almost naturally made him think of Becky Thalberg.

Where was she? Where had she been before all this mess started? So much had happened so quickly that Phineas could not remember all the details without concentrating. Oh yes, that's right. She'd stayed on at the paleo survey camp—she didn't care to see old Neville and his show because he played a little grab-ass with her.

Well, good for her, and too bad about Neville, he thought with a sad smile. Becky was probably safer than any of us, out there in the wilderness. When he called out to the survey camp after Mikaela he would ask for Becky too. After all, there was no reason they couldn't remain friends. He was finally starting to realize now that he had been acting like an ass, and every time he recalled his confrontation with Ian Coopersmith he wanted to crawl into a hole and hide.

Shaking his head, Phineas pulled back from his reflective thoughts and moved a bit closer to the first-aid station. Things had certainly been crazy and dangerous.

But the great ship had now leveled out. The constant acceleration had ceased when the engines suddenly cut off. An odd, after-the-storm serenity pervaded the atmosphere, and it seemed deathly quiet after all that chaos. Phineas surveyed the latest body count and estimated that his party had lost perhaps another twenty people during the demolition of the temple, and about half of their salvaged equipment. The terrace in front of the fallen temple looked like a city plaza after a blitz. Masonry dust still powdered down in pockets as everyone sifted through the debris and helped the wounded to medical attention.

Phineas had been cut across the thigh by a flying shard of stone, and as he stood in line to receive some attention from a hastily thrown up medic station he saw Kate Ennis walking toward him with Takamura and several others. Everyone appeared haggard and distressed, but there was a certain dignity in their faces that suggested to Phineas one of humankind's more noble characteristics—their adaptability to almost any condition.

His people had been through hell lately, he thought, but they still had that look of determination in their eyes.

"Phineas, are you all right? You're bleeding," Kate said.

"I know. A little freeze-pak and some tape and I'll live, I think." Phineas looked over at Takamura. "Glad to see that you made it, doctor."

"Thank you, Colonel." The physicist looked extremely concerned and quite dour. He cleared his throat nervously. "Colonel, I've got to talk with you right away."

Phineas moved up in the line toward the medic staff and nodded curtly. Even though he had been angered by Dr. Takamura's sarcasm, Phineas had to admit a grudging respect for the man. He was certainly a hard worker, and his own staff seemed to have nothing but respect for him. And of course, Phineas could remember Bob Jakes praising Takamura to the skies when they were engaged in the selection committee hearings for the Dragonstar project. It was just that there was something about Takamura . . .

"Excuse me, Colonel, I was talking to you," Takamura said once again. "Are you okay?"

Phineas smiled. "Sorry, Doctor. I was woolgathering, I suppose. Please, you were saying something?"

"Colonel, I'm sure you realize that this ship has accelerated under its own power, that it has vacated its

Lagrange orbital position.''

Phineas nodded. "Yes, Doctor, I've had my suspicions along those lines, although I have been consciously trying not to think about it. I'm sure you can understand what I'm saying. Have you confirmed this?"

"Yes, we have. Unfortunately," Takamura said.

"Do you have any more concrete information?" Phineas asked, although he wasn't sure he wanted to hear any more bad news at the moment.

"Yes. We were able to get some of our instruments running, and I've got some information I think you should know about."

"All right, go on."

"Those engines are generating more thrust than our instruments can measure, Colonel. They have accelerated the ship to seventy-five kilometers per second at a little more than one-half gee. We suspect that after the initial shock wave some kind of internal acceleration compensation was put into effect." Phineas said with a sincere, apologetic smile

"Could you please tell me what that *means*?"

"Sorry." Takamura seemed both surprised and pleased by Kemp's show of humility. "It means that if we maintain our present rate of acceleration we will eventually reach escape velocity from the solar system."

Even in his dazed state of mind, Kemp was shocked by the pronouncement. "Is that possible?"

"It is if it's happening," Takamura said. "Colonel, this ship is *moving*."

Phineas stared at the chief project assistant dumbly for a moment as he considered what this news really meant. How could this be happening?

"Phineas, are you okay?" Kate asked, touching his arm softly.

"Yes," he said, almost in a whisper. "Just a little stunned, that's all." He looked back at Takamura and forced himself to smile. "Tell me, Doctor, do you have any idea yet where we're going in such a big hurry?"

Eighteen

Although she had probably spent more time in the wilds of the Mesozoic preserve than anyone else on board the Dragonstar, Mikaela now felt oddly out of place there. As she handled the controls of the lead OTV in her small caravan, she realized that the primordial forest was not the place of her dreams—the fantasy land where she could conduct research and prepare monographs for the International Academy of Biological Sciences.

No, she thought as she looked out into the darkness of the forest, illuminated only by the powerful swath of her vehicle's searchlights. No, this was no fantasy land. It was more like horror land, actually. Especially now that she knew the Dragonstar was pulling up stakes with its human prisoners and was heading for parts unknown.

Her caravan had been traveling down from a high plateau when the ship's engines had kicked in and it had been a terrible experience. She'd had no idea what could be happening, and she was especially panicked when she couldn't raise anyone on the radio, no matter what channel she tried. Even Copernicus Base was silent. She had ordered the OTVs stopped on the last rise of the plateau, selecting a vantage point that, when she played the OTV's powerful searchlights downward, gave her a view of a river valley below. To the east, the river she had named the Bishop emptied into a large lake (christened Lake Kariskrona after her hometown). When the ship accelerated, Kariskrona had overwashed its banks and flooded a great portion of the surrounding scrubland. Mikaela watched the giant tidal wave sweep over the land, flushing out creatures large and small. Many of the smaller beasts were able to scurry up into trees, or were carried along on the surface of the water, but many of the larger dinosaurs had drowned.

She had waited out the initial effects of the acceleration until the engines suddenly cut off, leaving the Mesozoic preserve once again in relative quiet. Again she tried to raise someone on the radio, and this time she received a reply—from Lieutenent Barkham, the 'thopter pilot stranded at the ruins. He reported that the ancient buildings had survived the quake, and that Zabriskie had just dropped off the first three people from Ian Coopersmith's group back at the paleo survey camp.

"Oh, that's good," Mikaela said. "Were they okay?"

"Affirmative. But Zabriskie was running a little low on fuel so she transferred what was left from the tanks of my ship. She took off about 10 minutes ago."

"Tell me, have you heard anything from Hakarrh? From Colonel Kemp?"

"Not much, Doctor. Only that the whole bunch of 'em are leaving the Saurian preserve to come out here. All of a sudden everybody thinks this is the best spot to be on the whole ship, and all I did was crash-land my ship here." Barkham laughed weakly.

"I tried to reach them by radio, but there was no reply," Mikaela said.

"Well, I'd imagine they had some problems with the quakes. I expect they'll be getting in touch as soon as they can."

"I certainly hope so."

"Would you like me to give you a call from them?" Barkham asked.

"That would be fine, Lieutenent. As a matter of fact, please tell Colonel Kemp to call me on this frequency. I should be getting to the ruins within two hours."

Barkham agreed and signed off, leaving Mikaela to her thoughts as she signaled for the caravan to begin moving again. Slowly she led the three OTVs down from the grazing plateau into the flooded scrubland. The waters from Lake Kariskrona had receded, leaving the landscape mushy like a sponge but still solid enough to allow the OTVs to move with good speed.

They passed several drowned carcasses along the way, already attracting a crowd of carrion eaters to the spot. An entire herd of Ceratopsians had been trapped in an arroyo and drowned, and above them a stormcloud of insects was gathering, ready to descend upon the fresh meat. The sky was filling up with Pteranodons and other smaller species of Pterosaurs. These creatures were the vultures of their age, and their keening, scritching cries were like a dinner bell for all the nearby survivors.

Interestingly, Mikaela noted, with the sudden abundance of free meals in the aftermath of the flood, the predatory theropods such as Allosaurus, Tyrannosaurus rex, and their smaller cousins seemed to be totally oblivious to the line of strange-smelling OTVs. Many times they passed very close to a bipedal monster, searchlights splashing boldly over its body, reflecting coldly in its great walleyes, only to be ignored—either because it was dipping its bloody snout into the torn body cavity of a flood victim or because its nostrils were burning with the scent of recent death and it was fast on its way to a meal.

That was the most incredible part of observing the life cycles in the Mesozoic preserve: it was a never-ending ritual for the beasts, a ceremony of foraging and eating and sleeping and foraging and eating. The environment responded well to the demands placed upon it. The flora grew at a super-fast rate in the steamy, humid atmosphere. The herbivores consumed many times their weight in vegetation each day, and the carnivores ate the herbivores. It was a great relationship, a perfect understanding, even though there was very little communication, thought Mikaela with a wry smile.

As they moved away from the flood plain, Mikaela knew there would be fewer drowned, free meals lying around and that more caution would be necessary again.

She decided to try to raise the survey camp once again. Hopefully, they had survived.

"PSC," said a familiar voice. "We copy here. Come in."

"Hello, this is Dr. Lindstrom. Is everybody okay back there?"

"This is Becky, Mikaela. We had a few problems, but we're holding on." Becky briefed her on the attack, the quake, and its aftermath.

"I just spoke to Barkham, and he said that Zabriskie's on her way back for a second run," Mikaela said.

"We'll be watching for her. Thanks, Mikaela."

"Don't mention it. Please be careful."

Becky chuckled harshly. "I don't know if it really makes any difference anymore."

"Please don't talk like that," Mikaela said. "We can never give up."

"Yes, I know. But Ian thinks the Dragonstar is heading for another star system."

The words stung Mikaela. Up to that point, she had been telling herself that perhaps the IASA had started up the outboard engines, moving the ship to a more stable orbital window. But Becky had confirmed her unspoken, almost unformed fear of the worst. Oh God, if that was true, they would never see the Earth again.

"Oh God, I hope he's wrong," said Mikaela in a very soft voice.

"So does Ian, but I don't know—it's like I don't even care anymore," Becky said.

"You're just depressed," Mikaela said. "Hang on a little while longer and things will get better."

"They can't get much worse. All right, Mikaela, good luck. Hopefully we'll be seeing you soon. PSC out."

She signed off the transmission and again tried to raise the research lab without success. They must be having trouble with their receivers. Mikaela laughed aloud. Hell, they must be having trouble with a lot of things by now.

She had been controlling the lead vehicle absently as she used the radio, and she didn't immediately react to the thing that had lumbered into the path of her searchlights.

"Hey, Dr. Lindstrom," said the young voice of her gunner up in the bubble. "Watch out for this guy."

Suddenly Mikaela was back in real time and looking a Triceratops in the eye. The beast had emerged from the scrubland and rocks to the right, and when it spotted the approaching OTV it stopped, raising its crowned, horned head into the air, trying to get a scent on this strange-looking beast. The Ceratopsians were herbivorous, but since they were so well armored, they were not docile plant eaters like most of their type. If their disposition could be described, it would be called arrogant, as though they were always looking for a reason to get upset.

The Triceratops stood its ground, tilting its head so that one baleful eye might study this odd bubble-backed intruder. Mikaela eased down on the accelerator, stopping less than twenty meters from the creature.

"Shall I take it out?" her gunner asked.

Everyone else in the vehicle tried to squeeze around each other for a look at what was going on.

"No," Mikaela said. "It might be somebody's mother . . . or father, I can't tell from here."

"Well, what are we going to do, Doctor?" The trooper asked nervously.

"I'm going to try to go around it." She radioed her intentions to the other two vehicles and started moving again.

She steered to the left and cut a wide swath into the underbrush, grinding through the thick tangle of vines and tubers. The Ceratopsian continued to stare at the little beetle-shaped vehicle, waiting until Mikaela had almost totally passed by before making its move.

It advanced quickly on the lead vehicle. Mikaela expected it to lower its head and attack the side armor with its horn, but, surprisingly, the beast had other ideas. It gathered up a running start, then reared up on its hind legs in an attempt to sexually mount the OTV. As soon as the gunner saw what it was trying to do, he burst out laughing.

"Well, I guess it's somebody's father for sure," he said, and that kicked off everybody else in a wave of nervous laughter.

Even Mikaela could not keep from smiling as the Triceratops thrust itself repeatedly at the rear of the OTV. There was no logical reason why the beast would want to copulate with her machine, and no reason why it would normally mistake it for a female—darkness or no darkness.

The only cause she could imagine would be the same radiation that caused physical mutations in the dinosaurs and mental aberration in the Saurians. Perhaps it was the cause of the sexual confusion she now observed. The Triceratops continued to thrust at them with a steady thumping rhythm.

"Hold still, Doctor," someone cried out from the cabin. "He can't get a good grip on us."

More laughter.

"Isn't anybody going to squeal to make him feel good?" And that took them to the edge of pleasant hysteria.

Mikaela continued to churn through the underbrush at a slow speed, and the beast continued to chase and leap and thrust. He finally got the message that the OTV was not offering what might be called good sex, and at last gave up. This brought a round of applause from the passengers, obviously pleased to have something to break the tension and the monotony of their journey.

Checking the caravan's position on her monitor, Mikaela exhaled slowly. For some reason, she had not been able to let out all her tension and apprehension during the "sex" scene. And she knew why: just the thought of the entire ship hurtling off into deep space, actually leaving the solar system, made her feel physically ill. If she continued to dwell on it, the abject terror and feeling of desperation were going to drive her mad.

The monitor's readout informed her that she was less than fifty kilometers from the ruins. The crazy midnight journey was almost at an end. But then what? What would happen to them after that?

She didn't want to think about it.

"I don't believe any of this," cried Oscar Rheinhardt, security chief for Copernicus Base. He was a thin, ascetic-looking man with a pencil-thin mustache. He chain-smoked his cigarettes and had a cough like a howitzer.

"Well, I'm sure we all wish it were a bad dream, but unfortunately it is not," said Christopher Alvarez, who chaired the meeting of the Joint Chiefs. "This whole thing has been very bad for our public image."

Gregor Kolenkhov laughed. "Public image? Come, Chris, why don't you say it—we look like a bunch of fuck-ups. I'll bet the Third World Confederation is having a good laugh at this one, oh boy!"

"Is there anything else we can do?" asked Marcia Bertholde, a middle-aged woman of sophisticated manner. She had winced at Kolenkhov's words, but that was nothing unusual. She usually winced at whatever Kolenkhov said.

"I doubt it," Rheinhardt said, speaking beneath a billowy cloud of blue smoke. "The stasis field kept all ships and equipment at bay, and when its engine fired up, it jumped out of here like a rabbit with its ass on fire."

"How quaint an expression." Bertholde did not look amused.

"But very appropriate," Kolenkhov said. "The Dragonstar is now traveling at a velocity of between sixty and seventy kilometers per second, forty-eight degrees off the ecliptic. We don't have anything that could catch her, and even if we did, there's nothing we could do about it.''

"And you think it's leaving the solar system?'' Bertholde's voice sounded as though it might break.

"No question about it. We have Professor Labate tracking it with all available gear down at the observatory, but wherever it's going is purely academic now.''

"And it looks as though radio contact will continue to be jammed,'' Rheinhardt said. "Christ, we can't even tell them that we tried everything we could to help.''

"All those people on board,'' Bertholde said. "And Colonel Kemp is among them. I wonder if they realize what's happening to them.''

"I doubt if they could miss it,'' Alvarez said. "The gee forces when those engines first kicked in must have been impressive.'' The chairman shook his head sadly and cleared his throat. "Well, I know we could sit here and feel sorry for ourselves all day, but let's remember that the whole world is watching us now, and that we have an obligation to tell them what has happened. We have to prepare a statement for the media, so let's get going.''

No one spoke for a moment. The people around the table tried not to look into one another's eyes, not to see the hopelessness there.

"Doesn't anyone have any suggestions?'' Alvarez asked.

"Yes, I have one.'' Kolenkhov smiled sadly. "As far as the Dragonstar is concerned, I think we should tell the world to kiss it goodbye.''

"You'd better tell Colonel Kemp to come here,'' Mishima Takamura said to one of his assistants.

He had managed to coax some of his instruments, including the shortwave transponder equipment, back on-line. Somebody had strung some emergency lights around the ruins of the temple, and the scene had more the look of a late-night archeological dig than the refugee camp it was. The array of salvaged laboratory equipment seemed oddly out of place.

Seismic sensors were picking up a new series of vibrations in the hull. In fact, Mishima's ears were already beginning to detect a low-frequency thrumming. There were several monitors propped up in the debris—two of them giving number-crunching readout displays, the other with a dead-lens camera view of the stars and the distant Earth and Sun beyond the curve of the hull.

"Yes, Doctor?" Kemp's voice cut into his thoughts, and he turned to see the short, handsome man standing there at the threshold of some cleared rubble as though waiting to enter an office. The colonel's dress uniform was tattered and covered with dust. He sported an amateurish bandage about his left thigh and looked as though he should be posing for an American Revolutionary War painting.

"Something's happening again," Mishima said. "I don't like this one bit."

"Could things get any worse?" Kemp asked. "What do you mean?"

Mishima explained to him the resonances he was picking up and pointed to the indications that it was getting stronger.

"Any idea what it means?" Kemp asked.

"Not really."

Kemp slowly shook his head. "You know, I've been thinking—maybe we should try to break back into the crew section. Wouldn't it be possible to overcome the alien controls? Maybe we could turn this ship around and get ourselves back to Earth."

Mishima Takamura laughed lightly. "No offense, Colonel, but that doesn't sound very likely to me."

"Why not?"

"Well, for one thing, I doubt if we could break in there, unless the ship wanted us to, and second, we're not magicians, we're scientists."

Kemp seemed a bit irked by his reply. "Meaning?"

Mishima shrugged. "Simply that none of us could figure out very much of the alien technology before, so what makes you think we could now?"

"I always thought necessity was the mother of invention," the Colonel said. "I'm sorry, Doctor, I'm just not the type to give up so easily."

"That's a very admirable trait," Mishima said. "But I'm afraid I'm simply fresh out of ideas. Why don't we—"

Mishima did not finish the sentence. The low-frequency humming grew unbearably loud in an instant, and there was a monstrous sound that filled the enclosed atmosphere like a thunderclap. It sounded like a gigantic dynamo kicking in. The hull and everything in the interior seemed to convulse very slightly. One quick pulsing sensation, and that was all.

Looking quickly to the video monitor, Mishima saw the Earth, Sun, and stars smear across the screen in long lines of white light, followed by a spectacular redshift—beautiful streamers, like fireworks, that trailed across the screen.

And then everything was gone.

Kemp, Mishima, and a few others stared at the monitor, which now reflected a blackness so deep and complete that its only rival might be the feelings of desperation in all their hearts.

"Oh, no," Mishima said.

"Was that what I think it was?" Colonel Kemp asked.

"If you thought it was a redshift, then the answer is yes," Mishima said.

"Good Christ! You mean we've reached the speed of light? So quickly?"

Mishima pointed to the screen and shook his head slowly. "No, I don't think that's quite it."

"What do you mean?" Kemp sat down on a slab of fallen stone. There was a flatness in his voice that indicated he didn't really care anymore, that he was simply asking his questions automatically.

"Look, do you see anything on the screen?"

"No," Kemp said.

"Well, theoretically we should be seeing something called a star bow, but it's not there. Nothing's there."

"So what you're saying is that we're going faster than light? Hyperspace, and all that business?"

"And all that business. Yes," said Takamura.

Kemp rubbed his mouth nervously. "My God, you mean it's really possible? I just can't believe it."

Takamura shrugged as he stood up and started pacing about the area, running his hands through his dark hair, refusing to look again at the monitor. "Who knows? I may be way off base, but I have a feeling we're traveling FTL."

Kemp laughed nervously. "Some physicist you are! Working on feelings."

Mishima spread his hands in defeat. "What else is left to us?"

"Is there any way to know where we're headed, or how long it'll take to get there?" Kemp stood up and looked at Mishima.

Mishima shook his head and took a seat with an exaggerated display of weariness. "Not with the little bit of gear we have here. No, I'm afraid I can't tell you anything."

This seemed to irritate Kemp, and he too began pacing. "Damn it, there's got to be something we can do. I feel so helpless."

"That's because we are," Mishima said.

"No, there are things we have to do." Kemp looked at the black screen and shook his head. "God, I still can't believe this."

Mishima looked at him. "Do you have any ideas?"

Kemp stopped pacing and looked out into the air for an instant, gathering his thoughts, focusing in on the answer to Mishima's question.

"Yes, I've got a few. First, I think we should attempt to make contact with the Saurians again. They haven't tried to attack us since the riot, and besides, they're our only allies in this thing—we're all in it together."

Mishima nodded calmly. "Yes, I guess we are. Go on."

Kemp brightened, and his voice gained strength and conviction as he continued. "Secondly, we have to consolidate our forces, gather up all the fragments that are scattered around the ship.''

"The others are converging on the ruins. Should we go there, or should they all come here?''

"I don't know yet. Wouldn't that depend on how we get along with the Saurians?'' Kemp was staring down the wrecked, fissure-laden steps to the boulevard below the temple. The Saurian city lay shrouded in the darkness of evening. What thoughts were going on within the reptilian minds of Hakarrh?

"Yes, I guess it would," Mishima said.

"I'm going to ask Kate Ennis if she still wants to contact the Saurians," Kemp said.

"You're going to need somebody new to go with her. We lost Corporal Potlack, remember?"

Kemp nodded. "I know. I've already decided to go with her myself."

Mishima was surprised. "Do you think that's a good idea?"

The colonel smiled grimly. "No, but I think it's what has to be done, so I'm going to do it. We certainly can't just sit here and do nothing, can we?"

"No, I suppose not," Mishima said. Kemp had the right idea. The worst thing they could do was fall into a self-indulgent trap, feeling sorry for themselves.

"All right, then, Doctor. I'm going to round up Kate Ennis and be off. See if you can contact Captain Coopersmith, Bob Jakes, and Dr. Lindstrom. Tell them what we're about, and that it's imperative that we all join together on this thing."

Mishima nodded. "You're right. It occurs to me that none of the other parties may even be aware of what's happened. They have no way of knowing we've made the jump into hyperspace."

"Well, I don't think everyone should know about it yet," Kemp said, turning to leave. "I'll talk to you later, Doctor. I want to get started with the Saurians at dawn."

"All right, Colonel. But you're going to need a change of clothes before you get going. Let me see if I can scrounge up some coveralls."

"Oh, yes, I suppose that would be a good idea. Thank you."

Mishima signaled for one of his assistants, sending him off to find something more functional for Kemp to wear. He also directed Dr. Horton, who had become his communications specialist under duress, to try contacting the various outposts of humanity still scattered about the Dragonstar.

As Kemp went off toward one of the supply trunks his people had managed to drag out of the lab, Mishima Takamura allowed himself to reassess his feelings about the man. Sure, he was an egocentric bastard, and sure, he had a hell of a time seeing anyone else's point of view, and yes, he damn well had a bad habit of talking to everybody as though they were his subordinate officers, but underneath all that, Mishima was learning to see his good qualities too. Perhaps it wasn't going to be necessary to continue the hostilities, though Mishima wasn't wild about the idea of taking orders from Kemp all the time.

When he saw the colonel reemerge, wearing the standard IASA coveralls and an LS helmet, he hardly recognized him. He looked formidable enough, except for the pant legs being rolled up because they were too long. Mishima wanted to smile, because from a distance, Kemp reminded him of a young boy dressing up in his father's clothes.

He hoped the Saurians would not find him so humorous.

Zabriskie leaned out of the cab of the ornithopter, staring at him with a glazed expression. She was obviously fatigued, but Ian needed her to finish this operation. They had managed to squeeze three of the survey camp staff into the 'thopter's belly compartment, plus the fourth man in the shotgun seat. It would be a bit of a lift problem, but not enough to worry about. There were always some margins for error, Ian told himself.

"Good luck, Zabriskie," he shouted. "Hurry back,

and don't forget about the homing beacon.''

The pilot nodded and gave him the old thumbs-up signal. Then she pulled back on the controls, and the birdlike craft leaped skyward with all the grace of gooney-bird. Ian watched it rise up into the darkness, its searchlights boring through the night.

Turning to Becky and Murphy, he smiled weakly. "And then there were three."

"How much longer are we going to be out here, Captain?" Murphy asked. He didn't look pleased that he had missed the flight out. In fact, Ian thought he looked quite ill.

"About another hour or so and we'll be on the 'thopter ourselves," he told the trooper. "Don't worry about a thing."

"I'm not worried," Murphy said. "And it's not that I'm questioning your judgment, Captain. But I'm just wondering if we should be hanging around the camp with all this fresh meat around. Pretty soon everything's going to be coming back, I figure."

"That's why we set up the homing beacon," Becky said, pointing to the small electronic pack on her belt. "If we have to get out of here, the beacon will give the 'thopter our position."

"I hope so," Murphy said. "I've sure had enough of this duty." He flipped on the infrared scope of his weapon and walked back to his post. In the darkness, you could hear the rustling of fronds and the scampering tread of clawed feet as the scavengers slowly returned to their interrupted feast.

Nineteen

Arriving at the ruins was a cause for celebration, and
Mikaela was as ready to party as any of her passengers.
Everyone scrambled out of the OTV hatches as soon as
the caravan lurched to a stop within the walls of the
ruins. Mikaela was impressed by the tangle of vines and
undergrowth visible in the combined swaths of their
searchlights. The ruins were overrun with wild foliage,
and the night was thick with the sounds of predators
and their prey. It was a dark symphony of screams and
bellows, paeans to the triumph of the kill, the agony of
capture.

High atop the decaying stone pyramid, Mikaela could
see the torchlights of Lieutenant Barkham's group.
They were all waving and urging her group upward. In
the darkness, it was not an easy climb, but they made it
willingly, glad to be free of the stifling confines of the
Omni Terrain Vehicles. Mikaela thought it felt good
just to be stretching out her muscles.

It would still be several hours before the Illuminator
began to glow again, before the preserve was once more
filled with artificial day. How she longed for it to be
light! She had pushed herself through the longest night
of her life, and now it was almost over. Just take this

pyramid one crumbling stone step at a time and you'll make it, she told herself. The feeling of exhilaration at being free of the OTV passed quickly, and fatigue lurked on the threshold of her mind. A little bit farther and she could rest. She could hear the voices of the 'thopter party up above, cheering encouragement.

Finally she reached the last riser, the final step, and there were hands reaching out to her, pulling her up. A large, burly character with a thick beard stood in the center of the waiting group. He wore a flight suit with the name Barkham on it, but his features were hidden in the shadows. He smiled.

"Hi, I'm Daniel Barkham. I guess I've kind of been in charge here. I've heard a lot about you, Dr. Lindstrom. Nice to meet you."

Mikaela shook his hand and smiled. They exchanged pleasantries and began to help the stragglers up the face of the pyramid. When they had all gained the top, Mikaela's group was invited into the center of the platform that formed the top of the ancient building. Equipment and gear had been arranged in a large circle. Lanterns and flashlights cast a warm glow on everyone's faces. It reminded her of a camping trip or a group vacation, especially when she noticed how cheery everyone seemed to be.

Lieutenant Barkham approached Mikaela and invited her to take a seat next to a white-haired, heavyset man who looked familiar. "I think you two know each other," said the pilot.

"Dr. Lindstrom, I presume," said Bob Jakes with a smile. "Glad to see you could make our little party."

Mikaela had hardly recognized him in the dim light, with the beginnings of a beard disguising his face. "Are you all right, Dr. Jakes?" she asked, seeing his wrapped ankle.

"What, this? It's nothing. I can walk if I need to. Did you have any trouble getting here?"

She smiled. "Compared to the climb up, the jungle was a piece of cake."

"I know, but at least there won't be any hungry crit-

ters wandering up here in the middle of the night."
Jakes laughed easily.

For a moment neither of them spoke, and the silence was awkward between them. Jakes's expression
changed to something more serious. "Did Barkham tell
you that we just heard from the colonel?"

Her heart jumped at his words. "No, is he all right?"

"Yes, he's fine. They're holding on to a fort outside
the control section of the ship, but they haven't seen any
sign of the Saurians in a long time. Phineas is planning
to go down and try to make peace with them."

"Do you think that's a good idea?"

Jakes shrugged. "Who knows? If they're suffering
from some kind of radiation sickness or madness, I
don't think talking is going to do much good."

"Our tests indicated that not every species was being
affected the same way. Perhaps it was true with the
Saurians." Mikaela had a brief image of Phineas approaching the Saurians in a truce meeting when suddenly they all pounced upon him like wolves.

"Well," Jakes said, "I hope you're right. At any
rate, Phineas thinks that it's a hell of a lot safer to be
garrisoned behind the Saurian Barrier than to be
marooned out here in the preserve."

"He's certainly right about that," Mikaela said.
"Then it's a good idea to try to make contact with
them—it's something that must be done."

Jakes coughed, and nodded emphatically. "That's
what we all figured. They're going to head down as soon
as it starts to get light. Pretty soon now."

"What about Coopersmith?"

Jakes informed her that he would be coming in on the
next 'thopter run, and that they had only lost one man
during the night.

Someone handed her a cup of hot R-ration soup, and
she lifted the steaming container to her lips. It was the
first food she'd had since yesterday, and her stomach
growled as the aroma of freeze-dried chicken noodle
soup reached her nose. It tasted wonderful.

Looking at her watch, Mikaela estimated perhaps one

more hour until daylight. She was so thankful to be
safe, and so glad to know that Phineas had survived,
that she didn't care about all the bad things that were
still happening. She knew that if they all hung together,
they would make it. No matter what the problems might
be, she knew they could overcome them. She tried not to
think about the Dragonstar's engines firing, sending
them off to god knows where—that was a problem for
the physicists and the IASA engineers. They would
come up with something to bail them out.

"Do you see anything?" Kemp asked as he approached
a sentry on the barricades. The trooper was looking
through a high-powered scope down the steps of the
temple and panning across the boulevard.

"Not a thing, Colonel," said the sentry. "I started
sweeping the area ever since daylight started, and I can't
see a single one of them. I don't know what happened to
them. They must all be hiding from us."

Phineas shook his head. "I don't know, soldier. That
doesn't make any sense to me."

"Are you still going down there, sir?"

Phineas nodded. "That's right, we've got to try to
make contact with those guys."

"I heard everybody talking about it, sir, and I'd like
to volunteer to go with you . . . if you think you might
need the company, sir."

Phineas looked at the young man's name stenciled on
his breast pocket. CAVOLI, it said in block letters. "All
right, Cavoli," Phineas said. "I would appreciate that.
Meet me at the top of the steps in ten minutes."

"Yes, sir," Cavoli said. "Thank you, sir."

Saluting him crisply, Phineas smiled and shook the
man's hand, then headed back to get Kate Ennis and
their gear.

Kate was standing with Dr. Takamura, listening to
his instructions on how to use the portable radio. She
turned as Phineas approached and blinked her huge,
almond-shaped eyes at him. Kate could be an incredible
charmer when she wanted to be, and he could see that
Takamura was obviously falling for her.

Not that he could blame the dashing young scientist. Kate Ennis had eyes that lived a life of their own—they had a way of looking at you and making you feel special. Plus the woman had brains and courage and conviction. There wasn't much left out of the package, and Phineas had to admit that he had been having his own feelings of attraction for her. If he didn't already have a very satisfying relationship with Mikaela, he would definitely be in the running for Kate.

"Are we ready, Phineas?" she asked as she saw him approach.

Looking up at the Illuminator, Phineas nodded. "Yes. It's getting light enough to see what we're about now. I've got another volunteer, so let's get on with it."

"Good luck, Colonel," Takamura said, shaking his hand.

"Thank you, Doctor. I think we're going to need it this time."

Phineas guided Kate back to the edge of the barricade by the great set of temple steps. Cavoli was waiting for them, wearing a full complement of battle gear. His LS helmet visor was flipped down, and he certainly did cut a menacing figure.

"Any sign of them?" Kemp asked as they started down the steps.

"Not a trace," Cavoli said. "What do you think happened to them?"

"I haven't the foggiest, but that's what we're going to find out, I hope."

They descended the steps in relative silence. It was a somewhat treacherous journey because of the cracks and faults in the stone steps. Several wide fissures yawned up at them, but were easily avoided. When they reached the bottom of the steps and faced up the wide boulevard toward the mercantile center and the public parks, Phineas could not miss the utter quiet of the place.

The area seemed totally deserted. To the left of the boulevard lay the promontory where the priest-class Saurians resided.

Pointing up to the rock face and the switchback steps

cut into them, Phineas said, "All right, I suppose we should check those out first. If any of them are at all disposed to talk, it would be their philosopher-kings and not their roustabouts."

Kate smiled, and Cavoli just nodded silently. They all walked quickly toward the staircase that led upward to the living quarters of the priests. It was a grueling climb, and Phineas wished that he had kept to his exercise program a bit more stringently as they continued the ascent. Kate and Cavoli didn't seem to be having much trouble, however, so Phineas decided that he had better just tough it out instead of calling for a rest break.

"My God," Kate said. "This is higher than it looks."

They had reached the first of many landings that led off to several residences. Looking south and east, you could see the sprawl of the Saurian city in all its oddness—the open parks, the wide streets, the colored tents and spindly towers. And beyond it all, still shrouded in a steamy morning mist, the Barrier itself. It looked formidable even from the distance of more than twenty kilometers.

Cavoli and Phineas moved ahead, looking through the entrances of several residences and finding them deserted. This was not unusual, since the lower dwellings were of lower-echelon priests, and they would certainly be out on rounds at this early hour. Phineas wondered if higher rank had higher privilege in terms of when you woke up in the morning. He certainly hoped so.

They continued to ascend toward the top and had reached the second to the last level when Cavoli paused to look down over the landscape with his flip-down telegoggles.

"Oh my God!"

"What is it?" Kate asked. "What's the matter?"

"I just found out where everybody is," the trooper said. He unhooked the telescopic goggles from his visor and handed them to Phineas. "Take a look, Colonel—down there to the far left. Follow the Barrier off past the second park."

Listening to the whir of the goggles' auto-focusing, Phineas slowly panned along the Barrier. Beyond the tree-filled park he could see a huge mob of Saurians milling about in the streets and along the elevated ramps that led up to the Barrier. There were entire battalions of warrior-class Saurians surging about on top of the Barrier, and the guard towers, which were spaced evenly along the great wall, were bristling with Saurian archers.

The cause of all this activity could be seen a bit farther down the line. Good God! thought Phineas.

Maybe it was the initial series of tremors when the Dragonstar's engines kicked in. Or perhaps the series of vibrations and resonance factors that had pulsed through the hull had caused the problem. There was no way of knowing. But as Kemp peered through the tele-goggles he knew that he was watching what must be the most primal, most terrible nightmare of all Saurians, no matter what their class—a break in the Barrier.

No wonder they had abandoned their siege on the temple steps, thought Phineas. Somebody had sounded the alarm, and now they were all scurrying about the Barrier like rats.

As he watched the activity more closely, he could see that there were several teams of workers trying desperately to repair the damage—a great rending fault that had shifted the very foundation of the Barrier, twisting it so that it actually fell in upon itself.

To compound this problem, Phineas could see that the warriors were having their hands and claws full—several large carnivores had already noticed the break in the Barrier. A very large Therodont of some kind was out there, attracting plenty of attention. It pranced and roared, occasionally running toward the opening to the wall as though taunting the Saurians, who fired squaves and arrows at it with little or no effect. It seemed to Phineas that the big meateater was not terribly serious about trying to get through the gap in the wall. He looked as though he could, but he seemed to be merely playing for the moment.

A far more serious problem for the Saurians was a

pack of Saurian-sized carnivores that looked like a lean-legged, astonishingly quick version of Tyrannosaurus. There must have been seven or eight of them scampering about the rift in the Barrier, and even while Phineas watched, one of these rapacious little killers slipped through and began ripping and tearing at workers on a section of scaffolding. The warriors brought it down with a volley of arrows and spears, but not until the beast looked like a porcupine. If a whole pack of them ever got through, there would be wholesale slaughter.

He turned and handed the goggles to Kate. "Take a look at what our friends have been doing," he said sadly.

"Oh no," she said as soon as she focused in on the battle scene.

"I know. The poor sons of bitches are fighting for their lives down there."

"I feel sorry for them," Kate said.

"What?" Cavoli laughed with a hint of a sneer.

"No, really, I do," she said with conviction. "I mean, think about it. The Saurians have had nothing but trouble since we've come to this place."

"You know," Cavoli said, "I never thought about it, but you're right."

"However, Phineas said, "this may be just the kind of opportunity we need."

"You mean to escape while they're all occupied?" Cavoli took back the tele-goggles and trained them on the distant Barrier.

"No, of course not. This is our chance to help them, to show them that we shouldn't be fighting with each other and that we understand it wasn't their fault about the riot."

"It wasn't?" Cavoli asked.

"No," Kate said. "They've been affected by some kind of radiation leakage—we think it's been inducing some very grave psychological damage to them."

"I didn't know about that." The trooper shook his head slowly. "Poor bastards."

"Let's go back and get some reinforcements," Phineas said.

Kate smiled. "Just like the old cowboy movies—here comes the cavalry at the last minute."

Phineas grinned. "Yes, I suppose it would be something like that."

"You want to head back now?" Cavoli asked.

Phineas nodded and gestured to begin the descent from the platform by the steps.

But as they turned to go down, a sharp series of sibilant sounds reached them. The translator around Kate's neck announced a short message: "Wait! Please do not go away."

The sounds had emanated from the landing above, and all three humans looked up to see an older Saurian leaning over the railing, peering down at them with large greenish eyes. He wore the traditional lemon-yellow robe of his class, cinched at the middle by a woven belt.

"Please do not go away. I must talk to you!"

"Thesaurus! Is that you?" Phineas asked.

"Indeed. Who is it that knows my human name?"

The Saurian philosopher-king stepped off the landing and began slowly walking down the steps toward them. Cavoli trained his weapon on the creature, but Phineas ordered him to lower the automatic.

"Colonel Kemp. Phineas Kemp. I am a friend of Ian Coopersmith."

The Saurian emitted a rasping sound that served his race as a signal of pleasure. "Ah yes, Ian Coopersmith. Is he well?"

"As far as I know," Phineas said. "He will be joining us shortly."

The Saurian approached the three of them and extended both arms in a gesture of openness. "I wish to apologize for the behavior of my people. My class is so embarrassed."

"It's all right, Thesaurus." Kate Ennis introduced herself and then went on. "We understand the problem your people have been undergoing. We know that it's not the fault of the warrior class."

"No," said Thesaurus. "In fact, I spoke with Mishima Takamura about the fears I had. About the possibility that there might be trouble. And yet there was the large gathering, the killing. It is a very sad occasion for my people. I am humiliated for all of us."

Phineas could almost see the pain in the Saurian's eyes, and as much as it bothered him to touch the flesh of the creature, he reached out and took Thesaurus's hand. "Please," Phineas said, "do not worry. We want our two races to remain friends. I hope that you realize and that your people understand that we only fired upon them in self-defense."

Thesaurus hissed and barked. The translator untangled his speech: "Those of my class certainly understand. However, the agrarians are having difficulty doing so, and of course the warriors only wish to fight you now."

"Can you make them understand?" Kate asked.

"It is possible, but the warriors do not have much patience for speech, for learning. They much prefer action over words."

"Yes," Kate said. "I know a few men like that."

"What was that you said?"

Smiling gently, Kate touched Thesaurus on the forearm. "Oh, nothing. I was just making a small joke."

"I fear that I do not comprehend the humor of humans yet."

Kate chuckled. "That's okay. There are many humans who don't understand my sense of humor either."

The Saurian nodded his head, and Phineas wondered if it was a natural gesture or if he had learned it from being around the humans so much.

"Tell me, Phineas Kemp, why did you come here? And where do you now plan to go?"

"We came looking for you and your class," Phineas said. "We wanted to make peace so that we can solve our problems together."

"It seems to me a necessity that our peoples work together," Thesaurus said. "I am very happy to see you making the effort."

"We have discovered the problem you are having at the Barrier," Kate said. "Is it very serious?"

"Yes, Kate Ennis, it is very serious. The whole city is employed in defense of the rift in the wall. I also would go, but I am like many of my class: too old, and not enough strength."

"We were wondering why we could see none of your people from our place in front of the temple," Phineas said.

"The ground tremors caused the fracture," Thesaurus said. "My people believed that you humans caused the tremors to punish them for their behavior. Did you cause this to happen?"

"Oh no," Kate said. "The tremors were caused by the engines of the ship starting up."

"What is this you say?" Thesaurus sounded thoroughly confused.

Phineas attempted to explain what she had meant. Luckily, Thesaurus was one of the few members of his race who understood completely the physical setup of the Saurians' encapsulated world. Phineas recalled how, many months back, Thesaurus and several other high-priests had been taken out through the airlock-hatch down by the paleo survey camp and given a tour of one of the shuttles and a short flight around the bulk of the Dragonstar itself. It had been a strangely beautiful moment to see the Saurian priests' collective expression when they first gazed upon the stars, upon the infinte magic of space. Phineas recalled that it had been difficult to explain astronomy and cosmology, even to the philosophers of the Saurian race, but in the end the priests did seem to grasp many of the basics. But perhaps the most difficult thing for them to believe concerned the Dragonstar itself—that it was actually a giant spaceship, a vehicle designed to travel among the stars.

Phineas decided it would be enough merely to tell Thesaurus that the ship was changing position in the sky, but not that it was actually moving toward another star system. In fact, he doubted whether that would make much difference to Thesaurus. Just knowing that their entire world was picking itself up and going somewhere was enough of a shock. Especially when the priest learned that the humans had no control over it whatsoever.

Thesaurus nodded slowly. "Do you find this last

piece of news alarming?" he asked.

"Alarming?" Phineas said. "Well, yes, I would have to say we're not dancing in the streets about it."

"What?"

"Yes, Thesaurus, it is alarming," Kate said. "But we're trying to deal with the problems as best we can."

"Where is the ship moving? Away from your world? Away from the Earth?"

"Yes," Phineas said, trying to tell Kate with a meaningful look that he didn't want her to give the Saurian too much information. "The ship is moving away from the Earth, but we haven't learned where it is going yet."

Thesaurus nodded. "I see that this is a bad thing."

"Bad for now, yes. But it is only a temporary problem. Our scientists are working on it," Phineas said.

"Very well, Colonel Kemp," the Saurian said. "I must leave such matters to your people. In the meantime, we have a more immediate problem. Do you think your armies could help us to defend the Barrier while we repair it?"

"That is exactly what I had in mind," Phineas said. "I will contact them immediately."

The Saurian whistled and hissed appreciatively, and again reached out to grasp Phineas's hand. As he felt the cold, scaly flesh enclose his own, he felt a bit ill. Never knew he had such a bad case of xenophobia before. And there was no reason for it, really—Thesaurus was a very decent sort.

"We must go back to our people and get things organized," Phineas said. "There will be much to do."

"I understand," Thesaurus said. "Goodbye for now, Colonel Kemp."

"Won't you come with us?" Kate asked.

The Saurian paused before speaking, as though considering his reply. "Kate Ennis, I am old for my race. I have suffered from diseases and many battles in my time. I am not certain I could live through another— that is why the elders have allowed me to remain in my quarters, even in this time of great emergency."

"Thesaurus, if you are ill, our doctors can give you help," Phineas said. "You know that."

"That is very kind, Colonel. I would very much like to accompany you, but I fear I would slow down your progress. I do not move very well anymore."

Cavoli smiled and patted the Saurian gently on the shoulder. "Don't worry about that, sir. I can help you along."

"Again, you are most kind," Thesaurus said. He paused to consider. "Very well, I will go with you."

Kate smiled and reached out to hold the old creature's hand as everyone turned to begin the descent. Phineas led the way, followed by Kate and Cavoli on either side of Thesaurus.

"Do you know," asked the Saurian, pausing on the steps and looking very seriously into Kate's eyes, "if I might get the chance to see my first human friend, Ian Coopersmith?"

Twenty

"What's that?" Murphy cried. "Do you hear it, Captain?"

The trooper yelled across the treetops to a spindly redwood into which Ian Coopersmith had hoisted himself while it had still been dark. He had actually managed to doze off for an hour or so, before Murphy woke him up. There was the droning sound of an engine in the distance, punctuated by the telltale *whoomp-whoomp* of airfoils beating the moist air.

Opening his eyes with great difficulty, Ian looked across to the next tree, where Becky still slept, trussed up by the hammock he'd fashioned by the light of a flashlight.

"Captain, do you hear it?"

"Damnit, Murphy," he said harshly. "I bloody well hear it, and it sounds like the 'thopter, all right."

"Yes, sir," said the trooper. "Sorry, sir."

Ian waved him off and tried to collect himself. His exposed skin was welted with insect bites, and he was covered with a thick coating of sweat and dirt. He wanted a shower so bad he could scream, and he imagined that he smelled so awful that he must be projecting about a two-meter kill-radius. All around him the

Mesozoic forest was waking up, and the air was filled with the screeching of Pteranodons and the skittering noises of the little scavenger dinosaurs that ran through the undergrowth with the speed of jackrabbits.

The sound of the 'thopter was indeed growing close, and they would have to be getting down from their perches. Looking across at Becky, hoisted up in her own tree, he smiled. Even in the severe conditions of the last twenty-four hours, she still maintained her innate ability to look good to him. Sure, she was sweaty and smelly and dirty, but she didn't seem to wear it as badly as he did. Her long dark hair framed her face like a high-contrast photograph, and she looked sexy as hell dangling from the redwood limbs.

"Rise and shine!" he yelled out to her. "Time to go home, Miss Rebecca!"

Opening her eyes with a start, Becky seemed to suddenly remember where she had spent the night.

"Up and at 'em, lady," Ian shouted. "There's beasties about, and we've got a 'thopter to catch."

"Hey, Captain," Murphy shouted. "Is it okay to get down from here?"

Ian was getting annoyed with Murphy. The man acted like a child who needed to be told every single thing. Of course, there was a theory that any kind of military or quasi-military service attracted a certain personality type who enjoyed being told what to do and was thus relieved of the burden of doing his own thinking. Murphy was definitely that type of fellow.

"Yes," Ian said in an even voice. "We're all getting down now. I don't see any reason why you should remain hanging, Murphy, unless it might be by your neck."

"Aw, c'mon, Captain, I ain't that bad, am I?"

"You're getting there," Ian said. "Now, get down there and signal Zabriskie. She's going to be looking for us."

The sound of the ornithopter was growing very loud now, and Ian fully expected it to be overhead at any moment.

"You're very handsome when you get mad," Becky shouted over the din of the 'thopter. She had unhitched herself and was beginning to lower herself, mountaineer-style, to the earth. Ian smiled as he unsnapped his own harness and began to descend.

"I'm not mad," he said, walking up to her once they had both touched down. "I guess I'm just getting a little tangy."

Becky looked at him and giggled. "Getting a little 'tangy'?"

"Oh, you know, I'm feeling a little ripe around the edges, and that kind of bugs me. I'm sure I'm starting to smell like it too."

"Don't worry about that," Becky said. "We're all getting on toward the ripe side."

Ian smiled and tapped her lovingly on the arm. The two of them had been through plenty of scrapes together, and this one had the feeling of finally winding down.

Turning, Ian saw Murphy move out into the clearing at the edge of the paleo survey camp and commence a dance of some sort, which presumably would attract the attention of Zabriski better than the homing beacon that was bleating out its low-megahertz message.

The craft swooped down over the clearing and pulled up in a semi-stall, coming in for a landing. Its graceful, gull-like airfoils beat the air as it touched down. Murphy moved quickly to the equipment bay and took up a position guarding the craft's flank. Ian and Becky broke into a trot and approached the command cabin.

The hatch swung open and the haggard face of Sergeant Zabriskie greeted them. The woman's eyes seemed to have sunk deep into their sockets. Her cheeks were drawn and sallow. The pilot was a portrait of exhaustion.

"Before we go any further, Captain, let me go on record as saying I'm so tired I know I can't make another flight, okay?"

"You didn't have to tell me that," Ian said. "I'd say it's rather obvious at this point."

"She can't fly like this, Ian," Becky said. "What're we going to do?"

"She's going to get into the equipment bay with you and rest. I know how to fly one of these rigs."

Becky smiled and shook her head. "It figures. Is there anything you don't know how to do?"

Tell you how I really feel about you, thought Ian. He wanted to say it, but the words wouldn't come out. Instead he just smiled and said, "I guess not."

"Where do you want me, Captain?" Murphy asked.

"You can ride shotgun and keep an eye for anything funny. But help Zabriskie down first, and get her squared away in the bay."

"Yes, sir."

Zabriskie slipped out of the pilot's chair like a subject in a trance and allowed herself to be lifted up and slid into the equipment bay. Murphy climbed aboard, and Becky looked up at Ian before squeezing into the equipment bay.

"We'll be okay in here," she said. "Happy flying, Captain."

Ian shrugged. "Well, it's been a while since I've flown one of these things—and I've never flown one inside the ship."

"So?"

"So we might be in for a wild ride. But don't worry, I'll get us there in just a *few* pieces."

"I have a feeling you'll do better than that." Becky's smile was radiant and genuine, warming him like gentle sunlight.

"All right," he said. "In you go. We can talk more when we get back to the ruins."

Becky blew him a kiss and snuggled down in the equipment bay. Ian closed the hatch and climbed aboard, where Murphy was anxiously scanning the area.

"Okay, Murph, it's our turn. Let's go."

With Ian at the controls, the 'thopter jumped upward with an awkward leap, soon gaining purchase in the heavy atmosphere. He felt the machine fighting him as he coolly recalled all the little tricks to flying an ornithopter. Gaining altitude and confidence, he straightened out the aircraft and keyed in the coordinates that would bring him down at the site of the Saurian ruins.

The sprawl of the Mesozoic preserve slid beneath like an endless roll of thick, lush carpet. From his cruising height, it was impossible for Ian to see the prehistoric life that teemed within its foliage. The thought crossed his mind that if they were to crash-land down there, he didn't know if he could handle the pressure of simply surviving. He and Becky had done it once, but he didn't think he could do it again.

Just keep this bloody thing in the air, he thought solemnly, and you won't have to worry about that.

"It doesn't look too good over there, Colonel," Cavoli said as he flipped up his tele-gogs. "A big boy just came out of the jungle, and I don't think our buddies can stop him."

"Let me see." Phineas reached for the telescopic goggles. He and his party had paused to rest at the next lower landing because Thesaurus could not move very fast, and Cavoli had used the moment to check out the action along the Barrier.

One look told Phineas that the situation was worse than ever. While the warriors battled a fairly large carnivore at the very point of the fracture in the great wall, another predatory dinosaur, a much bigger one, had burst through the edge of the forest to see what all the commotion might be about. It was a very tall, tan-skinned Tyrannosaurus—larger than any beast Phineas had ever seen in the preserve. The Saurians already had their hands full and would never be able to stop this ravenous creature.

If even more of the beasts were drawn to the slaughter, the Barrier would be breached, and the Saurian city would be the new hunting ground for the carnivores. When he told Thesaurus what was happening, he thought the old Saurian might begin to cry, and Phineas wondered if Saurians were capable of such a thing.

"Give me that radio," Phineas said, reaching out to Cavoli for the equipment.

"What are you going to do?" Kate asked.

"I'm going to get some of our people in there to help," Phineas replied.

"But how will the Saurians know we're coming to help? Suppose they think we're attacking them? Kate asked.

"You're right. We've got to make sure that doesn't happen."

"I must take you to my people," Thesaurus said.

"He's right, Phineas," Kate said. "It's the only way. You can call for reinforcements, and then we'll go with Thesaurus to the Barrier. That way we'll get there before the troopers do."

"No, it's too dangerous," Phineas said. "Anything could happen down there."

Kate smiled. "Colonel Kemp, please. I'm a big girl, and I volunteered for this mission. I really don't want anybody telling me what might be too dangerous for me, all right?"

Phineas didn't even bother to reply, but simply nodded his head and managed a very weak grin. Radioing out on a Mayday all-frequencies band, he succinctly described the situation to whoever was listening and ordered as many armed people as possible to meet him at the break in the Barrier as soon as possible.

After a short pause, he received a reply from Mishima Takamura, who was dispatching everyone who was available. Phineas thanked him and signed off.

"All right, people, I've called in the cavalry. Now we've got to get down there and warn everybody that they're coming. I suggest we get moving as quickly as possible."

Ian Coopersmith intercepted the Mayday communication when they were within ten kilometers of the ruins. Looking at Murphy, he spoke above the whine of the engines. "Did you hear that?"

"Yeah, it sounds like they're in some deep shit, Captain."

"We're going to have to help them," Ian said. "How are the ammo banks on this thing?"

Checking the indicators, Murphy nodded. "You've got plenty of rounds. We going in?"

"Not 'we,' " Ian said. "Just me."

He leaned on the controls, and the 'thopter swooped wildly to the left, veering away from the ruins and establishing a new course which would bring it down at the coordinates of the broken Barrier.

"Wait a minute!" Murphy yelled. "What're you gonna do with us?"

"I'll drop you off behind the Barrier. It'll be safer that way."

"Aren't you going to need somebody to do your shooting for you?" Murphy asked. "I'm getting pretty good at popping these critters."

Ian smiled. Perhaps he had underestimated Murphy —or maybe certain situations bring out the best in some of us, despite our basic personalities.

Looking ahead, he could see the great, dark bulk of the Saurian Barrier materializing out of the steamy mist of the morning. Stretching far out to the east and west, the Barrier encircled the interior of the Dragonstar, sealing off the entire end of the ship and forming what was known as the Saurian preserve. As the 'thopter drew closer, Ian could see details of the Saurian countryside beyond the Barrier and beyond all of that he could finally see the flat, gray, metallic end of the giant cylinder.

Behind that impossibly huge wall lay the alien control section and the ship's engines. If only they could get back in there, and perhaps they could take control of everything again, Ian thought as he bore down on the Barrier.

As the 'thopter reached the Barrier, Ian headed west, following the Saurian wall.

"There," Murphy said. "Look at that. Do you see it?"

"Right," Ian said. Even from the distance of several kilometers, Ian had no trouble picking out the trouble spot. Like a cracked, festering wound, the break in the containment wall stood out from the rest of the architecture. It appeared as if gee-forces had caused the base of the Barrier to shift and twist, causing structural upheaval.

Leaning again on the controls, Ian forced the 'thopter down to a thousand meters and dropped the velocity to less than fifty kilometers per hour. As he closed the distance between his ship and the break in the Barrier, many more details became visible.

There was a great throng of Saurian warriors along the top of the Barrier on each side of the break. These defenders were raining down spears, arrows, rocks, and other missiles against a large carnivorous dinosaur that was trying to enter the Saurian preserve. In the center of the break in the wall a large body of Saurian warriors were also attacking the carnivore. The beast had been punctured and pummeled so many times that it staggered about as though drunk. Its maw and snout were a scarlet mess, smeared with the remains of unfortunate defenders. The beast was bleeding profusely, and Ian had to admire the plucky spirit of the Saurians to stand their ground against a nightmare like that.

"Drop her down," Murphy yelled. "Get me a good angle and I'll blow him away."

Closing the distance between the aircraft and the dinosaur, Ian brought the 'thopter in at treetop level, parallel to the Barrier. Directly in front of him, through the cockpit glass, the flat eye of the creature glared at him. Murphy let loose a volley of hollow-point, high-velocity slugs that ripped into its skull.

At the last instant, Ian pulled up the controls and the 'thopter leaped upward. Over the whine of the engines, he could hear the wailing of the beast as it collapsed at the base of the fracture.

"Nice shooting, Murphy!" he cried.

"Gee, Captain, how could I miss? Another couple of meters and we'd have been down his throat."

Ian wheeled back past the still heaving form of the beast to see ranks of Saurians—warriors and agrarians alike—cheering the 'thopter as it passed over their position. Already he could see the first shadowy, kitelike

figures of the scavenging Pteranodons gathering above
the bleeding form of the felled beast. They would be getting ready to swoop down and steal a few pieces of hot
meat, thought Ian with an ironic grin. You had to act
fast in a place like this.

"Captain! We've got another one down there!"
Murphy yelled.

At the same time, Ian heard Becky's voice cutting
through the din. "Ian! Ian! For God's sake, what're
you doing?"

Leaning out of his seat, Ian looked back for an instant to the underside of the 'thopter. The equipment
bay hatch was open, and Becky was hanging out of the
hatch yelling up at him.

Instead of trying to scream over the noise, he pointed
downward to the scene on the ground and hoped she'd
understand where they were and what was happening.
Then, following the pointing arm of Murphy, he saw
that a very large Tyrannosaurus had crashed out of the
trees to the east of the break in the wall. Although it was
some distance away from the break, it wouldn't take the
beast very long to get there.

Becky was still screaming at him, and he was certain
that it was no fun to be tossed around in the equipment
bay while he played tactical fighter pilot with these
monsters. There was only one thing to do, and he had to
do it fast.

"Hey! What're you doing?" Murphy yelled.

Leaning on the controls, Ian brought the 'thopter in
low over the Barrier and searched for a good place to
land. There was a flat area, an entrance to a park,
beyond the ramparts and the assembled fighting pla-
toons. Lower and lower he eased the craft, not looking
at Murphy until the ship was idling on the turf.

"Got to get them out of the belly," he said. "Go on,
Murph, give them a hand."

Becky was already scrambling out of the tight
quarters as Murphy jumped down and ran around to
help. A crowd of Saurians slowly was closing in on
them, looking very wary and apprehensive. It could be a

very touchy situation, and he wondered if it was a good idea to leave Becky on the ground with little protection.

"Ian, what do you think you're doing?" she screamed. "Were you trying to kill us in there?"

"Of course not, my dear," he said with an impish grin. "Now come on and get out of there, both of you. I've got some business to take care of."

"Ian, please be careful," Becky said.

"Captain Coopersmith. Ian. My God, Ian, what're you doing here?"

Turning away from Becky for an instant, Ian looked up to see Phineas Kemp running toward him. Trailing behind were three others—a commando, that journalist, and . . . good grief! it looked like Thesaurus.

"Greetings, Colonel. Nice to see you again," Ian said, reaching out to shake Kemp's hand. "I've decided to give you guys a hand. You look like you could use it."

"C'mon, Captain," Murphy said as he climbed into the cabin.

Waving him to silence, Ian looked at the hobbling figure of the Saurian being escorted over to the aircraft. It *was* Thesaurus.

The crowd of Saurian warriors drew closer to the aircraft; several had raised their weapons. They stopped, however, when they saw Thesaurus approaching the humans with no fear or trepidation. Turning to confront the warriors, Thesaurus held out his arms in a cruciform position, barking out a series of commands that the translator announced as simple orders to leave the humans alone, telling the slow-thinking warriors that the humans were indeed friends. The lemon-robed Saurian then turned back to regard his first human friend.

"You are a brave human, Ian Coopersmith," Thesaurus said as he approached the open cabin of the ornithopter.

"It's good to see you again," Ian said. "I've come back to help my friends."

"Captain," Murphy said again.

"I know, I know," Ian said, then turned back to Becky, Phineas, and the old high priest who had become his friend. "It looks like I've got to go."

With a smile at everyone, and a wink at Becky, he closed the hatch and lifted off. The 'thopter responded nicely, as he was now growing more accustomed to the controls. The machine practically grabbed the air with its airfoils, moving like a swimmer pushing the water past his body.

"All right," Ian said with a smile. "Let's go get that big boy."

Reaching a cruising altitude just above the ramparts, Ian was shocked to see what had happened in the short time he had squandered by dropping off his passengers. The Tyrannosaurus, which had presumably been attracted to the scene by all the noise and the smell of blood, had closed the distance between the forest's edge and the gap in the Barrier.

It was an abnormally large animal—larger than any predator Ian had ever seen in the preserve. It was a light tan color with some minimal striping, and it stood out against the lush greens of the forest behind it. Taller than any other theropod, the creature leaned forward, balancing its weight with a thick, heavy, but extremely fluid tail. As it approached the rift in the wall, a small squad of warrior-class Saurians ran out through the rubble to meet its charge.

Like a chicken hunting and pecking in a barnyard, the beast opened its jaws and plucked the Saurians from the ground, tossing them up into its cavernous maw. It moved with surprising quickness, and the storm of spears and arrows that rained down from the ramparts seemed to have no effect on it.

Its pillbox head seemed too large for the neck that supported it like a gun turret on a swivel mount. As the 'thopter approached it for the first time, the beast's attention was diverted from the opening in the wall for an instant and it turned a glistening yellow eye up to assay them.

Murphy fired his automatic into the thing's head as

they passed, but the weapon sputtered into silence after a terribly short burst.

"Need another clip," he yelled in frustration, digging into the utility pouch on his belt. "Get me around for another pass."

Ian nodded and pulled up on the controls as the Tyrannosaurus looked away from them and again strode forward toward the piled-up debris. Methodically, it began to sweep the area with its tail, pushing aside the smaller pieces of the broken wall. It pushed away the larger fragments with its powerful hind legs. The beast appeared determined to stride right into the Saurian preserve.

Whipping the 'thopter out of a tight turn, Ian brought the craft up for some additional power in its attacking dive. He had been keeping his attention mainly on the position of the beast below them. And that would prove to be his only mistake.

He had forgotten about the flock of Pteranodons that had gathered above the sight of the bloodbath. They were carrion eaters, the vultures of the Mesozoic. Their circling, gliding patterns above an open clearing in the Mesozoic preserve served as a clear marker that death was down below.

It happened so fast that Ian had no time to react. In one instant the airspace was clear; in the next, a swarm of the reddish, leathery-winged, pencil-headed reptiles filled the window with their furious flapping.

"Watch it, Captain!"

Murphy's warning came too late. Yanking the controls hard to the left, Ian tried to avoid the flying reptiles on instinct alone. The ornithopter careened into the center of the flock, and with the force of a concussive shell, one of the creatures exploded through the window. Like crystalline snow, the fragments peppered Ian, momentarily blinding him. The 'thopter rocked dangerously as another of the Pteranodons impacted on the rotors of the engine. There was a sickening crunch and a quick series of crowlike caws, screeches of death closing in on the beast.

It was that fast, and the aircraft had cleared the flight of reptiles, but the damage had been done. The once steady whine of the engines had been reduced to a ratcheting, knocking sound; the airfoils moved with a twisted, battered slowness which Ian knew would not keep them aloft for very long. He yanked up on the controls and threw the craft into a stall, then tried to fall out of the maneuver to increase his glide factor.

"We've had it!" he yelled to Murphy. "She's not going to stay up."

Murphy only stared at him with a sick expression on his face. It was a look of fear mixed with a touch of disbelief. Ian was certain he wore a similar expression. Is this it? Is this how it's going to end? he wondered.

The 'thopter tilted dangerously to one side as the left airfoil collapsed in upon itself, no longer able to handle the stress factors and support the weight of the fuselage. Ian scanned the scene on the ground below and knew what he had to do. The Tyrannosaurus had cleared the majority of the debris from the rift in the Barrier and was fighting its way toward the opening despite the valiant but futile efforts of the Saurian warriors.

"I'm taking it in!" he yelled to Murphy. "Get ready to jump!"

"Jump? Are you crazy?"

"Jumping is safer than riding it home," Ian cried. The controls were stiffening up as the engine knocked and coughed out its last few bursts of power.

The flight path of the 'thopter tightened into more of a dive than a glide, and Ian knew it was going to be a rough landing. He looked over at Murphy, who was hanging on to the frame of the cabin with a white-knuckled grip.

"Get ready to jump," Ian cried.

"Screw you!"

"Now! Get out of here *now*!" Ian said.

Murphy ignored him, and Ian did the only thing possible in the situation. Grabbing a handle above his head, Ian vaulted up out of his seat with a gymnastic move and kicked Murphy across the chest with both feet. It was a quick maneuver which sent the trooper sprawling back and out of the ship less than twenty meters from impact.

The move gave Ian just enough time to get back into his seat and wrestle with the controls for one last course change—the last one he would ever need.

Becky may have screamed when she saw the body falling from the diving 'thopter. She couldn't remember. The helmeted figure plunged spread-eagled into a copse of ferns and cycads just within the Barrier and disappeared from view. In the next instant, the ornithopter, tilting crazily, flapping limply at the air like a wounded bird, wheeled downward and cut a sharp angle away from the trees, heading straight for the rift in the Barrier wall and the nightmare creature that now approached it.

Becky held her breath as she watched the ornithopter rush headlong into the Tyrannosaurus. The impact of the crash shattered the command cabin like an exploding eggshell, flinging Ian through the air like a rag doll. The force of the crash against the great beast's body slammed it backward with incredible force. And the whirling, twisted airfoils sliced through its neck as cleanly as the blade of a guillotine.

For a single, frozen moment, the head of the Rex remained stable. Then a fountain of bright blood erupted from the incision in its neck. It tottered backward, a dying scream gurgling weakly in its throat as the great head slid slowly from the neck. It dangled by a few untouched cords of sinew and shredded flesh as the beast collapsed to the earth.

For an instant the scene remained deathly quiet, before the assembly of Saurian warriors and agrarians erupted into a chorus of barks and hisses and tail thumping. The scene had been so spectacular, so unbelievable, that it seemed fixed in time like a photograph in Becky's mind. She had been stunned by the visual impact of the event, and the full realization of what she had seen was only now beginning to sink in.

"My God," someone said in a soft whisper.

Ian, thought Becky, Ian had been thrown clear!

Suddenly she was running toward the crash, and it

was as though her movement was a signal for everyone else. Phineas and the others moved quickly behind her, and the hordes of Saurians—warriors, agrarians, even the philosopher-priests—closed ranks and ran toward the site of the crash. Becky ran ahead of the pack, and she could see that the felled Tyrannosaurus, wrapped in the twisted wreckage of the ornithopter, formed an effective barricade against the break in the Barrier. Nothing else would be able to get through—at least for quite some time.

Passing the crash site, she looked toward the area where Ian had been thrown—a slapdash of crude scaffolding which the Saurians had been using to repair the Barrier. Part of the primitive latticework of planks and supports had collapsed, and it was in the midst of this debris that she saw him.

Lying on his back, with his head twisted at a terrible angle, Ian Coopersmith stared up past the ramparts, beyond the edge of the Barrier. Thick rivulets of blood seeped from the corner of his mouth, his nose, and ears. He did not move; his eyes did not blink.

She rushed to his side, crying out his name over and over, trying to fight back the tears, trying to ignore the frantic pounding in her breast. Easing herself down next to him, careful not to collapse any more of the scaffolding, Becky reached out and took his hand in hers. The color was fading from his face; his eyes were glazing over.

"Ian, can you hear me? Oh God, Ian, why did you do it?"

Although he did not reply, his eyes blinked and he smiled a small wry smile.

Becky quickly assessed the situation, and she knew he was in very bad shape, with a concussion and probably a skull fracture, internal hemorrhaging, back injuries that probably included shattered vertebrae in the neck. Ian Coopersmith was going to die.

The thought ate through her like a terrible acid. She could feel the tears welling up, burning the corners of her eyes. "Oh, Ian. Why?"

With what seemed like a great effort, he turned his

head, slowly and with obvious pain, until he was facing her directly. His lips trembled as he fought to form the words.

"Becky . . ."

"Yes?" Just hearing his voice made her cry harder.

Reaching out, Ian touched her arm and tried to squeeze it, but there was no strength left in him. Becky could hear the sounds of a great crowd encircling them, but she ignored their presence, and thankfully no one approached. She felt that she needed a few moments alone with him.

"Becky . . . I must talk," he said, his voice a gurgling, coarse rattle.

"No, Ian, save your strength."

Another forced smiled. "For what? You're a doctor, my dear. I shouldn't have to tell you what's in store for me."

"Ian, please, don't talk like that."

"Becky . . . I know this is not a very good time to tell you this . . . but I'm afraid it's my last chance."

She watched him as he forced the words from his lips. His breathing had become ragged, and the hemorrhaging had increased. Her image of him had always been one of strength and competence and common sense, and it hurt so bad to see him lying helpless before her. She knew there was nothing she could do for him, and she felt cheated that she'd never get the chance.

"Why did you do it, Ian?" Becky fought back the tears, but they surged down her face, stinging her cheeks.

"Forget that. It had to be done." He coughed up some blood, which momentarily choked him, then his breathing evened out a bit.

Becky stroked his hair and kissed his damp forehead.

"Becky, I must tell you this one thing." He coughed once, then continued. "Ever since the first, I think I've loved you, but I could never say it to you, or even . . . even say it to myself."

"Ian, it's all right. I understand," Becky couldn't control her tears any longer. They rolled off her face to spatter on the side of his cheek, mingling with his blood.

"I feel better now that it's out," he said with great effort. "Hold me, Becky."

"Oh, Ian," she said, shifting to lie gently across his chest. "Oh Ian, I've loved you too. I guess I was too dumb to admit it too."

He did not reply. She sensed a subtle change, a difference that couldn't be explained. "Ian?" she whispered softly, suddenly afraid to pull back from him, afraid to look at him. "Ian?"

Oh, no! Not yet, she thought. Please, not yet!

But when she forced herself to look at him, to check for a carotid pulse at the base of his neck, she knew what she would find. His eyes were still open, and there was a slight smile in the corners of his mouth—and he was dead.

Twenty-one

They found Murphy hanging unconscious in the fronds of a giant fern. When he woke up, he told them that Ian had kicked him out of the cabin, thereby saving his life. It was just one more little thing that would help to memorialize Coopersmith as a hero, thought Phineas Kemp. The air was filled with the sounds of urgent industry as he supervised the rebuilding of the Barrier, along with several of Takamura's staff and a group of the Saurian priests. Phineas was very busy, but he couldn't seem to get Ian's death out of his mind—nor Becky's tearful reaction to it all.

After Coopersmith had died, there had been a large commotion among the Saurians—especially the warriors and the agrarians. It seemed that Coopersmith's sacrificial gesture had done more than merely block the Barrier and kill the invading beast. Far more importantly, Ian's unselfish martyrdom had demonstrated to the Saurians that humans could be trusted after all.

The concept of giving one's life for the benefit of others, however, was a very alien one for the Saurian warriors. Apparently it was an act that had never occurred to them as a way of solving a problem. Phineas had watched Thesaurus spend a long session explaining the concept and the inherent nobility of the act to a large assemblage of warriors. The speech seemed to impress them, because they all jumped up at its conclusion and began barking and hissing and slamming the butts of their weapons against their chests. It was a fantastic display of enthusiasm and support, and he wished that Ian could have seen what reptilian emotions he had stirred up.

Considering all the problems still facing them, Phineas thought calmly, things were shaping up a little better. If work continued at the present rate, the repairs to the Barrier would be completed within twenty-four hours. With IASA troopers and their automatic weapons patrolling the ramparts, there would be no more threats from the dinosaurs, and the Saurian preserve would be a safe place to base their operations.

"Good evening, Colonel," said the voice of Mishima Takamura.

Turning around, Phineas looked at the young scientist. "Everybody checked in yet?" he asked expectantly.

Mishima smiled and nodded. "The last OTV is rolling in now."

Phineas shook his head in mock exhaustion. "Good. At least we've finally pulled everybody together."

"Yes," Takamura said. "But I keep wondering what we're going to do now."

"That's a good question, but I'm not going to worry about it for now. First things first. I think we should call for a meeting and address our problems to the group. Don't you agree?"

Takamura took a seat along the railing of the scaffolding, looked down over the construction that was furiously going on below them. "Hell, yes! Everybody's got a right to know what's going on around here." He looked at Phineas with a stern, serious expression that made him appear older than his years. "I don't know about you, but it makes me feel very uneasy looking everybody in the face and not telling them what I know. I feel like I'm lying to them by keeping quiet."

Phineas nodded. "I know what you mean. We've got to tell them soon."

"I'll talk to Thesaurus," Mishima said, "and see if

we can use one of the rooms in their nursery buildings. It should be big enough to fit all of us, don't you think?''

Phineas shrugged. "I don't know. I've never seen any of their nurseries."

"Oh, that's right," Takamura said. "You haven't spent much time around the Saurians, have you?"

"Is that supposed to be a cutting remark, Doctor? I thought we had worked our way past that stage." Phineas still didn't know what to make of Takamura.

"No, I'm sorry, Colonel, it's just that I'm a bit surprised that you could be in charge of a project such as this and seem to ignore such an integral part of it as the Saurians."

Phineas sighed. "If you want to know the truth, I find them more than a little bit repulsive. I never had any great attraction for reptiles—you know, frogs and snakes and stuff like that."

"I see."

"Which reminds me," Phineas said. "Do you think we are still in danger from them? What with the radiation and all that?"

Mishima shook his head. "No, I don't think so. From what I've been able to piece together, it seems like the radiation and the mutations were simply by-products of the changes taking place on board, an effect of the ship's automated systems turning on again."

"Do you think we will be able to get any kind of control over this ship?"

Takamura grinned wistfully. "Who knows? That sounds like the number-one project for me and my people, though."

Just then a trooper appeared at the far end of the rampart. "Excuse me, Colonel," he said. "I've got a message for you from Dr. Lindstrom."

Phineas felt his pulse jump at the mention of Mikaela's name, and suddenly he didn't want to talk to Takamura any longer.

"She's back? Where is she?"

"Down by the gates, Colonel. She said she'd like to see you there as soon as possible."

"Thank you, Corporal," said Phineas, saluting him off. Turning to Takamura, he extended his hand in friendship. "Let's get that assembly set up as soon as possible, all right, Doctor?"

"I'll get right on it, Colonel."

Her skin glowed like polished ivory in the light of the lantern as she rolled off him, staring at the roof of the tent. Even with her blond hair cut short, Mikaela looked fantastic to him. Her body was lithe and athletic—narrow hips, tiny waist, high pert breasts—and her capacity for lovemaking seemed inexhaustible. For pure physical excitement and gratification, she was unequaled.

"You're unbelievable," said Phineas.

Mikaela giggled and looked at him with her electric blue eyes. "I've been saving it up. I feel like I've been living in that OTV for a month."

"It certainly was nice of the Saurians to let use their tents, wasn't it?" he asked with a smile.

"Well, we're all in this together now, and we've got to make camp somewhere. The outdoor bazaar seemed like a logical choice—the stalls and vendors' tents make perfect cabanas."

Phineas laughed. "Is that what we're in? A cabana?"

"Well, you know what I mean. Besides, who cares where we are as long as we can be like this." She kissed him lightly on the forehead and brushed her fingers over his limp penis.

Phineas stirred instantly. "My God, Mikaela . . . again? I mean, I'm not complaining, mind you, but I need some time in between to rest."

"You men are all alike," she joked.

"I don't think I like the sound of that."

"Is the colonel getting jealous?"

"Now look here, Lindstrom, you women don't have to worry about getting it up, you know. You'd feel differently if that were the case."

"I think it's all rather symbolic, don't you?" she asked.

"Whatever are you talking about?" Phineas was suddenly confused.

"Well, think about it—men worrying about their silly erections is a perfect symbol for all the other dumb things they worry about. Promotions, achievements, commissions, records . . . God, they're always trying to get *something* up. Higher and higher. Bigger and better."

"Are you complaining, my dear?"

Mikaela giggled softly. "No, I'm just trying to be the devil's advocate, I suppose." She looked at him warmly and kissed him again. "I guess what I'm really doing is smoke-screening."

"Really? For what?"

"Phineas, I'm scared."

"You're not alone in feeling that way."

"But that doesn't make it any better." Mikaela looked him squarely in the eyes. "Tell me, what's really going on? Why is the ship moving? Where is it going?"

"I'm not supposed to say anything until the assembly later tonight," Phineas said. "So you'll have to promise to keep your pretty mouth shut."

"I think I can be trusted. I mean, how many people can I tell in the next hour or so?"

"All right, I'll tell you what I know, but you're not going to like it."

Everyone had come to the large room at the appointed time. It was a circular enclosure like an amphitheater, divided up into many smaller cells or boxes, each set upon rising platforms. The female Saurians employed rooms like this to raise their infants, but Mishima had no idea what actually took place in their nurseries.

This evening the boxes were occupied by all the humans who had survived the chaos of the last several days. Mishima Takamura had counted 106 people, and he was shocked to learn that so many had died. He stood in the center of the room with Colonel Kemp, Dr. Jakes, and Dr. Lindstrom, looking from face to face, trying to read the emotions that burned behind their eyes.

The room was totally silent now, and it seemed as though everyone was afraid to speak. Mishima had just finished explaining everything he knew about the events so far.

He had just told them that they were trapped in a ship that had made a faster-than-light jump into hyperspace, that the Earth and the solar system were probably thousands of light-years away by now, and that there was no way of knowing the ship's destination or the duration of the flight.

The news was absorbed by the group of survivors with an eerie, stunned silence. Mishima shifted his weight from one foot to the other and looked at the others in the center of the room, then back to the assembled group. He could sense anger in them, and frustration, and of course fear. They looked at him and Kemp and the others as though they were somehow responsible for the present state of affairs.

Finally someone stood up near the back. A young woman who had worked in the Paleo Camp.

"Yes?" said Mishima.

"How certain are you that what you've told us is true, Dr. Takamura? I mean, are we one hundred percent sure that we've left the solar system?"

A murmur rippled through the crowd, and Mishima could sense their hope, their desire that perhaps the scientists could be wrong, that just maybe this was all a big mistake.

He shook his head slowly. "I'm sorry, but all of our tests tell us the same thing. Instruments running independently of each other are providing the same data. As far as I can tell, what I've told all of you is inescapably true."

Another quick murmur went through the crowd. Then came a question from an IASA trooper assigned to the Tactical Base. "Well, sir, if that's the case, do you mind my asking just what we're all going to do now?"

"He's right," someone else shouted.

"What now?"

A chorus of angry, frustrated voices joined in to become unintelligible, and Mishima motioned for silence. Colonel Kemp stood and approached the center of the room, waiting until the crowd noise died down before speaking to them.

"We realize how you all feel. I feel the same things. I know that you are all feeling lost and helpless, but let's not forget that we represent some of the best examples of our species, and that we are a damned competent bunch of people. We still have a job to do—and that's to make the best of what looks like a pretty bad situation. The way I look at it, we don't have much choice."

This sparked off more murmuring and discussion within the crowd, but Mishima sensed that it was more orderly now. There was less panic and hostility.

A young man from Jakes's research team stood up and began to speak. "That sounds like a good idea, Colonel. I propose that we form some task forces to map out just what things we can do, and then start selecting groups, or committees, or whatever you want to call them, and get into action."

"Yeah," said another man dressed in trooper's coveralls. "That sounds good to me."

The discussion broke up into smaller islands of conversation once again, and Colonel Kemp waited for it to die down before continuing. "It seems to me that we're on the right track with that kind of thinking. We've got to think of ourselves as a little world-nation here. We're on our own now, and we must plan for our future—whatever it might be. We have to set up a series of contingency plans."

"Could you be a little more specific, Colonel?" asked a middle-aged woman who worked with Mikaela Lindstrom's group. "What kind of contingencies are we talking about?"

Kemp cleared his throat. "There aren't too many, actually. One, we somehow manage to take control of this ship and get back to Earth; two, we come out of hyperspace in the foreseeable future and face whatever is waiting for us; or three, we never come out of hyperspace."

Another wave of murmuring, louder and more distressed than before, coursed through the room. Hostility radiated from the crowd like heat. Kemp tried to quiet the crowd, but they ignored him until their frustration and their words had been vented. Finally, when the noise subsided, the questions commenced again. The colonel tried to field them as best he could, getting help from the other senior staff members whenever he needed it, but Mishima sensed some genuine problems.

The conflict came to a head when one of the scientists from Jakes's research team stood up and spoke calmly but with conviction. "Colonel, I think we are overlooking a very basic fact here. A fact which is extremely germane to our situation."

"All right," Kemp said. "What's that?"

"We should not forget that we are totally on our own now. We are cut off from the Earth and all her ties and obligations. In essence, we are a tiny little nation." The man paused for dramatic effect, and Phineas interrupted him.

"What exactly are you trying to say?"

"Simply this: I feel that we may be making a mistake by continuing to accept the power and authority structure which existed when we were still connected with the Earth."

"What do you mean?" Mikaela Lindstrom asked defensively—she already had a good idea what the man meant.

"I mean that there is no IASA in hyperspace, Doctor. I mean that I have very strong doubts about listening to a man whose mistakes have left us in this practically hopeless situation."

"Now see here!" Kemp shouted, his face flushing instantly with anger.

The crowd erupted into a wild and passionate discussion, everyone talking at once, and no one able to hear anyone else. Things escalated into shouting matches and then threats. Mishima and Mikaela attempted to quiet the crowd, but it was a difficult process. The scientist who had started this round of chaos had obviously touched a raw nerve in many of the survivors, and Mishima knew it was an issue that would demand some kind of quick resolution. The group would never be able to function and work and live together with this kind of dissension and distrust.

Finally the shouting subsided into talking, and finally into a soft murmur. Mishima had everyone's attention. "It's obvious that we have some problems here," he said. "Let's try to solve them instead of fighting, all right?"

"That's right," said Colonel Kemp. "I agree with the suggestion that we may be making a mistake by retaining the old authority structure. I for one am willing to stage free elections—right now if everyone wants them."

Bob Jakes stood up and said essentially the same thing. The survivors discussed it among themselves, and several people stood to offer suggestions.

It was a long and grueling process, but eventually a plan and a structure of government were hammered out. The group came up with a largely democratic structure of committees, answering to a ruling council of elected representatives. There was to be no single authority figure, and all decisions would be made by the council unless the majority demanded a referendum vote on major issues.

Nominations were taken for committee heads, and for the members of the ruling council. Not surprisingly, Jakes, Lindstrom, Mishima, and Kemp himself were among those nominated for the positions. Ballots were created, and a general election was held. For purposes of decorum, all nominees were asked to leave the room during subsequent discussion and voting. After the nominees had cast their own ballots, they left the Saurian nursery and gathered outside on the steps to the building.

"An interesting turn of events, isn't it?" Jakes said, trying to keep things light, but it seemed to Mishima that no one else was in the mood to smile or joke.

Especially troubled by the entire electoral process was Phineas Kemp. He had not spoken or even looked anyone in the eye since the revisionist talks and action had begun. If the colonel didn't win a seat on the council, Mishima wondered how the blow to his ego would effect him.

They waited almost an hour before someone invited them back into the meeting room, announcing that the ballots had been counted and the results were now official. Mishima and the others took their seats, and the election officer read off the names of the winners of the committee chair positions. There were few surprises, and Mishima personally felt that the group had demonstrated wisdom in their choices.

Next, the names of the winners of seats to the ruling council were announced: Robert Jakes, Mikaela Lindstrom, and Mishima Takamura were among the five people named, but Colonel Phineas Kemp was not.

Twenty-two

Mikaela Lindstrom was arguably the closest person to Phineas Kemp, and even she had a difficult time gauging the effects of the election and his "fall from power," as he had come to call it. For the first few days there seemed to be a period of reorientation for everyone. There was much organization to be done, tasks and assignments had to be recognized and given out, priorities established, and methods of accomplishment tested and worked out.

Being a member of the council was an exhausting experience during those first few days, and Mikaela felt that she hadn't been able to give Phineas the attention he needed during that time. She had become fairly friendly with Rebecca Thalberg, and she kept telling herself that she would have to sit down with Becky sometime and have a serious woman-to-woman talk about the care and feeding of a particular IASA colonel.

Phineas had attempted to busy himself in the construction project along the Saurian Barrier, and Mikaela assumed that it would be the best thing for him to do—have a project that would keep him occupied. There was also the major work of establishing a small human settlement in the city of Hakarrh. Thesaurus and his minions had generously donated one of the outdoor bazaar sites, complete with tents and stalls for the humans, and there was much work to be done in getting the area habitable. Phineas had selected a gaily colored tent for himself and Mikaela, and he spent the evening hours attempting to build furniture for their new home.

Mikaela noticed that while everyone referred to their situation as though it were a very temporary thing, their actions belied such notions. It appeared as though everyone was digging in and setting up for a life among the Saurians that might last indefinitely. It was one of those things that Mikaela suspected everyone must be thinking about but choosing not to discuss.

Everyone except perhaps Phineas. In the evenings, when they would sit down and talk by the heat and light of the lanterns, he would speculate on where the great ship was going, when it might pop out of ultramathematical space and back into the galaxy, and what might be waiting for them. There was also something about the way Phineas talked of these things that disturbed Mikaela. Phineas spoke as though he truly believed he was responsible for every bad thing that had happened.

It was as though there was a great cancerous guilt growing inside him, threatening to consume him. And that scared Mikaela very much.

And so, when she arrived at their tent one evening and didn't find him there, she became extremely worried. Asking about in the immediate area gained her nothing. No one had seen him all afternoon. Calls to Takamura and Jakes and Becky Thalberg only served to cause them to worry along with her, since none of them had seen Phineas either.

Takamura inquired at the construction site by the Barrier and learned that Phineas had left the job recently and had been seen entering the Mesozoic Preserve.

Now Mikaela was panicked. There was no reason for Phineas to go into the Preserve. She took out the OTV, entering the forest in search of Phineas. Perhaps an hour of artificial daylight remained when she entered the thick cathedral-like vault of tall trees and fronds.

Using the vehicle's infrared heat-imaging sensors, she was able to pick up the trail of a warm body that had recently passed through the area. Her instruments told her that the body was approximately Phineas Kemp's size, and she had to hope that she was following him rather than a human-size dinosaur.

The heat imager followed the trail as a bloodhound might follow the scent of a fugitive. Mikaela watched her instruments carefully, but she also watched the amount of light still available. If she didn't find Phineas wihin the hour, she would have to return to Hakarrh. Even in the OTV, she didn't want to be out in the Mesozoic Preserve at feeding time—not if she had a choice in the matter.

She spotted him fifteen minutes later.

He was moving with an aimless, slow, shuffling walk across a small meadow. Mikaela stopped the vehicle and watched him as he headed for an outcropping of rocks at the edge of a ridge. He didn't appear to be paying any attention to his surroundings, and she wondered how he had wandered this far without running afoul of a predator. When Phineas disappeared behind the rocks, she reached for the OTV's hatch.

That's when she heard the shot.

It was single report, a soft *crack* that was muffled somewhat by the thick foliage and vegetation.

Oh, God! No! she thought as she raced the engines up to speed and ripped the vehicle across the meadow, heedless of anything except reaching him. The crazy bastard! The egocentric, crazy bastard!

Stopping at the base of the rocks, Mikaela jumped down and headed for the rocks. As she cleared the first ranks of the formation, she saw him. He was sitting up, leaning back against the rocks with the revolver still in his hand. His eyes were open, and he was staring at her in surprise.

"Mikaela! Good Christ, you scared me. What're you doing here?"

She stepped forward and exhaled slowly, trying to stop trembling. At the base of the rocks where Phineas

sat was the carcass of a Comsagnathus—a small bei-
pedal dinosaur no more than a single meter in length. It
looked like a miniature Allosaurus built for speed and
quickness. There was a bullet hole in the center of its
skull, looking like a dark, third eye.

"The bugger tried to jump me," Phineas said, pointing at the tiny predator's body with the barrel of his
gun. "I had to pop him one." He laughed nervously.

"Phineas, I was looking for you. You scared me."

He laughed again, this time with more obvious effort.
"Listen, I scared myself."

"It's not safe out here, Phineas. We've got to get
back."

"I know. We will. Don't worry about that. But let me
finish what I'm trying to say. I might not be able to
later."

She felt reassured by the way he talked now. They
were close to the OTV. It would be all right to remain
there a little bit longer, despite the cry of carrion eaters,
still far off but inevitably closing in.

"All right," she said. "Go on."

"I came out here because I didn't know what I was
feeling anymore. I didn't know what I was going to do
with myself."

He looked at her with the expression of a lost little
boy, and her heart went out to him. She wanted to take
him in her arms and hold him, but she knew that he had
some things he wanted to say. It would be best not to interrupt him.

"It's not hard for me to understand why they voted
me out, Mikaela. I've been a real fuck-up lately, I know
that. But it has been hard for me to live with it, with not
being a leader anymore. Not being a decision-maker.
It's what I'm used to, damn it."

He looked at her, and there were tears in the corners
of his eyes. It was a side of Phineas Kemp that she had
never seen.

"I've always been a chief, Mikaela. And I'm afraid I
won't be able to make it just being an Indian. I'm very
much afraid."

"It's okay to be afraid," she said, coming to his side. "We all have things we're afraid of."

"I'm learning that, but I'm a slow learner, I think."

She looked at him, kissed him tenderly, then pulled back to look at the gun. "Were you really thinking of using that?"

Phineas shook his head. "I don't know. I don't think so. Every time I thought about actually pulling the trigger, actually trying to imagine myself doing it, I just couldn't get the picture right. It just wasn't *me*, you know?" He laughed sadly. "Who knows, maybe I'm even afraid to do that."

"That's not fear. That's just good sense. We need you, Phineas. I need you."

"Sometimes I can't imagine why."

"Because you're you, that's why." She smiled and kissed him again. "Sure, you're feeling lousy right now—you've been rejected, and you're the kind of person who has not had much rejection in your life. You've never realized that there are millions of us that live with it all the time. You'll get used to it, Phineas. It's not the end of the world."

He smiled for the first time. "Somehow that old cliché doesn't sound right under the circumstances."

"Phineas, don't talk like that."

"Well, really, what's going to happen to us? Don't you ever wonder why this ship started up again, and why it whisked us off to God knows where?"

Mikaela nodded and put her head on his shoulder. "Of course I do. Everyone is wondering about the same things," she said. "But it's no reason to give up."

"Who said anything about giving up?" Phineas stood up and pulled her close to him, kissing her gently. Somewhere in the forest there came the cry of a beast.

"We should be heading back," Mikaela said. "It's getting to be feeding time."

They walked slowly back toward the vehicle, but Phineas paused and looked around, as though appreciating the vastness of the Mesozoic preserve for the first time.

"What's the matter?" Mikaela asked.

"Nothing . . . and everything." Phineas laughed softly. "This is a hell of a crazy place, and I almost let it beat me. I wasn't ready for all the things that happened this time around, but I'll be ready the next time."

"Are you sure there'll be a next time?" Mikaela asked.

"No," said Phineas. "But I sure as hell hope so!"